MIND IN CHAINS

The Mind Sleuth Series Book 3

Bruce M. Perrin

This book is a work of fiction.

Names, characters, places, and incidents are products of the author's imagination or are used fictitiously. Any resemblance to actual events, locales, or persons living or dead is entirely coincidental.

First Edition.

Cover Art by Courtney M. Perrin

Visit the Author at

BruceMPerrin.blogspot.com

Mind Sleuth Publications

ISBN-13: 978-1-7320835-2-3 (paperback)

*For my family and
their boundless love and support*

Table of Contents

Medicine is a science of uncertainty
and an art of probability.
WILLIAM OSLER

SEVEN YEARS EARLIER

Martha Wilson pushed the silent alarm button, not sure exactly what it did. As far as she knew—and she knew a lot since she had worked at the hospital since it opened five years ago—it had never been used. But all her training said this was the time to find out.

At first, nothing happened. But after a few minutes, Jorge Caballa peered around a corner. "Nurse Wilson. What can I do for you?"

Martha blinked, surprised. Nothing against Jorge, but she had expected a more urgent response, something more official. Sure, Jorge had been in the military, many years ago, followed by a career in the police department of one of the many small towns that surrounded the city of St. Louis, Missouri. After that, he had moved some 70 miles to this more rural setting, taking what he called his "retirement job" when the hospital opened. Martha just wasn't certain, however, if that term meant work he did in retirement or a position that was part of it. She had seldom seen him do more than read a magazine or stroll the halls.

"One of the newborns is missing," she said.

Jorge stopped midstride, his brow wrinkling. "Where did you see it last?"

Martha blinked again, wondering if Jorge was going to ask all the questions one might when searching for a set of lost car keys or a misplaced TV remote. "In the nursery, twenty minutes ago. But Mil and I have checked everywhere. She's not in the hospital."

Perhaps those were the magic words because Jorge pulled a walkie-talkie from his belt. "Al, we need an Amber alert now. Hold for description." He looked at Martha.

"Female, black, not yet named," she replied. She pulled a card from her pocket. "Length …."

Jorge stopped her with a raised hand and spoke into the walkie-talkie. "Black, Baby Jane Doe. Last seen," he raised his wrist to look at his watch, "at 1:47 PM."

"OK, hold a moment," came the voice from the speaker.

"Stats on that card?" Jorge asked. Martha nodded and handed it to him. His head started shaking almost the moment he took it.

"Description?" came the question over the speaker.

"Dark hair. Brown eyes. Length, 20.2 inches. Weight, 7.9 pounds. No distinguishing features. I'll round up the newborn pictures, get them to you."

"OK. I'll get this out," said Al on the radio.

"If she's gone …." Martha stopped, the thought behind her words stealing her breath. For the last 20 minutes, all of her attention, her total reason for existence had been the search for the missing baby. But now, with the alarm passed to the authorities, she felt lost, helpless. She swallowed hard and then dropped into one of the chairs lining the hallway. "Those details aren't going to help much in finding her, will they?" she asked so softly Jorge had to bend over to hear.

"No," Jorge admitted. "Probably not. By the time we could take her weight, we'd be in a position to use something better. Like DNA linking her to the mother. But anything might help."

Martha nodded, watching as Jorge paced, a hand rubbing what was left of his gray hair while the other still clutched the walkie-talkie. The radio crackled to life. "Amber alert's out. Expect the locals in about 15 minutes, state and maybe the feds to follow. Bring everyone down to Security."

"Will do," replied Jorge. Turning to Martha, he asked, "Who else has been involved?"

"Mildred Saks helped search. Alicia Riggs, my super knows. And a bunch of others I ran into in the halls," she said, standing from her chair. "And

Towanda Jenkins, the hospital administrator—she knows, too. I called. She's coming back from lunch. Should be in your office in ten minutes or so."

"OK, let's get Ms. Saks and Ms. Riggs. Where are the parents?"

"In their room, 357." Martha frowned, as they turned toward the nurses' station where she hoped to find her coworkers. "The parents don't know yet."

"That's fine. Better they hear it from Ms. Jenkins in the privacy of her office." Jorge pulled the walkie-talkie to his face. "Al, send someone to 357 for the parents and take them to Riggs's office, but remind them what's up."

As they turned into the wing with the nursery, Martha slowed and turned to Jorge. "They'll find her, won't they?" Jorge said nothing for a moment, so she added, "The truth."

Jorge sighed. "I can't really say. Is there an angry ex-spouse somewhere? A childless neighbor? All I know is that the police will run down every lead before they give up."

"But if it's not friends or family?" Martha asked although she thought she knew the answer.

"Then you've done everything you could. Getting this on the air in 20 minutes is a good start; the first few hours are the most important. After that, the chances start going down fast. And after a few days ...." He shook his head but didn't finish.

Martha shuddered and squeezed her eyes closed. These were facts she had heard before, but they had been only meaningless statistics at the time. Now, they tore at her heart, the pain worsening with each tick of her mental clock.

Two hours later, after meeting with the local police who had no news about Baby Jane Doe, Martha couldn't control her emotions any longer. She started sobbing.

Six hours later, the interviews were complete, and Martha took a taxi home, afraid to trust her driving. She went to bed, hardly speaking to her husband. The next day, she called in sick. And the day after. And the day after that.

To Martha, the news was always the same. There were no ex-spouses. The neighbors either had children or were retired with their children now raising their own. Video cameras had caught the comings and goings from the maternity wing at the hospital, but everyone belonged. Simply put, there were no suspects, and the trail, if there ever had been one, was ice cold.

After ten days passed and there was no news about Baby Jane Doe, Martha went to work only to resign. She couldn't face another expectant mother, knowing she had lost a human life left in her care.

FRIDAY, MAY 3

11:17 AM – A House in Independence, Missouri

I was starting to sweat. Overnight, light rain showers had moved through, and now the morning sun was pushing the mercury upward. The level of humidity was following the same trajectory, but the weather wasn't totally to blame for my perspiration. I had never done what I was about to do, and the anticipation had my heart drumming in my ears, my hands balled into sweaty fists. I closed my eyes and took a deep, reassuring breath. It was time.

I checked the street and driveways from the shade of a maple tree, finding them as deserted as I had expected for a weekday in this residential neighborhood, only a few miles from the boyhood home of President Harry S. Truman. But even so, there might be some retiree—an old lady with a house full of cats, an aged man with a collection of guns—peering through their shades, wondering what I was doing. Having the police show up now would never do. I screwed up my courage and walked up to the house I had been watching.

Relax. You have nothing to worry about.

But my thoughts had no sway over my emotions. I reached out and quietly tested the doorknob. It moved freely, just as I had expected. The people who lived around here were so trusting. I dropped my hand, stepped back, and took another breath, knowing this was my only option. I turned the knob again and quietly opened the door, revealing a living room to the left, a hall to the right, and part of a kitchen counter and dishwasher through an arched doorway straight ahead. I stepped forward and peered around the edge of the door. A woman was there, drying silverware. The quiet of the scene was broken by the clatter of knives as she dropped them into a drawer.

"Hi, Maggie," I said, raising my voice to be heard over the noise.

"Sam," she said, spinning around. A smile came to her face as she laid the spoons and forks on the counter, then stepped over and gave me a hug. "I didn't hear the door."

Although it was quiet enough in the bedroom community where Margarite and Thomas Veles lived—Maggie and Tom to their friends—I still wondered about their practice of leaving the front door unlocked. But I had been scolded enough for knocking, so I wandered in whenever I found it open.

Just like family.

The thought produced a mix of elation and disbelief because that was what I was about to become. In fact, Nicole—Tom and Maggie's daughter— and I had made this trip from St. Louis so that we could tell our parents. We'd already made the stop at the farm where I had been born and raised, telling my folks. They were excited about the news, of course, but it would be different here. Her family wore their hearts on their sleeves, which was quite different from my upbringing. So, while I wasn't worried—well, not too much anyway—I wasn't sure what to expect.

I believed her father liked me in the same gruff, cynical way he felt about almost everyone. But if he had reservations, they would be more than offset by Maggie. In her, I had a staunch ally.

It hadn't always been that way, or at least, that was what Nicole had told me. According to her, after my first visit nearly a year and a half ago, Maggie had started crying. In truth, I really couldn't blame her. At the time, my right arm had been in a sling and the parts of my face not covered in cuts and scrapes showed bruises that were just starting to turn greenish-yellow. To make myself a little more presentable, I'd attempted to shave left-handed, resulting in a fresh set of nicks. And to top it off, the last of the painkillers I'd taken for my injuries were just leaving my system, so I don't remember exactly what I said to her. At that moment, I'm sure Maggie was wondering what she had done wrong for Nicole to even take a second look at me.

But that was history. And after another 17 months of visits to my soon-to-be in-laws with not so much as a paper cut, they had come to accept me. In fact, the tables had turned so far that according to Nicole, her mother's favorite admonition had become, "you should be nicer to Sam." And while it was true that Nicole was a direct, tell-it-like-it-is woman and that could sometimes produce raw feelings, over the long haul I appreciated her approach to our relationship. I never had to wonder if she meant what she said or look for hidden meaning in some cryptic phrase. Add that to the fact that I found her consistently fascinating and cute as hell, and I was completely captivated by her.

"I still don't know why you two came in during the week?"

"Something about that art store that's not open on the weekend," I replied to Maggie's question. Fortunately, I had overheard Nicole's end of the phone conversation, all the little white lies, when she told her mom to expect us. But that begged the question, why was she asking me when Nicole had already told her?

"So, where's my daughter?" Maggie asked, stepping back to look at the door, then me.

"At Jenn's. Something about work."

What am I thinking? My on-the-fly rationale was about as lame as could be. Nicole was a biomedical engineer, enthralled by the technology and helping people; Jenn did something in marketing or public relations. I wasn't certain, but I doubted they ever talked about work longer than ten seconds. Even their pastimes had little in common. Nicole favored reading and art, while Jenn's distractions involved friends – shopping, gambling, movies.

If Maggie wasn't suspicious before, she was now. She stepped back, her eyes narrowing. "They're doing what?"

"Something about a party Nicole is supposed to help host at work," I said, surprising myself with the plausibility of my impromptu fib. But I also felt bad about it. I liked Maggie, and the ruse was already troubling my conscience. But if I broke the news of our engagement without her, Nicole probably wouldn't speak to me for a year. So, I changed the topic. "We've been doing some interesting stuff at work."

"Oh?" Maggie said, one eyebrow rising.

I suspected the change in topic was already working, quieting the alarm in her head ... or maybe just burying it under a layer of perplexity. Although in a completely different realm, my career in cognitive science applied to training was nearly as technical as Nicole's. Perhaps more so, if you considered I was trying to work with the biggest black box in existence—the human brain. But regardless of which of us faced the bigger challenge, Nicole's and my work would never be a topic of conversation around the Veles's dinner table. Tom and Maggie were proud of their daughter, but they didn't share her or my fascination with science and technology.

Unfortunately, my inner calm lasted only a moment as Maggie asked, "So, Jenn is off work today, too?" She was undoubtedly wondering why two of her four daughters had taken the same day off and why they were talking at Jenn's house after Nicole and I had driven four hours across the state of Missouri to see her and Tom. Good questions all, for which I had no answers.

I stuck my hands in my pockets, walked over to the kitchen table, and sat. I wasn't tired; I was stalling, hoping something would come to mind. Unfortunately, nothing did except another change in topic. "Yeah, I guess so. Tom around?"

"At his brother's. He'll be back soon."

"Good."

Maggie's eyes narrowed as she studied me again. I pulled my phone from a pocket, thinking that would reduce the chance she would read something in my face. But before I even had it turned on, I put it back. As many times as Nicole and I had joked about trading texts for talk, social media posts for conversation, she'd know something was wrong if I started fiddling with my phone now. "Plant a garden this year?" I asked, rubbing a hand over my forehead.

Maggie had returned to the silverware but laid it back down with my question. She turned fully toward me. "Sam Price, just what ...."

Like her daughter, Maggie only used my full name when I was in trouble. Fortunately, the sound of the front door interrupted her as I released a silent sigh of relief. In a moment, Tom came in, saying, "Look who I found in the driveway. Daughters number 1 and 2." It was a running joke as if he couldn't remember all four names. Nicole and Jenn followed him through the kitchen door. "How was the drive in, Doc?" he asked, using the nickname that everyone used. Everyone, that is, except Nicole, Maggie, and my mom.

"Uneventful. The best kind, Tom," I replied, standing to shake his hand.

Tom believed in tradition, and I didn't expect these types of formalities to end when Nicole announced our news. But still, it would end that feeling I was walking on eggshells around Maggie. Unfortunately, Nicole didn't feel the same sense of urgency. She wandered to the refrigerator to get a drink.

I reseated myself at the table, Tom sitting across from me and taking up a newspaper that was lying there. "Let's see what's going on in the world."

Jenn came in and sat beside me. Despite the year-and-a-half difference in their ages, she and Nicole could have been twins. They had the same light brown hair, matching fair complexions, and identical deep-brown, doe eyes. In fact, the first time I met Jenn, I did a double take. She had just opened her parents' front door to my knock, and I wasn't certain that Nicole hadn't altered her hairstyle a bit, maybe lost a little of her tan. Fortunately, a small voice said something wasn't quite right. That along with Jenn's puzzled look saved me from embarrassment. Of course, since I wasn't even to the point of giving Nicole a casual peck on the cheek at the time, my discomfort would have been limited to using the wrong name.

My eyes returned to Nicole, but she was still in no hurry to break the news. She took a sip of her drink, then walked over and looked at the paper her dad was reading. "Hmm, upper-seventies today. Sounds nice. Sam, maybe we should go for a hike?"

"OK," I said slowly. Tom was still looking at his paper, but Maggie's gaze was tracking back and forth between us. I'd had a couple of close calls in my life—complete flukes in my line of mostly desk-bound work—but this was as nerve-racking as either of them. If this went on much longer, I'd have to excuse myself to use the bathroom.

Nicole turned to her mom. "Got your garden started yet?"

I gasped. I hoped it was silent, but from the corner of my eye, I caught the motion of Jenn turning to look at me and knew it wasn't. And now, Maggie was going to say, "Sam's already tried to distract me with that question. What's going on with you two anyway?" The fact that I had raised Maggie's suspicions but hadn't completely spilled the beans would probably mean Nicole's displeasure with me would only last a month.

But perhaps Maggie read the dynamics and decided to spare me. Or maybe she knew what was coming and was letting her daughter build the suspense. But whatever the case, all she said was, "I've got my early vegetables in. Are you planning on finding space for a garden of your own?"

"Probably not," Nicole replied. "It would be my luck that the tomatoes would rot on the vine ... while I'm on my honeymoon."

Maggie dropped the last fork on the floor and hurried across the room to hug her daughter. It seemed to take Tom a moment to understand the implications of Nicole's words—at least, that was the way I chose to interpret his hesitation because I didn't want to consider the alternative. But after a moment, he let his paper fall, took my hand again, and said, "It's about time."

What does that mean?

But the thought disappeared as it now made little difference. Our news was public, her parents were happy, and I was relieved. Now, I could come in the front door unannounced without a concern ... just like family.

SUNDAY, MAY 5

11:22 AM – The Evangelical Church of the Rock

The Reverend Micah Eastin raised his arms to his sides, his black, knit shirt under the dark, blue blazer stretching tight across his chest. His gaze drifted slowly across the congregation. Sally Hoker's boy—was it Joel—had lain down in the pew, and now the heels of his shoes were drumming against the wood. She grabbed his collar, pulled him up, and whispered something in his ear. He sat like a statue ... at least for the moment.

The Reverend's gaze moved on. Emily Brady was holding her crying baby girl close, trying to bounce her without really moving. It wasn't working, and Pat reached his hands toward his wife. She shook her head, moved to the end of the pew in a crouch, and left the nave. Piping his sermon into the basement nursery had been one of the best decisions he had ever made.

His look reached another, older couple. They were new to the church. The man was stooped by years of hard labor, his wife a mere wisp of a woman. Reverend Eastin thought he recognized the overly solicitous behavior they showed each other. He'd seen it before, many times, just before one of a long-married couple was to die. He would talk to them after the service.

It was a good crowd. In excess of 300 if Reverend Eastin was right, and he had, over the years, become quite adept in gauging the church's draw. When he had started, he was lucky to bring in 30. His current flock was also a good cross-section of the people who lived in the surrounding towns and on the nearby farms, albeit one that was slanted toward the older generations. The draw of St. Louis, some 55 miles to the north and east, was too much to hold the kids. But that was fine with the Reverend because the older generation was more devout, more urgent in their search for eternal life. His younger followers, while fewer in number, would grow into that mold. And their ranks would swell, as their peers came to recognize the impermanence of life.

The congregation quieted. He ran a hand through his thick, brown hair and smiled at the group. "Welcome friends and neighbors. We are truly blessed by this beautiful spring morning." The room was filled with nodding heads, and he heard a few, quiet "amens."

"If you would," Reverend Eastin continued, "look to your left." Heads turned hesitantly; he waited for everyone to comply. "Now to the right." The gazes swung in unison. "Aren't those stained-glass windows beautiful? Truly, works of art." This time, the nods were more forceful, the amens a bit louder.

"But make no mistake, brothers and sisters, beyond their beauty, we—each and every one of us ..."—he paused, letting his pointing finger sweep across the room—"we are surrounded by evil."

Over the years, the Reverend had spoken of many evils from his pulpit: the cavalier treatment of sex in popular culture, rampant crime, bullying in the schools. But in particular, he took pride in identifying social ills before they became national headlines, and today, he had just such a revelation for them. True, it was an extension of a malady he had spoken of before—several times. But in its growth, there was greater malevolence, and with that came the capacity to incite his flock to more ardent stewardship.

"A few years ago, I stood before you and told you of the coming opioid crisis." Heads nodded. "Reverend Eastin, you ask—how bad has it become since your early predictions? It's bad. Bad enough that we can expect nearly a thousand deaths across our great state this year alone. And why? Because the men of medicine who peddled this drug put greed before truth. They told us opioids weren't addictive. I hope they repented their evil ways. I hope they did because otherwise, a special place has been reserved for them in Hell!" It was the first time Reverend Eastin had raised his voice, and the calls of amen matched his volume.

"Is change in this epidemic before us, you may ask? I say, it is not. Nothing will change because despite all the evidence—the addiction, the betrayals, the deaths—the men of medicine will not allow it. They continue to foist their false beliefs upon us. In fact, if the group assembled in this house of worship represents the norm for our state, we will be told over 215 times in the coming year, 'here, take this drug, it'll fix everything.' And under their breath, the men of medicine will whisper, 'and it will make you its slave.' Two hundred and fifteen times! That's the number of prescriptions for opioids the 300 of us could expect if we represent the state's norm. Thankfully, we're not average."

Although seventy prescriptions per one hundred didn't necessarily mean that over two hundred in his flock were users—some individuals would receive several scripts, while many would get none—Reverend Eastin still recognized the number as a good wake-up call. And with it, he expected accusatory glances to sweep the room. They all knew each other's business, as well as their aches and pains. He even considered asking the congregation to keep their eyes on him during this part of the sermon. But in the end, he decided it better to let the emotional indictments fall where they may.

"Brothers and sisters, don't misunderstand my message. The bible speaks of physicians, but it also speaks of the role of faith in the healing process. 'And the prayer of faith will save the one who is sick, and the Lord will raise him up,' says the Book of James, Chapter 5, verse 15. Seek His guidance through prayer as part of a healing regimen. Not as an afterthought, but as a guiding light. It only makes sense, doesn't it?"

Reverend Eastin paused, letting the reasonableness of his words take root. When the self-assured glances and shared nods-of-the-head ended, he continued.

"While the opioid epidemic is a plague on humanity, it is only a small part of the evil that we are about to witness." His volume had dropped, and he could see his congregation lean forward in the pews. "Because I tell you on this fifth day of May that we are about to witness a new movement in medicine. A movement that proclaims that faith is irrelevant because all things are possible through drugs and the surgeon's knife. It's no longer just opioids to mask your senses; it's a medical, get-out-of-jail-free card for every human transgression. If these men of medicine prevail, you'll be able to buy, here or abroad, from a sterile hospital or a backstreet alley, any medicine, any treatment you need to prop up your failing body. And all the while, this façade that is your physical manifestation will be hiding a soul that is rotting from within, from a mix of greed and lies and lust."

It was time to make these abstract concepts real. The Reverend pulled a piece of paper from his pocket and held it up for the crowd to see. "It's a ten-dollar-off coupon from the biggest, retail pharmacy chain in the United States. And what's it for? An emergency contraceptive. Take it within three days and the Sixth Commandment is obsolete. You don't even need a doctor's prescription; just ask at the counter. This is exactly what this movement seeks—sanctioned, commercial immorality based on medicine."

Even though this was information any of them could find in their evening paper, every head in the congregation was shaking. Reverend Eastin never doubted the power of denial.

"And if the pill doesn't work, there's always the abortionist's knife. True, we—you and I—we have fought the good fight against abortion in this state. We've stood shoulder-to-shoulder in protest until we were ready to drop. We've written letters to our representatives in government until our hands cramped. Unfortunately, much of what we've accomplished is to force our young women across state lines. Last year, nearly half of the 7,000 abortions performed in the state of Kansas involved women with Missouri addresses. How many more unborn were killed in Illinois? We don't know; that state doesn't even bother to count. But I say to you, we are a beacon of hope to our neighbors. Don't let this medicine-is-all movement dim our light."

Reverend Eastin paused, letting the murmured words of determination fade. "Lest you believe this evil lives only in the big cities back east or the sprawling metropolises out west, let me correct that misperception. One of the chief proponents of this movement has called St. Louis home for the last six years—Dr. James Conroy, Jr. He tells a heartbreaking story of the death of a sister after a botched abortion. Truly, a sad tale and he uses it to justify killing the unborn. But never once does Dr. Conroy mention the sanctity of the two lives that were lost that night. He is blind. He has made a pact with the devil. I ask you to pray for him because his days on earth are numbered!"

The Reverend shouted, the congregation leaning forward to embrace his indignation, not avoid it.

"I will," said Layton Tyler from his regular spot in the third row. Reverend Eastin smiled and nodded at the man. He could always count on Tyler, and a dozen more like him, to take up his causes.

"You may be asking yourself, but what can we do, Brother Eastin? I say to you, your voices shall be heard. Even though the battle for minds and souls will be waged in the cities and towns across the nation, the war will be won in Washington, DC. There, we have a voice in Dr. Jerry Tibbs. But unfortunately, Brother Tibbs lacks the means to extend our fight against opioids to the broader hypocrisy of the medical community. His odds will be worse than David facing Goliath with his sling empty of stones. We must arm him. So, brothers and sisters, we will need that additional five dollars, or ten, or a hundred, if we are to turn back the forces of Satan. I ask you to dig deep, find it in your hearts and your souls and your pockets to assure our victory."

Volunteers began passing through the room, collecting the congregation's offering envelopes. And along with those regular donations in their yellow sleeves, bills started appearing from purses and billfolds. Reverend Eastin nodded at the assembled group, now believing this clash with medicine could be the rallying cry he had hoped.

MONDAY, MAY 6

1:22 AM – The Campus of St. Louis University

shadow slid across the lawn, the ghost of a cloud floating on the breeze backlit by a half-moon in the night sky. In its wake, Sister Constance could just make out clumps of tulips, more of their petals now adorning the ground than their stems. Beyond them, a row of peonies was taking up the task of bringing color to the university campus, their sweet, spicy smell mixing with the odor of damp earth, mowed grass, and car exhaust. A dog barked in the distance. A large vehicle, probably a truck, rumbled down Highway 40, three blocks to the south. Closer, Constance heard footfalls, probably male by the gait. She couldn't see him but he smoked; the smell of a cigarette drifted to her nose.

Sister Constance had been in hiding since 10:30, her senses now finely tuned to the faintest sound, the subtlest movement, the slightest smell. So, when the band she wore on her wrist vibrated, she flinched, even though she had been waiting for its signal since arriving. At last, it was time.

She got up and moved slowly toward a building about 20 yards to the east, her black-clad figure ready to melt into the shadows at the slightest provocation. But finding no need to hide, she reached the structure in moments. She moved silently along its edge, keeping in the shadow produced by the moonlight and the dim rays of a floodlight mounted on the roof. Her hand trailed along the wall, feeling the cool, rough texture on her fingertips. The building was four stories, made of brick outlined with white stone. Ahead, there was a structure of similar style but only two floors. A one-story passageway connected them. She stepped into the U-shaped recess formed by the two buildings and their connector. She looked outward. Straight ahead, there was an open area with grass and a large tree, its long, slender branches drooping toward the ground. She knew the scene well. Everything was right, exactly where it should be.

Constance turned and faced the shorter of the two buildings. She tugged on the straps of the small backpack she wore, rocked back, and then raced forward. Just before reaching the wall, she leaped, planting her right foot at nearly the height of her five-foot, ten-inch frame. Momentum carried her forward, her right leg and both arms coiling against the structure. Then, in a single, fluid motion she spun and leaped back toward the wall behind her. This time, the increase in altitude was only about two feet but still upward. She spun again, gaining even less, but with that final leap, she should reach the top of the passageway.

But as luck would have it, her last foothold was just above the joint between two bricks and her foot slipped. The fraction of an inch she lost sealed her fate, and she fell back to the ground. Looking up, her body started to tremble with a rage directed inward. She slapped her face with her right hand, the viciousness of the blow bringing tears to her eyes. She pounded her fists against her legs as if punishing them for letting her down.

After a moment, her self-control returned. She retraced her steps to the starting point and tried again. This time, she succeeded, with almost the full length of her fingers gaining purchase on the top edge of the passageway wall. Pulling herself up over the edge, she dropped down to the surface of the roof and rolled to her back. It was warm, the heat stored there from the daytime sun. It seeped through her clothes, letting her muscles relax. After a few moments, her heart rate had returned to normal. She cautiously peered over the edge, checking for the signs that would dictate her next actions. No one was in view. The world was silent; even the locusts and crickets seemed to have called it a night. It was the best of all the possible situations she had practiced.

Constance crawled across the roof to a window located on the four-story building. After cleaning part of the glass with a hand, she pulled a suction cup from her backpack and attached it to the window. A heave upward failed to move it. She tried again with the same result. The window was locked. She removed the suction cup and turned it backward, placing the metal, pump handle against the glass. Then, she drove her hand into the rubber cup. The glass cracked but didn't break. With a second blow, the pane shattered and dropped to the floor inside the building.

Constance dived to the surface of the passageway roof, quickly securing the suction cup in her backpack. She listened. Nothing. The world still slept. After a moment, she peered over the edge of the roof. Still, no one. A check through the shattered window yielded the same information; all was clear. After removing a few shards from the window frame and laying them quietly on the roof, she pulled herself through.

Constance knew three ways to get to her goal and four ways out. With no one in sight, she took the quickest, easiest route and was soon standing outside a door with familiar numbers—332. To its left, there was a small table. A tray with some papers rested on its top, an empty shelf below. To the right sat two chairs. Everything was there, just as it should be.

She laid her backpack on the floor and carefully removed a small package wrapped in brown paper. Her fingers probed its back, finding a soft spot in the otherwise solid surface. Pulling the box to her ear, she pushed, careful not to tear the paper. The expected soft click reached her ear. She placed the box on the open shelf. Now, she only needed to exit the building and go home to her reward. It was what she lived for.

5:22 AM – The Campus of St. Louis University

The night sky was starting to brighten, although sunrise was still more than a half-hour away. As he climbed the stairs, Dr. John Huether could just make out the lawns and gardens outside the windows on each landing. The sidewalks that crisscrossed the campus seemed an ethereal network, dim bands of gray concrete connecting spheres of brilliance under the streetlights.

Huether exited the stairwell and walked to his office, briefcase in one hand, a large coffee in the other. He placed his drink on the floor so he could dig through his pockets for his keys. He wasn't a morning person; he'd need that liquid kickstart if he was going to do anything but yawn in this morning's meeting. But the loss of a couple of hours of sleep was nothing. They were a mere trifle in what he had already sacrificed to reach this point in his career. First, his long hours of research had cost his marriage. Then, his kids had turned their backs. Now, he only saw them around Christmas when disinterested civility became the replacement for holiday cheer. Even his colleagues at the university had become aloof, the cost, he believed, of his looming victories.

Huether glanced at the table outside his office, its tray filled with papers from anxious students. How many of those pages, he wondered, would be excuses, requests for extensions to work that was already overdue? Or past assignments "accidentally" re-submitted, giving the tardy another day or two until he brought the error to their attention. And even with their manufactured delay, most of them still wouldn't finish. Didn't they know, he'd seen it all before?

Today's meeting with Ridgeway Pharmaceuticals was the first step in leaving all that behind: the jealous colleagues, the procrastinating students, even his demanding ex-wife. And perhaps, it was even the means for him to make it up to his kids; he'd like to try. Today's confab had that potential because it was the first of three with a major drug manufacturer, all interested in the new delivery system he had designed for flu vaccines.

True, treating the flu wasn't sexy. But the fact was his system might save as many as a third of the 36,000 lives lost each year to the illness, as well as millions of dollars in lost productivity. Those kinds of numbers made up for a lot of humdrum in his research. They drew national attention and, more importantly to him, brought new career opportunities. He had already narrowed the field to three of the major players, and within a few weeks, that number would be one.

Huether propped the office door open with his briefcase so he could retrieve the students' papers. But as he did, he noticed a package. His eyes narrowed. He had heard stories of under-the-table "signing bonuses," but he doubted they were true. It seemed ludicrous that a pharmaceutical company would give him an inducement without any type of commitment on his part. But after confirming the name on the package, he scooped it up with the papers and brought it into his office. There, he placed it on a bookcase across the room, taking the papers to his desk.

After retrieving his coffee and briefcase, he dropped into his chair and glanced at the first paper. It was actually the assigned work, although it was so short, he couldn't imagine it would warrant anything above a C. He took a sip of coffee, looking across the room. His thoughts were pulled along with his gaze. He needed something besides caffeine to wake his mind, and there sat the package. And since he had nearly memorized the promotional materials on Ridgeway, it was the better option.

He stood and walked to the bookcase, picking up the box to examine it more closely. It was heavier than he had realized earlier. Then, ironically, he brought the package to his ear just as a soft tone emanated from within. The sound, however, never registered in his brain as the package exploded in a brilliant ball of flame. A fragment of metal propelled by the blast ripped through his jugular vein, and he crumpled to the floor. Had he been conscious, he might have prolonged his life by pressing on the wound, slowing the flow of blood, but his mind was filled with darkness.

In the seven minutes it took another early riser to find him, Dr. John Huether bled to death.

7:43 AM – An Apartment in the Soulard Neighborhood

FBI Special Agent Rebecca Marte opened a bleary, blue eye to stare at the phone ringing on her bedside stand. She'd only been asleep for about three hours after pulling a late night conducting an "assessment." According to the Attorney General's guidelines, that designation for an FBI operation permitted, among other things, physical surveillance of public activities based on "an authorized purpose." And that purpose was easily established for the Council for the Right. The stream of denunciations of black Muslims that emanated from their home base some 30 miles west and south of St. Louis had become increasingly vile and hate-filled over recent months.

Rebecca doubted that many of the local businessmen and farmers in the Council had met a black Muslim. So far, she hadn't found even one, but that didn't keep them from hating. The topic of discussion last night, however, had been the spring weather and its probable effect on crops. The assemblage knew their livelihoods hinged on the unpredictability of Mother Nature, and they'd put their vitriol aside for the night to lament their dependence. In fact, Rebecca's only, semi-relevant observation for the evening was that membership in the Council evidently came with the right to harass the catering crew, of which she was a member for the night. She was certain she'd find a handprint on her butt if she looked, and it had taken most of her willpower to keep from beating the crap out of a couple of them. But then, the FBI tended to frown on such behavior.

Rebecca blinked, trying to read the phone with one eye. Had she forgotten to put it in the do-not-disturb mode before falling into bed still in her catering uniform? She thought not, meaning that the caller was one of the handful who could bypass that block. She sat up, and after using both eyes to decipher the display, she found her boss's name. "Special Agent Rebecca Marte," she said. While her boss didn't demand the formality, he had once handed his phone to a district director after dialing her. The director didn't think much of her greeting, "Spit it out, Chuck."

"Rise and shine, Rebecca," came Chuck Wheeler's deep baritone over the speaker. "Long night, drinking with the boys down south?"

"Not funny. More like a long night carrying trays of beer and wings to frustrated, middle-aged men. It'll be a week before I get the smell of smoke and buffalo sauce out of my hair. And they're not even supposed to be smoking."

Wheeler snorted. "I'd say, cut your hair, but you don't have much left."

Rebecca ran a hand through her short, light-blonde hair. Even without a mirror, she knew it now had that spiky, just-out-of-the-shower look she wore around the office. She didn't really care for the style and it was probably unnecessary, but it had slowed some of the handsy recruits at the FBI

Academy and she had stuck with it. She'd seen what an office romance had done for her dad when her mother left the police department where they both worked, putting both her and her dad in the rearview mirror. She wanted no part of that drama. A nice, boring, yet loyal accountant was closer to her ideal. Well, that and being good in bed.

"So, all quiet then?" asked Wheeler.

"It's always possible that someone's stirring up trouble in the backrooms, but if so, I didn't see it. You'll get my report. But I doubt you called at the crack of my dawn for status. What's up?"

"Yeah, sorry about the timing, but things have unraveled with your wanna-be Unabomber. She just graduated to the big time."

"Shit," Rebecca mumbled over the phone.

A small part of her displeasure stemmed from the nickname Wheeler had adopted—"wanna-be Unabomber." True, there were some similarities between the infamous domestic terrorist, Ted Kaczynski, and Sister Constance, notably their preferred instrument of violence. They both mailed or hand-delivered bombs to their intended victims. But most of her irritation came from the implications of the moniker. The Unabomber had evaded an FBI-led joint task force composed of 125 agents for nearly 18 years. Rebecca found it unacceptable to suggest such a thing might happen again.

The nickname also glossed over vast differences between Kaczynski and Constance. Where he worked from the shadows of his isolated cabin in Montana targeting leaders in technology and industrialization broadly, Constance and her "Crusaders for Common Sense" operated in a limelight that grew daily, and their hate focused solely on people with medical expertise.

The group's public persona had been built on social media. They didn't maintain a website; even with the most convoluted and highly encrypted routing, that site would be tracked back to them eventually. Rather, they used readily available, public hotspots and one of the growing number of laptops you could buy for a few hundred dollars—always purchased with cash. They would set up an account and broadcast their message in a series of posts, tweets, and emails, the latter directed to the media. The machines, often covered with fingerprints, were left behind in the bookstores and coffee shops where they were used. Constance and her cohorts appeared convinced that this forensic evidence couldn't be linked with their identities, and so far, they were right.

The social media accounts were taken down as fast as they were discovered, of course, but even with the quickest response, it was too late. The public had started routinely searching online for any mentions of Sister Constance, her group, or her infamous tagline, "Stop Playing God with Medicine," so even a two-minute delay was 119.9 seconds too long. And the number of these morbidly curious fans would skyrocket if Rebecca interpreted her boss's words correctly.

"So, we have a body this time?" she asked. Constance's first two attempts had been near misses. The FBI probably wouldn't have even known they were dealing with a potential serial hate killer if the Crusaders hadn't publicized the fact.

Rebecca could hear Wheeler blow out a long breath before he answered. "Yep, 'fraid so. A Dr. John Huether at St. Louis University. He had some type of dual teaching and research appointment. The research was on flu medicines, and supposedly his results had the potential to be a game changer. I'll text you the address."

"OK," replied Rebecca. "Constance already take credit for this one?"

"She has, which is probably the only reason we're talking. If forensics had to find all the similarities, it would have been a while. But the Crusaders lit up the Internet within minutes of the attack. Must have had it all typed up in advance." Wheeler paused a beat. "I'm calling in Clements to give you a hand."

"OK," Rebecca said slowly, wondering what her boss's pause had meant. Then, she got it. "I'm still going to have the lead, right?"

"With just you and Clements, sure. But if the powers that be want someone more seasoned in the lead of a bigger team ...." He didn't get a chance to finish.

"Damn it, Chuck."

Wheeler knew what was coming and headed her off. "Easy, Rebecca. We're looking at three prominent individuals being attacked, leaving one dead. You've done great so far, and I'll make a case for you keeping the lead."

"And the powers that be, as you call them, will never leave this in my hands, will they?"

Wheeler paused again, with Rebecca hearing a second sigh over the line. "Probably not," he said after a moment.

"OK. And thanks for being straight with me. I'm heading out to SLU."

She broke the connection, afraid her irritation might come through. It was pointless to shoot the messenger. She even admitted to herself that he was probably right. She was less than a year out of the Academy and had never led a team … unless you considered her and her sometimes partner and full-time mentor, Senior Special Agent Gus Clements, a team. But just because her boss was right didn't mean she liked being demoted.

7:35 PM – A Lambert St. Louis Airport Hotel

In the waning light of day, her reflected image in the hotel's window was ghostly. Dressed in black, the pale, white skin of her face and neck was almost translucent in the fading rays. Her eyes were dark orbs, hidden in shadow. The spectral image was spoiled, however, by a mane of frizzy, red hair, its fiery color dimmed little by the fading daylight.

Sheila Moore silently berated herself for her disheveled look. Although she had been in and out of the Midwest several times in the last six months, she still hadn't mastered the vagaries of its ever-changing weather. The unruliness of her hairdo was the result of getting caught in a brief shower that morning, although the remaining humidity might have been enough to undo her coiffure anyway. At least now she owned a warm coat, that lesson learned from one of her first excursions. The light jacket she wore on the flight from her home in Arizona did little to offset the windchill of the unpredicted Minneapolis snowstorm when she landed.

Moore turned from the window and scanned the crowd waiting outside the hotel ballroom. The gathering was large, one of the biggest she had seen for this talk, and she had witnessed many of them. She pushed her way through the throng, the maneuver serving double duty. She wanted to be near the doors when they opened, but the move also brought her closer to a five-foot-tall poster of the reason she was here.

The man who stared back at her from the wall made her heart beat faster. She remembered the first time they had met. It was only a handshake, but the electricity in his touch had taken her breath away. She felt it now as if his hand was caressing her, leaving a tingling wake in its path over her arm, across her neck, up to a cheek. She shivered with the imagined caress.

Moore moved closer to the picture, though she had no need to study it. The man wasn't traditionally handsome, with short, curly brown hair, a neatly trimmed beard, tanned skin, and black-framed glasses. But to judge him from external appearances was like declaring a geode nothing but a rock, when in fact the plain surface hid a dazzling secret in its crystalline core. The man's inner beauty came from his intellect, and Moore couldn't match it. Few could. But she possessed a yin for his yang. It was her passion. The heat of her emotions, her love was the perfect complement for the power of his mind.

The time for the doors to open was quickly approaching, and Moore abandoned decorum. She started elbowing her way to the front, her drive fueled by the knowledge that the seat she occupied during the show would be as close as she got tonight. She wanted to see him after the show, even if only for another handshake. But she knew she wouldn't, knew she couldn't. And with the lights in his eyes, he wouldn't even know she was there. And yet, perhaps he would sense her, feel her love reaching out to him. She could hope.

Progress was slow, and Moore looked upstream. A man was making his way through the crowd, apparently trying to leave. Despite the mass of humanity pushing against him, he appeared serene. His green eyes calmly surveilled the crowd, seeking the path of least resistance. He paused, a hand coming up to push a shock of brown hair off his forehead. He adjusted his path slightly, now heading directly for her.

"I think you're going the wrong way," she said when the man broke through the last of the people between them.

"Not if you're leaving," he said simply. His hand went to his hair again, making Moore wonder if this was a nervous tic. He had, after all, done it twice in less than a minute. But with his face radiating such self-possessed confidence, she decided it was a signature mannerism, like the way some women toss their hair when speaking. His hair falling on his forehead gave him something of a naughty-boy look. His muscled arms and fitted shirt further promoted that impression.

On a whim, she extended a hand. "Sheila Moore. And I think you're going to miss a good show."

"Reverend Micah Eastin," he replied, taking her hand. But rather than shaking it, he held it flat on his palm, like it was a delicate flower to be admired.

Moore blushed, recalling the description she had just applied to this man of the cloth. And yet, it fit. Her hand felt cold as she pulled it from his. "I would think the uplifting message you would hear tonight would be right up your alley."

"Yes, it is something that would ... arouse my congregation, but I don't need to hear every word to know that. I did, however, want to get a sense of his following, and I have. Ms. Moore," he said, slightly bowing his head. "It was a pleasure to meet you."

"And you," Moore replied.

Moore's eyes watched as the Reverend walked away. His looks stirred her emotions, and his oddly formal mannerisms intrigued her. And yet, he couldn't hold a candle to the man she had come to see.

She continued forward. Finally, the doors to the ballroom opened, and with a final push, she was inside. Once again, it was time to see Jimmy, as she thought of him.

Same Time, Same Place

Dr. James Conroy, Jr., paced across the narrow hallway behind the hotel's main ballroom. Five steps, just like it had been the first time he made the trip. And just like that trek, he took a deep, cleansing breath before turning to complete the loop. As he neared a curtain covering the ballroom's entrance, he listened to the words drifting through the dark red fabric.

"It's an honor and a privilege to introduce tonight's speaker." Conroy started another lap.

His pre-show anxiety, although unpleasant, was normal. He'd even decided if it ever vanished completely, it was probably time to quit. But since he had only one more show, on Thursday, his jitters would outlast his onstage career. In fact, for that last rally, it would be much more than the usual butterflies, but that was a concern for later. Right now, he had a show to do. He paused at the wall, took his calming breath, and turned.

During the course of many people's lives, they had felt the sting of medical help just beyond their reach. Whether it was a treatment banned in this country, a drug priced out of their financial reach, or a roadblock of endless paperwork, people had found themselves helpless, devoid of hope in the face of a massive bureaucracy that was the United States healthcare system. Tonight, he would remind them of those slumbering emotions. Tonight, once again, he would tell his story. And though the images he would describe were 32 years in his past, they formed a vision that was never far from his thoughts.

* * *

His sister's voice tugged at the corners of his sleeping mind. "Jimmy, wake up."

A fourteen-year-old James Conroy, Jr., turned his back. "Leave me alone, Diane. It's the middle of the night."

"Jimmy, you have to wake up. I need you." His sister's voice was soft, almost breathless. The presence of their parents just down the hall might explain some of that. But he heard something else in her tone—an urgency? A fear? He rolled to face her. Her outline appeared in his open door, illuminated by the dim glow of a hall light beyond. Her tall, slender figure was bent as if pressed down by some unknown weight. He stared into the gloom, but her face was lost in shadow. "What is it, sis?"

"I need you to ... to drive me to the hospital."

"What are you talking about?" he asked, shaking his head, wondering if the sound of his heart beating in his ears could all be part of a dream. "I'm not even old enough for a learner's permit."

"You can do it," Diane replied softly.

She turned, looking back through the door. As she did, Jimmy caught the reflection of a sheen of sweat on her face. He sat up. She turned back, steadying herself with a hand on the doorframe.

"You don't look good. I'm getting Dad."

"No, you can't. He'd kill me," Diane whispered. She stepped into the room, her hand shooting out to grab his arm. But the sudden move threw her off balance, and she dropped her hand to the bed to keep from falling. Her arm trembled with the effort. She inhaled deeply and released a long, ragged breath. "I need to go to the emergency room. They'll fix me up, and we'll be home before Mom and Dad know anything."

Jimmy stared, seeking understanding in his sister's face, but finding only darkness. "I don't know, Diane."

"I've got the money and I'll be fine ... if you get moving. I'll be in the car." Diane started toward the door, shuffling her feet. The night was cool, as October evenings in the Missouri Ozarks could be. But even so, the long coat she wore spoke of a snowy winter day, not the cool night air from his open window. She disappeared into the hall.

Jimmy stood and then dropped back to his bed. He raised a fist to his mouth, biting his flesh as if the pain might bring an answer. He should wake his dad. He'd know what to do. But he couldn't. Diane had always been there for him, whether it was something with their parents or school ... or even girls. He couldn't let her down. And if there was another answer, Diane would have thought of it. She was the smart one.

Jimmy got up quietly and pulled on a pair of jeans, T-shirt, and tennis shoes. Tiptoeing down the stairs, he found the light on in the entry hall, the front door still ajar. Diane must already be in her car. He started for the door but stopped short, noticing a dark spot on the wood floor. He looked closer, learning only that it was wet; the hall light reflected back into his eyes from its surface. His gut, however, already knew what he would find when he dabbed at it with a finger. Even so, his heart rate spiked when he saw the bright crimson on his pale skin.

Jimmy looked back toward the room where his parents lay sleeping, his breath catching in his throat. He started for the stairs, only to stop and turn back to the door. Surely, it was just a matter of an hour or two at the hospital and Diane would be fine, just as she had said. Jimmy left the house, closing the door quietly behind him and hurried to Diane's car.

Diane was already sitting in the passenger seat, so Jimmy slid behind the wheel, closed the door, and started the engine with the keys he found in the ignition. His fingers came away sticky. In the glow from the dashboard, they looked black, but he knew better. He cracked the door, needing to see his sister's face, needing to know this was the right thing to do. But before he could ask, he saw more blood dripping to the floor mat from the hem of her coat.

Jimmy drew back, his hand flying to his face where it left a trail of red across his cheek and chin. "Diane, there's blood everywhere."

Diane turned to him, her face ashen, her eyes glassy and unfocused. "An abortion .... Something went wrong," she said so softly Jimmy could hardly hear.

Jimmy started trembling, his eyes becoming moist. "I can't do this. I have to get Dad."

"No time. Drive. Now." Those four words took the last of Diane's energy, and she collapsed against the car door.

Jimmy glanced back at his home, wiping tears from his eyes. He could wake Dad and they'd be on their way within minutes, but he wasn't sure Diane had even that much time. He put the car in drive and sped down the street toward the hospital.

He hardly had the car in park before jumping out and running into the emergency entrance, yelling for help. The sight of a fourteen-year-old covered in blood galvanized a medical team, and within moments, Diane was loaded onto a gurney and moved into a treatment room. Jimmy identified himself and his sister, but the admitting nurse balked when he promised to pay in cash. 'Where are your parents?' she wanted to know.

Jimmy hated to betray his sister, but he couldn't do this alone. He gave the nurse the information she sought and was then shown to a waiting room. Some of the staff came out to console him, but he ignored them all. He sat in a corner, his head in his hands, his lips trembling as he fought against the tears.

How could this have happened? He had his suspicions.

His sister had only broken up with her longtime boyfriend a few weeks ago. A pregnancy she refused to terminate seemed the likely cause. But if so, why had she changed her mind? And where had she gone for help? He glanced at his surroundings, his tears of pain now laced with anger. Where was her old boyfriend? Where were these doctors and nurses when she needed them earlier? If anything happened to her .... He couldn't finish the thought, didn't want to consider the possibility.

"Jimmy, are you all right?"

"Mom." Jimmy jumped up from the chair and ran to her, no longer able to fight the tears. "How's Diane?" he managed to ask between sobs.

"Your dad's talking to the doctors, but I'm sure she'll be fine." Jimmy recognized the emptiness of her words, even without the crack in her voice. "Go wash your face in the bathroom."

"But, Mom, I want to wait for Dad."

"It'll only take a second. Now go, before you get blood on anything else. And bring back a damp paper towel." Jimmy pulled back from his mom, seeing the smear of red on her shoulder. He dropped his head and shuffled to the men's room.

He scrubbed the trails left by blood-laced tears from his cheeks, dampened a few paper towels and left the bathroom. As he came into view of the waiting area, he saw his mother collapsed into the arms of his dad, her shoulders shaking in time with the sobs that reached his ears. James Sr., perhaps sensing the presence of his son, turned. His eyes were moist, the muscles working in his jaw as he fought the despair that had overtaken his wife. He raised a hand to his son, welcoming him to their embrace.

Jimmy, however, couldn't accept their comfort. He dropped the towels in the hall, turned, and ran from the building.

* * *

Guilt and shame had kept Conroy from talking about his sister's death for years. But when catharsis came six years ago, it had been sudden and unexpected, over dinner with a woman he hardly knew. That evening meal became a night of self-recrimination and tears, as he slowly and painfully unburdened his soul. And when it was over, all his earlier days of political activism felt unfocused, ineffectual. It was as if his sister was whispering in his ear, "there's a better way. They need to hear your story." And so, for the last six years, he had told it.

Conroy approached the curtain covering the entrance to the ballroom, hearing familiar words, "... followed by two years on a presidential science and technology panel investigating stem cell research." His introduction was drawing to a close. One more lap would cover comments about his testimony before Congress and his work with a Missouri representative on House Bill H.R. 7872. He turned and started for the back wall, five steps away.

His story always rekindled forgotten memories in his audience, but with Sister Constance's killing of Dr. John Huether this morning, he thought his message might stir even deeper, darker passions. That appeared to be the case, as both tonight's and Thursday's shows—the latter in a much larger venue downtown—had sold out within two hours of her attack.

The final lap ended, and Conroy peered through the curtain at the standing-room-only crowd in the 500-seat ballroom.

"And now, I give you, Dr. James Conroy, Jr." It was showtime.

Conroy wiped his hands on his pants legs and stepped through the curtain. The sea of faces he had studied only moments ago faded to apparitions behind the glare of the stage lights. But they were there. He could feel them. He could hear them—usually not words, but he knew their thoughts in the low murmur of the crowd, the shuffle of their feet, the readjusting of their positions. And occasionally, a confidence from the front row would reach his ears. "He's taller than I thought." "Now, we'll see if he's as good as everyone says." "A lot more people here than I expected."

Conroy said nothing, moving his gaze across the space, right to left, then back. Letting the crowd's anticipation build was just the first, small step in his fully choreographed dance. After a moment, they quieted. Still, he waited, three seconds, four, five. He could feel the tension in the room grow. He raised his hands into the air and shouted his trademark phrase, "We must take back our health."

The applause was loud but hardly the frenzied response he'd get to the same words when the evening was done. He knew that for a fact; he'd seen it too often in the past to have doubts.

"We're the greatest nation on Earth." The remark elicited a few scattered claps, as he anticipated. "There's a car in every garage. No, make that two ... or three. There's a chicken in every pot unless, of course, you're planning a visit to KFC." A chuckle or two. "We're five percent of the world's population, and yet, we consume twenty-five percent of its resources. We want for nothing ... except our health."

Now, the room was silent. He had their attention.

"So, how bad is our healthcare, you ask? If we're not number one, we're second, right? No, sorry. Top ten? Nope, off again. Surely, we're in the top twenty, you say. But you're still wrong." He paused, waiting for some of the unrest to dissipate.

"Let's look at life expectancy. You all want to live a long, happy, healthy life, right?" A murmur of agreement passed through the crowd.

"And yet, we aren't. Not compared to our neighbors across the globe. Of course, you're thinking that these nations where people live longer—they're all small, rich lands that can afford the best healthcare, right? Wrong again. Chile's per capita income is less than half of the United States, but their citizens live longer. How about the United Kingdom? The financial discrepancy is less, but they too outlast us by years. Our neighbors to the north, Canada? Same story. So, just where do we rank in terms of life expectancy? North of 30. Did you hear me? The citizens of more than thirty nations live longer, healthier lives than we do. Countries that are rich and poor. Big and small."

He paused again. The fraction of his audience that was primarily analytical in disposition would be pondering those numbers, forming their own conclusions with the data he had provided. But the thoughts of the vast majority would be starting to wander. Numbers didn't stir most people, so now he'd give them something to engage their emotions.

"So why, you're asking yourself, aren't we doing better? I won't lie to you. The reasons for our shortened life expectancy are many and varied: the stress of our rat-race lives, our poor diets, the lack of exercise. But each and every one of you ...." He paused, letting his accusing finger point track across the room. "You control those things. You can take a day off when you need it. You can order the salad in place of those cheesy fries. You can take the stairs and skip the elevator. Those factors are not the problem.

"The problem is, what you don't control. You don't control your own healthcare. As strange as that sounds, it's true. You've surrendered that responsibility to backroom politics and special interests. You let others dictate the treatments you can receive and the ones beyond reach. You allow big pharma to tell you what it costs. And don't even think about getting drugs from another country. That is, unless you want to wade through mountains of bureaucratic red tape or risk time in a prison cell. We have surrendered our most basic human right to care for ourselves and that's wrong. We must take back our health."

The applause was a bit louder this time and somewhat longer. Slowly, they were warming to his message, right on plan.

"And what do we get when we surrender the rights to our health? Waste, fraud, and abuse!" He paused a beat, imagining the news stories under that rubric that would be coming to the audience's minds.

"We've created government behemoths to oversee our nation's healthcare that are so immense no one could manage them. No wonder we have abuse and fraud. It's easy money. No one will notice a hundred thousand here, a million there, ten million somewhere else. And what does this vast health bureaucracy look like? One special interest group or government agency targets a specific socioeconomic need, while another wants to help people of a certain age, and a third focuses on a geographic region. How can we allocate health services to so many, distinct slivers of the population—rich or poor, young or old, black or white—and not have overlaps with excess existing next to pockets of neglect? We can't and we don't. And so, inequality and inconsistency in healthcare are the rule, not the exception."

He waited for the applause to end.

"Fraud, however, is the root problem, but perhaps not the type of fraud you're thinking. I'm talking about the lies we've let the politicians tell us for far too long. We've looked the other way when they've said, 'we know what's best for you.' They don't. They know what's best for themselves and the organizations that have bought them."

The strength of the audience's response increased again. It was time to galvanize the worries that now cluttered their thoughts.

"Giving someone else responsibility for our health only leads to tragedy," he said softly, forcing the crowd forward in their seats to catch his words. "I was only fourteen when I learned this hard, brutal fact. By making a simple, nearly foolproof, medical procedure—an abortion—available only from a backstreet butcher, my sister bled to death sitting in a car seat next to me. Of course, you may ask, why didn't she seek our parents' aid. And, yes, she should have; I should have. But curing teenage naiveté is a much taller order than simply taking back the rights to our own bodies."

Conroy returned once again to the night of her death, recounting the details of her appearance in his room, her pleas for help. He spoke of his sweaty hands on the steering wheel, driving faster than any fourteen-year-old should. He painted a vivid picture of his mother collapsing in his father's arms, a young doctor looking anywhere but their faces as he broke the news. And when Conroy finished, he paused again, this time as much for himself as the crowd. The cracks in his voice, the moistness in his eyes had not been feigned. He still felt the pain. He always would.

For their part, the crowd was silent, save the sounds of a few sniffs or a soft sob. They shared some of his agony.

When he had first started giving these talks, he had expected his audience to lash out against the current laws on abortion. He had been sorely mistaken. The religious and societal beliefs surrounding those laws were simply too deeply ingrained for a single talk to precipitate more than an evening's unease. He had come to accept that. And in its place, he had adopted a broader goal—to start a national discussion on the rights and responsibilities of personal healthcare. Simply put, if all the splintered concerns of the public could be brought together in one place, they would show medicine and big pharma for what it was—the largest, self-serving, special interest in the world. Concerns about humanity were lost in the race to be first-to-market, blocked by the barriers to foreign competition, overlooked in the administration of clinical research, and on and on.

"That's my story," Conroy said softly when he finished. "I'm sure yours is different. Maybe it was Aunt Betty dying of breast cancer because she couldn't afford to travel to a foreign country for treatment. Maybe it was a son, Johnny, denied a full life because a research company with an experimental treatment for autism hadn't yet jumped every hoop of every oversight agency known to man. Or a drug company, supplying a life-saving medicine that increased in cost 500, 1,000, 3,000 percent in one year. It happens. And much too often.

"But tell me. Since when does 'do no harm' apply only to doctors? Doesn't the government, the insurance industry, the drug companies—don't they harm us every time they say, 'trust us. We know what's best.' And all the while, they're lining their pockets. Of course, the politicians and the regulatory agencies should keep the scam artists at bay, make sure we have the best information science can provide on effectiveness and safety. They need to inform and educate. But after that I say, get the hell out of our way because we must take back our health."

The applause was longer and louder than ever. It was time to close, give them something to remember, something to talk about around the watercooler tomorrow at work. And for that purpose, last night he had penned a new ending to his talk. He thought it was good. Soon, he'd know.

"Is this change going to be hard? No, it's not. It's going to be a war!" Some rumbles returned, and Conroy waited for the crowd to settle.

"And if you don't know what I'm talking about, you must have canceled your subscription to the paper, turned off the TV, and stayed offline all day because medicine is under attack by a group with the name of the Crusaders for Common Sense. Common sense? It should be crusaders for nonsense. Crusaders for the senseless murder of prominent doctors and medical researchers. They slaughter people who could make a difference in our lives and the lives of our children. And once those pioneers are gone, those great minds that would have illuminated our future are extinguished, we have no recourse except to accept a shorter, less fulfilling existence."

Conroy paused. The sound of a single cough somewhere off to the right came to his ears; otherwise, the ballroom sat in silence. The tension was palpable. It rolled off the crowd in waves he could feel.

"Is this your war? Damn right it is. Because if we don't push back just as hard as the Crusaders—not violently, but with the same full devotion to cause—there'll be more Aunt Bettys dying of cancer and Johnnys suffering from debilitating conditions. Is that what you want? I say, no. I say ... we must take back our health!"

His words had touched the collective nerve he sought. The crowd rose to its feet in thunderous applause and shouts of resolve. Soon a chant of "take back our health, take back our health" broke out. Conroy held his hands extended in the air for several moments, bowed deeply three times and left the stage.

Over the years, he had finely tuned his expectations. He had come to believe that an hour from now, no one would remember his words beyond his trademark rallying cry. He didn't think anyone would bequeath their estate to medical research just because of what he had said. He didn't expect to see a headline on the nightly news that read, "Thousands of Conroy Followers March on Washington."

But as he stood in the back hallway, giving the crowd a moment to stew in their own indignation of rights stolen and responsibilities surrendered, he realized this meeting violated all his preconceptions. The din from beyond the curtain was deafening, the calls for reform fervent. He peeked through the cloth, finding a scene that was simultaneously humbling and chilling. At this moment, the mob could do anything. The story of Sister Constance and the Crusaders was working out better than he had ever imagined.

TUESDAY, MAY 7

11:14 AM – The Biomedical Engineering Associates Building

Nicole Veles stared at the open journal in front of her, not sure who she was trying to fool. She hadn't read a word of it in the last 30 minutes. She was too nervous. But it made little difference she wasn't reading; she had studied this particular paper so many times, she had it memorized. Her gaze drifted to a book lying face down at her elbow. A woman's piercing, dark brown eyes looked back at her from behind wire-rimmed glasses. Her lightly tanned face was framed by short, black hair with just the first touches of gray. In this picture, a slight smile played at the corners of the woman's mouth, like she knew something Nicole didn't. Of course, of that fact, Nicole was certain.

The woman on the cover was Nicole's next client, a medical researcher who stood on the cusp of greatness. She had turned her back on a life of wealth and privilege to study and treat the maladies that accompanied premature birth, working in some of the world's most beautiful and exotic locations. She had also toiled in some of its harshest and most unforgiving.

Nicole picked up the book and placed it on the shelf above her desk. Although she admired the woman greatly, it was best not to come across as a starry-eyed schoolgirl, even if that bore some resemblance to how she was feeling. And in fact, "schoolgirl" would have been appropriate only a couple of years ago, but not now. Now, she was a biomedical engineer with all the responsibilities the title implied.

The sound of footfalls reached Nicole—a man and a woman by their gait. Then, she heard the light tenor that could only be her supervisor's voice. It was time. She stood, rubbing her hands over the knees of her pants as she did, not sure if her palms were actually sweaty or if it had been an unconscious reaction. Her boss and the woman entered. He had a sheaf of papers in his hand. She was carrying a large, well-worn, leather briefcase.

"I'd like to introduce Ms. Nicole Veles, one of our up-and-coming biomedical engineers," her boss said to the woman. "And Nicole, this is—"

"I know," said Nicole, before thinking about the fact she was interrupting the man who evaluated her job performance. "Dr. Laura Greenwood, renowned cellular biologist. It's a great honor to meet you."

Greenwood's eyes twinkled as a soft laugh escaped her lips. "You have the occupation correct, but renown? I'm not so sure about that. It's nice to meet you, Ms. Veles." The women shook hands.

Nicole thought about telling her why, in her estimation, the adjective fit perfectly, but that would only increase the gap between them. Instead, she said, "Please, call me Nicole." Easy familiarity among collaborators was the better stance.

"I'd be pleased to, if you'll call me Laura."

Nicole nodded, warming in the woman's smile and easy manner.

As her boss spoke, covering the final details on building hours, parking, and the like, Nicole had a chance to observe Greenwood. The eyes that were piercing on a book cover now radiated intelligence and confidence. She had a presence as if anything she sought was now within their collective reach. She was also tall—probably a half-foot or more over Nicole's five-foot, six-inch frame—and broad. She wasn't obese; she was just ... big.

Her supervisor paused in his welcoming spiel, checking the papers he carried. Nicole's eyes were naturally drawn to the shuffling pages, but after a moment, she glanced back at Greenwood, finding the biologist studying her surroundings. Her surveillance, however, appeared anything but casual. There was an intensity in the woman's stare as if she was cataloging every item in sight for its worth to her research. But the look vanished when her boss spoke, making Nicole wonder if she had imagined it.

"Nicole, I have A27 reserved for the two of you." Then, turning to Greenwood, he added, "It's just a small office, but it'll give you two some privacy for discussing the specifications. Nicole said it best when she said it's an honor for us to be working with you. I'll leave you two to get acquainted." He shook Greenwood's hand, nodded at Nicole, and left.

"So, shall we check out our new home for the next few days?" asked Nicole.

"Absolutely," replied Greenwood. "Lead the way." Nicole scooped up her laptop and the women left.

"I was surprised and, frankly, thrilled to hear I'd be working with a female biomedical engineer," Greenwood said, glancing sideways as they walked down the hall. "I'd have to check the numbers to be sure, but women in your field may be even rarer than female cellular biologists."

Nicole laughed softly, saying, "Maybe so."

"Something funny in that?" Greenwood asked.

Nicole felt her face warm, now realizing her amusement must have been louder than she thought. "It's just that ... well, that comment sounds like something my fiancé would say. He's always checking the statistics."

"You're getting married? Congratulations. Set a date yet?"

"Not yet. We just got engaged less than three weeks ago. Told our parents this weekend."

"That's wonderful. How'd you meet?"

"At his work, actually. I was there on loan—just for a day—but within 15 minutes, I knew I was interested. He, on the other hand, hardly noticed me. But when I was summarizing my thoughts on the project at the end of the day, it was like he saw me for the first time. Maybe it's my imagination, but he started rummaging around on his desk and I could swear, he was looking for my resume."

"And the rest is history, as they say?"

Nicole hid a laugh behind a hand. "Well, sort of. It took a second project, and then we ended up apart for a couple of months when he was on a work assignment. But yeah, after that, it all clicked. He's the sweetest guy with this quiet, intense curiosity. It encompasses about everything ... including me and what I do. Makes me feel like we're partners both emotionally and intellectually." She paused, feeling her face screw up in a wince. "Oh, god, did I just say that out loud?"

"Why? Isn't it true?" asked Greenwood.

"It is, absolutely. But that was the same phrase I used when I described him to my sister and she broke out laughing."

"Don't worry, your secret is safe with me. So, he's a biomedical engineer, too?"

"Oh, no. He's a cognitive psychologist, at Ruger–Phillips. In broad terms, he studies learning, memory, and training technologies." Greenwood stopped, Nicole continuing another two steps before she realized she had left her companion behind. She turned back to look at Greenwood.

"Really?" said the woman, her eyes widening. "A cognitive psychologist and a biomedical engineer? That must make for some interesting talks around the dinner table."

Nicole didn't try to contain her amusement this time. "I'm not sure that's the most common reaction. Even my family's eyes glaze over whenever either one of us starts talking about work. They just wave a hand, then ask about the weather in St. Louis. So, interesting table talk? Can't say I've heard that comment often."

"Well, that's your family's loss, in my opinion," she replied, as the two women started down the hall again. "It's not so much the nuts and bolts of either of your jobs, but the promise of the combination of them. He knows where skills get stored in the brain and how. You develop the mechanism to implant them there. Voila. Instant aircraft pilot or brain surgeon from the team of Veles and .... I don't think you mentioned his name."

"Sam. Dr. Sam Price."

"Instant skill from the team of Veles and Price. And by the way, don't let him have top billing when you reach that pinnacle." She grinned and Nicole returned the expression.

Greenwood rubbed her chin with a hand. "I only know Ruger-Phillips by reputation and theirs is a good one. How's he getting along there?"

"Great," replied Nicole. "He likes the work, and they keep him really busy—research, proposals to customers, conference papers, that kind of thing."

"Conferences?" she said, raising an eyebrow. "He likes giving papers?"

"Likes might be too strong of a word, but I understand he's pretty good at it," Nicole said. "Sometimes I worry …. Sorry, I'm getting way off topic—again."

"That's OK. We're just walking. What were you going to say?"

Nicole paused to choose her words, knowing she was biased when it came to Sam. "He's fairly quiet. But when he talks, he can make the complex sound simple. And if you ask a question, he'll ramp up the technical until you're satisfied. It's a style his company values, which is what bothers me. I'm a little worried they might want to keep him on the road all the time, giving talks, meeting with potential customers, things like that. I've met a couple of people there who do that, and it doesn't seem like much of a life."

Nicole stopped almost mid-stride. "I'm sorry. I just criticized how you've lived much of your life."

"No need to apologize, Nicole, because you're right." The women started down the hall again. "A business life on the road is almost no life at all. But when you're just starting out and trying to make a reputation without aligning yourself with a company like Ruger-Phillips, there's no alternative. Fortunately, now I have the credentials to do almost everything online or with email. Funding and regulatory agencies don't need to shake my hand anymore."

"Sounds like you're in a good place in your career," replied Nicole.

"I am," said Greenwood brightly. "But I do have one disappointment in how things are going here."

Nicole was fairly sure Greenwood was joking, but apparently, she wasn't certain enough to keep the worried look from her face. Greenwood smiled, put a hand on her shoulder, and squeezed softly. "I'm worried I won't get to see Dr. Price give one of these famous explanations of his."

Nicole chuckled, mostly from the teasing but a bit from relief. She also wondered if her client's joke had been a hint. "Would you be interested in getting together, the three of us, maybe for lunch or dinner?"

"If it's not too much trouble, dinner would be great."

Nicole ran through the logistics in her mind. They'd be finishing up their work on Friday. But since Greenwood would have about a 70-mile drive home, she wouldn't want to delay her departure.

"How about Thursday night? I'll have to check with Sam to be sure, but I know he's free."

"Wednesday?" Greenwood asked, raising her eyebrows. "I have another commitment on Thursday."

"Same caveat, but I'm sure Wednesday will be OK, too. Any idea where you'd like to go?"

Nicole glanced at her companion who was grimacing in an overly dramatic way. "After this chat, you're probably going to find your boss and ask for a less whiny customer. But to be truthful, I'm pretty sick of eating at restaurants. It's gotten so bad that I look for hotels with mini-fridges so I can make sandwiches in my room."

"Ouch," Nicole replied. "Dining on bologna sandwiches sitting on your hotel bed? You're destroying my fantasies about being a world-class, medical researcher. But I can cook ... well, at least a little."

"Thank you, thank you. Make it something simple. Something you and Sam would eat if I wasn't there. And I'll bring the wine. Any thoughts as to the menu so I know what to get? Or am I rushing things?"

Well, there goes Mexican food. At least, Nicole didn't think wine and tacos went together. That left a half-dozen other dishes she could manage with lasagna topping the list. "Italian?"

"Perfect," said Greenwood. "And I promise, no more favors not related to work for the rest of the project. Cross my heart."

The women arrived at the room they'd been assigned, Nicole announcing the fact by saying, "Here we are." She opened the door, and the two walked in.

"Everything I'll need," said Greenwood after looking around for a moment. "I know it's a bit early, but I got up at the crack of dawn to drive in. Breakfast was a long time ago. Lunch? Or should I go alone and let you find your boss to file that complaint?"

Nicole smiled. "There'll be no complaints from me. Lunch it is. You can leave your briefcase here. I'll lock the door."

"Great," said Greenwood. "We can take my rental car. All right if we run by your place while we're out? That way, I won't be more than fashionably late on Wednesday."

"Absolutely," replied Nicole, thinking she might end up with a friend as well as a client from this job.

12:32 PM – The St. Louis FBI Field Office

Special Agent Rebecca Marte focused on the sound of her footfalls on the sidewalk, pushing thoughts of Sister Constance and the Crusaders for Common Sense from her mind. That there was a case-breaking clue hiding somewhere in the evidence was unlikely, but like many, she had found that insights often came when her mind was elsewhere. So far, it hadn't wandered. The lunch that was to free her thoughts had been spent reflecting on Constance's last known movements: the place she had hidden on the university campus, the wall she had scaled, the halls she had trod, the man she had killed. Rebecca hardly tasted the sandwich that had disappeared from her plate.

She slowed her pace back to the FBI field office and let her gaze wander over the roads and buildings, cars and signs in the area. The Drury Inn had trimmed their lawn, that fact revealed by the telltale, green clippings against the light gray of the sidewalk and the scent of freshly cut grass. It seemed early to be mowing, but the appearance of an adjoining lot changed Rebecca's mind. It had a ragged look, as thick clumps of grass blessed with a little extra nourishment were scattered across an area slowly making the transition from brown to green. The sun fell on her back, the warmth of its rays penetrating the dark blue blazer and white shirt she wore. Some of the tension in her neck and shoulders dissolved. She ran a hand through her short, blond hair and took a deep breath, recording the details of the day in her memory. She did so lest the next time she noticed the world, it was due to the onslaught from heat and humidity in the middle of July.

A man in shirtsleeves approached on the sidewalk, no doubt enjoying the mild spring day as well. Although Rebecca couldn't see it, he was apparently wearing a headset; either that, or he was laughing at the jokes of an imaginary friend. He looked mid to late twenties. He was an inch or two taller than her five feet, eleven inches, with brown hair and a light complexion. There was certainly nothing objectionable in his appearance, although Rebecca had stopped thinking of men as "attractive" based solely on looks. What men were beneath the shell was so much more important, a fact she had discovered in high school, relearned at college, and had reinforced nearly every day on the job.

Rebecca watched the man approach, and from a distance, he returned her gaze. Her interest was piqued. After a moment, she heard, "OK, talk to you later." The call was over, and he wasn't starting another. She stopped, now adjacent to the employee entrance to her building, waiting for the man to pass. And if he was the quiet type? Rebecca decided on, 'Nice day, isn't it?' It was casual but nearly demanded a reply, and then, she'd see what happened.

But as the gap closed, the man glanced at the FBI building, then her. His eyes narrowed. He stepped from the sidewalk and started angling across the street. She'd seen guys flee before, but it usually came after she mentioned her career. But loitering in front of her place of employment apparently had the same effect.

"You know, there are laws against jaywalking," she called out. He glanced back, his frown deepening. He hurried on without a word. She knew she shouldn't hassle him, but her flicker of interest had become annoyance. He had it coming.

Rebecca entered the building and climbed the stairs to the Criminal, Cyber, Response, and Services Branch on the second floor. She wound the way to her small, interior cubicle and dropped into the chair behind her desk. Now in her work environment, her mental gears shifted. Gone were the thoughts of spring and the chance of finding a friend who was neither in law enforcement nor wary of it. But also missing was any insight about Sister Constance. Perhaps it would come in her dreams ... that is, if she ever got more than three hours of sleep at a time.

She started her computer, brought up a video file, and then fast-forwarded to the part she wanted to see. She had watched this section of the clip at least a half-dozen times, and she still found it difficult to believe. But as she positioned the mouse over the command that would show it a seventh time, a voice came from the opening to her cube.

"We're gonna be in bigger digs real soon."

"And when that happens, the Crusader case won't be mine," Rebecca said, turning to face Clements. "All over the news?"

"Yeah, still the lead at noon. And the trailers for the evening news. The two failed attempts barely caught anyone's attention but with blood in the water ...." Clements didn't finish; he didn't need to. Rebecca knew the phrase "serial hate killer" and "domestic terrorism" would be on everyone's lips, even if technically, serial didn't fit yet. But there was no denying that the Sister's messages reflected that intent.

"Here, watch this," said Rebecca. Clements moved to look over her shoulder.

Clements snorted. "Watch what? Can't you lighten the picture?"

"It just grays out and gets fuzzy if you do," Rebecca replied, looking back at her mentor. "She's in the shadow of a building. You'll see her when she moves."

Clements leaned forward, squinting at the screen. Rebecca turned back to the monitor just as Constance started moving. At first, she was little more than a somewhat darker spot moving across a wall that was uniformly black. But as the spot neared a passageway between two buildings, the feeble rays from a roof-mounted light revealed a dark, human form. The figure paused.

"What's she doing?" asked Clements.

Rebecca shrugged. "Getting ready?" At that moment, Constance burst forward, reaching full stride in two steps. Just before she would have crashed into the wall of one of the buildings, she leaped into the air.

"No way," said Clements, as her feet left the ground. And indeed, after leaping between the walls of the two buildings and then reaching for the top of the hallway between them, she fell back to the earth. "Damn, she almost made it. And the roof of that passageway is what—almost two-and-a-half times her height?"

"Fourteen feet, give or take a few inches depending on where you measure. And she makes it the second time." They watched as she did.

"Is that as hard as it looks?" asked Clements.

"It's not easy. We had a local parkour trainer check it out. He had a whole list of things that made it a tough scale—rough ground, uneven wall surfaces, the height. But it was the depth of the recess that he really hated. It's only eleven inches. He hit his elbow against the back wall on his third try and gave up."

"And you didn't goad him into another attempt, saying even a woman could do it?"

"I wasn't there," replied Rebecca, leaving the implications unstated.

Clements snorted again, then walked over to a chair near the wall of her cube and dropped into it. He crossed one arm over his chest and rested the elbow of the other on it while his fingers massaged his forehead. Rebecca had come to think of this position as Clements's thoughtful pose. After a moment he said, "I think you told me that Constance cases her scenes carefully. Is that really the easiest way into the building?"

"Without setting off an alarm or involving someone else—like stealing someone's entry card—yeah, that's about as simple as it gets. She couldn't even use a rope to scale that wall because there's nothing there to hook. Once again, she was well prepared, right down to the days, if not weeks of training to make that jump. And the window she got in?" Clements nodded. "One of the few that wasn't replaced when they rehabbed the building a couple of years ago. The new ones are covered with ..."—Rebecca checked her notes—"an acrylic sheeting, making them about 50 times stronger than glass. She knew exactly where to go."

"Any other video?" asked Clements.

"When she leaves. The only cameras inside the building are on the first floor. And she simply walked out when she was done."

Rebecca clicked a tab on the video viewer and started the clip. A young, black woman walked down a hall. You could almost see the muscles in her legs and shoulders rippling under the tight, black clothes she wore. Pausing just below the camera, she looked up and smiled. But it wasn't an everyday, life-is-good smile. It was elation.

"You know, it's too bad she's a wannabe serial killer. She has a great smile."

"I hate that taunting shit too much to admire it," replied Rebecca, biting off each word. "She's mocking us. She's sure we can't find her even with all the physical evidence she's leaving behind—pictures, fingerprints, even some blood from the second case."

"And that hasn't changed, right?" asked Clements.

Rebecca scowled in response.

"And you're trying to get in the international databases, too?" Clements asked.

"The key word is 'trying.' So far, it's been slow going. That'll probably change now."

"Probably." Clements resumed his thoughtful pose. Rebecca wondered if he was reaching new depths of contemplation; he was kneading his forehead so hard that his fingertips were turning white. When he dropped his hand, he said, "We seem to be getting slower at taking her posts down. The news had several minutes of what appeared to be scrolling text. Never saw that before."

"I know the story there. Constance went higher tech on this last message. She set up a laptop as a web server, connected to the Internet service at a downtown coffee shop. You'll have to ask IT, but I understand it's not that hard to do. She left the computer running a webpage off batteries for a couple of hours. The staff found it just before the police arrived, so all of Constance's fingerprints were probably smudged, not that we need them."

"Same—" Clements started, but Rebecca cut him off.

"We even have video of her going into that coffeehouse. This time she winked at the camera," she said, her tone dripping sarcasm. "Wanna see?"

"That's OK," replied Clements. "I was going to ask, any change in her profile? I just caught the highlights of her message on TV."

"I'm getting the full review, but their first impression is that there's nothing new. They're still saying well educated, articulate, high IQ. Her athletic prowess is obvious. She's probably spent all or most of her life in the Midwest, which of course is one of the reasons why approval to search the foreign databases has bogged down. Social, but most likely single." Rebecca paused a beat. "How the hell do they figure that?"

"Not sure." Clements shrugged. "Maybe they figure no spouse would go along with this insanity. Anything else?"

"There's a lot more detail—things like she's extremely knowledgeable about medicine." Again, Rebecca paused. "That still feels weird to me. Talks like a doctor but thinks medicine will be the death of us? And, yeah, Chuck has reminded me—several times—that the Unabomber was a math professor, and yet, he railed against technology."

Clements shook his head. "I wish he wouldn't make that comparison either, but he has a point. Constance wouldn't be the first to learn her hate from the inside. And you've got that on your board?"

"It's there," Rebecca said, sticking a thumb toward the whiteboard across the cube from where he sat. He wandered over.

Clements knew her organizational strategy, and accordingly, he started at the center of the board. He worked his way slowly to the right, tapping a couple of fingers against his chin as he read. That side contained the "facts" of the case or as close as one had in a criminal investigation. And some of those data were extremely accurate, like Constance's height. The FBI had enough pictures of her with backgrounds that could be measured to know it within a half-inch or so. After finishing that side, he returned to the center of the board and repeated the process to the left, covering everything from fairly well-founded inferences near the center to the wild guesses on the far edge. The scheme was basically one Rebecca had learned from an instructor at Quantico and had modified for her own use.

"There's an assumption running through your analysis," Clements said. "Or, at least it seems that way. Like you're trying to make everything fit one person."

"Yes and no," she replied. "If there are two or more people, I think the centerline could divide them. The right side is Constance—gender, height, weight, physical skills. The left side would be Constance and the person in the shadows, if there is one. I realize it's easier to think of several people: the near Olympic athlete, a computer type for setting up their broadcasts, a doctor who's gone over the edge. But it's not required, I don't think. At least, not yet."

"No, you've taken the right approach," said Clements. "Keep it one person until we're proved wrong, even though I think we're getting close to that point. I mean, who says things like 'arrogance-fueled medical atrocity,' can discuss state-of-the-art gene editing, and can scale a 14-foot wall wearing a backpack? There's hardly enough hours in the lifetime of a 20-something-year-old for all the training and education implied in that."

"Tell me about it," replied Rebecca. She snapped her fingers and walked over to the board. "I almost forgot to add something about local medical school graduates. School could explain a couple of things: Constance's medical expertise and her detailed knowledge of some of these buildings. But so far, nothing. Most of them moved away after graduating, and we've found nothing on the rest."

"Still worth the look," replied Clements.

As Rebecca was adding an entry to her board, a possible motive for Clements's interest came to her. "Are we doing this so I have everything I need to brief my successor?"

Clements rubbed his chin, his gaze tracking around the cube as if in search of the right words. "I'll make a case for you leading."

She was shaking her head even as he spoke. She had come to accept the inevitable after the phone call from her boss. Nonetheless, she appreciated Clements's gesture.

"But, yes," continued Clements slowly, "if it comes to a handoff, make sure you cover everything on the board during the briefing."

"Any idea who it will be?" asked Rebecca.

Clements turned to look at her. "Probably Hawkins."

Rebecca took a deep breath, turned away, and slowly shook her head. "Just my luck."

Rebecca's dislike of Special Agent Bradley Hawkins wasn't news; everyone knew the she-said, he-said story. She said he introduced himself as separated. He said he and his wife were just in a rough spot and had said so. Now, Rebecca cursed the day she had decided to relax her no-law-enforcement boyfriend policy for that "lying sack of shit," as she now thought of him.

"OK," she said after another sigh. "I'll tie it up all nice and neat for Agent Hawkins. All he has to do is find an attractive, black, world-class athlete with a genius-level IQ who thinks we should go back to the days of roots and berries for all our cures. He'll probably start by checking his websites."

Clements frowned. "Check what?"

"You know, all his dating websites?"

Clements guffawed, then turned and left.

1:03 PM – The Biomedical Engineering Associates Building

Nicole opened the door to room A27, and she and Dr. Laura Greenwood entered.

"That was a great suggestion for lunch," said Greenwood. "I doubt I would have ever tried that place without your recommendation, but it was excellent."

"Thanks, Laura." Nicole knew she was grinning—had been for most of the lunch—but she couldn't help it. Greenwood had been so complimentary of everything. "But I guess it's time to get to work." Nicole gestured to the chair behind the desk.

"No, you take that," said Greenwood. "You'll be taking notes, and typing on your laptop will be a lot easier at the desk. That gives me the rest of the room for pacing while I talk and draw pictures on the whiteboard. I usually need it—both the space and the board. So, I take it you've been doing a bit of homework?"

Not sure exactly what she meant, a frown must have replaced Nicole's smile. Greenwood explained without being asked. "I saw an old copy of *Brain Cell Biology* on your desk. So, what did you learn from hours poring over dry medical journals?"

Nicole nodded, then sat behind the desk, opened the laptop, and powered up. Her settling-in production was more elaborate than necessary, but the biologist's question had caused some of Nicole's nervousness to return. She felt something like she did before an oral exam by a particularly tough professor but even more so. She was about to summarize the life's work of a woman who was revolutionizing the treatment of abnormal brain development in preterm babies. And now that they were in their working quarters, some of the intensity Nicole thought she had seen earlier was clearly evident in her client.

She looked up at Greenwood who was still standing on the other side of the desk. "I actually got interested in your work several years ago from a story in the local paper. You mentioned that some of your inspiration came from research completed right here, at the Washington University School of Medicine in St. Louis."

Greenwood nodded, but she remained silent. Her eyes never left Nicole's face.

"The school was researching brain development in newborns, looking at the areas that showed most of their growth and maturation after birth. The idea was that these areas would give us clues about what might go wrong in babies that are born preterm."

"Well, it's nice to finally meet someone who got something positive from that story," said Greenwood. She pulled a chair from the corner of the office and placed it next to Nicole, then sat. She was sitting close enough that Nicole had to turn slightly to see the woman's face.

"Do you happen to remember the correlation the researchers drew between brain changes after birth and evolution?"

"I do," said Nicole, not certain why the woman had asked but glad she could provide the answer. "They found the areas that change are the same ones that distinguish apes from man. In other words, the brain of a newborn is similar to the brain of a lower primate." Nicole paused. "Is that why some people didn't react well to you drawing parallels between your research and the Wash U study?"

"You're very generous to use the phrase 'didn't react well'," replied Greenwood, matter-of-fact. "Irrationally livid is how I think of their responses. But then, in the Midwest, it might have been a reaction to evolution as much as anything I said. It's hard to believe how many people still don't believe in evolution in any form."

The scientist's face screwed up for a moment as if she had just swallowed something bitter. "Anyway, at the time, I was planning to return to the Midwest after nearly ten years in Florida. I thought the mention of a local institution might garner some goodwill, but obviously I hadn't considered my audience. Suddenly I was calling people's little bundles of joy nothing more than monkeys. It was a PR nightmare. Now, I stick to the work of Martin Schwab and his colleagues when I talk about inspiration."

"Like the study by Schnell and Schwab?" Nicole asked, hoping she could bolster her credentials in the eyes of her client.

The question had the desired effect, as Greenwood's head jerked back. "You know that research?"

"I think I remember the basics," said Nicole, now realizing she had unintentionally volunteered to be quizzed further. "They identified a protein that inhibited neuron growth in primate spinal cords. Then, after discovering an antibody that neutralized the protein, they used it to treat rats with spinal cord injuries. With the protein out of the picture, new nerve pathways grew and the animals regained lost functions."

"And how does that relate to my work?" asked Greenwood.

"Basically, you want to do the opposite in primates."

"OK," said Greenwood slowly. "And why would I want to slow cortical development rather than speed it up?"

"As I understand it, premature birth places demands on a preemie's brain that it's ill-equipped to handle. So, you want to temporarily impede neuron growth, giving the rest of the body time to mature while the more primitive parts of the brain keep the baby alive. Then, when the treatment is removed, the demands from the heart, lungs, and limbs are better regulated, and the risk of disabilities may be reduced."

Greenwood chuckled, and for an instant, Nicole wondered if she had misunderstood the woman's research.

"The inquisition is over," said Greenwood smiling. "Knowing my research and the work by people like Schwab is in no way a prerequisite for what we'll be doing. But I wanted to get a feel for your background, and you've certainly done a lot more than give this area a cursory look. Thanks, because your preparation will make my job a lot easier."

Nicole tried to keep her grin from returning but knew she wasn't completely successful. Now that Greenwood had admitted her purpose, Nicole realized why the give-and-take had felt so familiar. She'd had professors who preferred it as a means to gauge their students' mastery of a topic. And it was certainly more revealing than asking if everyone had read the chapter, which always received a unanimous response in the affirmative.

"And I particularly like the way you've cast the forward-looking nature of my work," continued Greenwood. "So many want to say I'm researching treatments for autism or attention-deficit disorder and that's just not true. Not yet anyway." Greenwood touched two fingers to her lips, staring for a moment far beyond the office wall that was only a few feet away. Then, she turned back to Nicole. "Well, maybe someday, when we've jumped through all the regulatory hoops."

"You've run into issues there?" asked Nicole.

"Oh, no," Greenwood replied, placing a hand on Nicole's arm. "Nothing like that. It's just that approval is a bureaucratic paper chase. The first cases where Schwab's methods were used in rats were in the late 1980s, but it wasn't until about 2010 that they could start the human trials. And that was in Europe, which tends to move more quickly than we do. It's tough, thinking about all the suffering that could be avoided if we could streamline things."

"Well, hopefully, your procedure will gain approval quickly. Aren't nearly ten percent of all births in the United States premature?"

"Now look who's quoting statistics," replied Greenwood. "Must be your fiancé rubbing off on you."

Nicole felt her face warm. It was true her life had changed because of Sam, was still changing, and all in good ways. She loved his quiet, measured approach to life and his intense curiosity about life in general ... and her, in particular. His eyes lit up with the details of her day. But his reaction was the same when she spoke of work, a topic that had put all of her previous boyfriends to sleep—if she dared talk of such things at all. It was a passion for another she wasn't sure she'd find until it happened. And now, she wondered if it showed in her words and actions. But that was a question for another time and for someone other than a business client.

"I was wondering," Nicole said instead, "just how much can you slow brain development?"

"We can stop it."

"Really?" Nicole hadn't expected anything this dramatic.

"Yes, for all practical purposes. Change would be so slow as to be nearly undetectable. But interestingly, the protocol has the opposite effect on the rest of the body. We're not certain about the mechanism, but it may be related to the stage of development when treatments start. When we pause brain development at a more primitive state, the biological clock runs at a pace appropriate to it. The human body matures at about the same rate as that of a lower primate."

"So, a month of treatment with no brain development ...," started Nicole.

"Yields about six months of growth in the rest of the body," finished Greenwood.

The cellular biologist got that faraway look again. Nicole started to ask if there was something wrong when the woman spoke. "Of course, this is all based on an extremely small sample. We'll be in a much better position to answer these questions when we have all the data from your new instrument package."

Greenwood raised her eyebrows as if inviting concurrence. And Nicole wanted to give it, although she knew there were challenges. Perhaps her hesitancy spoke to Greenwood, as she asked, "You're not nervous, are you?"

Nicole hesitated and then admitted, "Maybe a little. The challenge is in the scale. Human preterm babies are small, but the primates you're working with? Their preemies are hardly bigger than my thumb. The equipment exists, but getting it packaged and integrated with an interface that supports your methods, the sequence you use when you work? That'll be the challenge."

"And the way you just described the project is exactly why I need someone like you," responded Greenwood. "My current setup is an octopus of wires and readouts. It's more of a hindrance than a help in getting the job done. I'm constantly recalibrating and sifting through applications to find the functions I need. You can turn this mess of hardware and software into a well-oiled machine."

"We can," said Nicole. "I'll handle the hardware, and together, we'll document the steps in your protocol. Then, I'll have a software engineer package all of the applications and create a menu that follows the workflow. When we're done, it'll feel like a single app."

"Perfect," said Greenwood. "You ready?"

"I am. And let me suggest we start with the perfect case, the one where everything goes right. After that, we'll branch out to the complications."

Greenwood rose from the chair and stepped over to the whiteboard. "The perfect case," she said and started drawing.

After a moment, Nicole realized the scribbles were supposed to be a preemie. She ducked her head, pretending to type on her laptop a moment to cover her amusement. Perhaps it was too much to think that such a brilliant scientist could draw anything better than a stick baby.

6:23 PM – The Central West End Neighborhood

I pulled the order of Moo Shu Shrimp closer to my face, sheltering it from the light rain that pattered against the hood of my jacket. I'd had the foresight to grab it for the walk from my apartment to the restaurant and then on to Nicole's place, but the realization of how much easier it would be to carry this load with an umbrella had escaped me. Now, I had to protect our dinner from the elements with my bowed head and hunched shoulders.

Ah, that smells good.

The spicy aroma of the food just inches from my nose brought several thoughts to mind. The obvious one was the empty feeling in my stomach.

Nicole and I generally dined closer to 5:30, but work had kept me late. And yet, as strong as that biological drive was, another thought swamped it. It was the thought of Nicole. This particular meal was the first we had ever shared and had been repeated often over the intervening 18 months. The scent brought back those memories in a kaleidoscope of images and a feeling of warmth. I was certain time would never erode the sensation.

I climbed the stairs two at a time and let myself into Nicole's apartment. She was sitting at the kitchen island, bent over a Sudoku puzzle. "Thank goodness. I'm starving." She tilted her head to the side, and I placed a kiss on her cheek before dropping the package on the counter. She jumped up and pulled two plates from a cabinet. I retrieved silverware from a drawer.

"How was your day?" I asked.

"Good. Shorter than yours ... obviously."

"Yeah, sorry about that," I replied. "We had some new, three-dimensional displays come in. I had to make sure they got set up. And first look, they're better than the last but still not there. The scenes look good, but there's a bit of delay in updating if they're complex or you move your head too fast. Probably end up with some sim sickness if you use them too long."

"And you got all that from a first look?" she said, as she spread some plum sauce on one of the Moo Shu pancakes and started rolling. "You didn't leave me here starving so you could play with your latest electronic toy, did you?"

The slight smirk on her lips said "teasing," so I replied in kind. "I was thinking about playing longer," I replied, emphasizing the verb she had used. "But the manufacturer suggests no more than six hours at a time."

She gave a single, quiet laugh, shaking her head. "My day was excellent."

I waited for more, but food appeared to be consuming her attention.

"Mmm," she said after a bite. "I suppose it's not polite to make noises while you eat, but mmm."

We both ate, Nicole ending the lull in the conversation after a few minutes by asking, "Are you going to be able to make it to dinner tomorrow night?"

What?

I stopped with my second Mu Shoo roll inches from my mouth, turned, and looked around the room as if seeking the person to whom she was speaking. Other than an occasional business trip, I'd hardly eaten anywhere else for the last year. One of us asking the other to dinner had long since been replaced by planning menus together, so my confusion was only partially feigned.

"Is this a trick question?"

"No, it's just that I started work with Dr. Laura Greenwood today. She sounded interested in having dinner with us, so I invited her. You available?"

"Sure," I replied. I scoured my memories. "Is she the one you're designing those instruments for? The stuff for primate preemies?"

Nicole nodded, her mouth full of food.

"She connected with the zoo?" I asked.

Nicole swallowed and stared at me a second. "No. Dr. Laura Greenwood? She's a cellular biologist."

My blank stare was apparently enough to let her know that I still didn't see the connection, so she explained. After a few moments recounting how Greenwood wanted to adjust brain development to bring it and the body in sync, Nicole finished by saying, "I know it'll be years before her research is put into practice, if ever. But she may hold the key to several developmental disabilities for preterm babies. You gotta admit, that's exciting."

After a moment, I said the only thing that came to mind. "Wow."

"I thought you'd be impressed," Nicole replied, a knowing smile coming to her lips.

"Yeah, really. I'm surprised I haven't heard of her. Laura Greenwood?" Nicole nodded. "I'll have to read up on her a bit before tomorrow."

I meant it. I mean, how often do you have a soon-to-be-famous cellular biologist come to dinner?

WEDNESDAY, MAY 8

9:18 AM – The Biomedical Engineering Associates Building

Nicole stepped out of the front door of her building, looking up into the dark gray overcast of the morning sky. She turned to the east, finding no one on the sidewalk. To the west, it was the same story. She looked across the street. There wasn't much there: a small grocery store to the left, a parking lot ahead, and a four-story office building to the right. She was getting worried. Greenwood's rental car was in the part of the lot reserved for visitors, but the woman was nowhere to be found.

They had started at 8 o'clock, right on schedule. After about 40 minutes, Greenwood had asked to take a break, saying she needed a few minutes alone to collect her thoughts about the next step in her procedure before they discussed it. Nicole had stayed in their temporary workroom, cleaning up the notes she had taken. But when Greenwood hadn't returned in a half-hour, Nicole had become concerned and started looking. After several circuits inside her small building, she had moved the hunt outdoors. Where else could she be?

Nicole walked east, turning at the corner of her building and looking down the sidewalk. No missing cellular biologist. Since the west side of her building abutted another structure, the back was the only place she hadn't looked. When she got there, her search was rewarded. There stood the woman, her smartphone held out in front of her.

"Surely you can find better scenery to photograph than the back of my building."

Greenwood jumped at the sound, bringing her smartphone down as she turned. "Nicole."

"Sorry, I didn't mean to startle you," Nicole said. "I sometimes get lost in thought, too."

Greenwood brought the phone back up. "Ah, no wonder you came looking. I didn't realize how long I've been gone. There was this large bird, maybe a hawk? I couldn't get a good picture and got carried away trying."

"I'm not enough of a bird watcher to know what they are either, but I've seen a couple of them," Nicole said. "I'm surprised they've adapted so well, except the parks and residential areas around here are teaming with rabbits and birds. I guess that's what they eat?"

Greenwood shrugged. "I'm not sure either, but I've slowed us down enough. Shall we get back to it?" She started for the building's back entrance.

"We should walk around to the front," Nicole said. Greenwood stopped and turned to her, raising an eyebrow.

Nicole cleared her throat, feeling a bit like she was about to divulge a company secret. "The building's owners have been fixing the outdoor lunch area." She raised a hand to the temporary, wooden fencing just to the right of the entrance. "The surface was starting to crumble. But the job has left the back sidewalk and the area just inside something of a construction zone. We're in A27, up front, so you won't have to deal with that mess."

"Is the door locked?" asked Greenwood.

"No. But if my boss caught me leading you through that obstacle course, he'd be none too happy."

"Well, we wouldn't want that," replied Greenwood. The women headed back to the front of the building.

"I don't think we discussed a time for dinner," said Nicole. "Is 6:00 too early for you?"

Greenwood hesitated. "That's normally when I eat, but would it be possible to move it back an hour to 7:00? I have a call that may run late."

"No, that's fine," replied Nicole.

"I worked on a project in Italy, a long time ago," said Greenwood. "I never could adapt to their dinnertime—8:00 or later. And then, the meal lasts for two or three hours. You take a table in an Italian restaurant and it's yours for the evening."

"Now, that's how I picture you—at some exotic location, having late dinners after a day of treating newborns."

Greenwood chuckled. "Yeah, that job was great, but as I said, it was a long time ago. My last business trip was about two years ago, to Omaha. Like the old joke goes, I spent a month there one week. But I'm not complaining. I've visited some great spots during my career."

When the women reached the front of the building, Greenwood paused. "In addition to being an excellent, wildlife photographer ..."—she cleared her throat dramatically to emphasize the irony—"I also do a mean selfie. Mind if I take one of us?"

"Us?" Nicole asked, letting her voice slip into wide-eyed, schoolgirl mode again. She pushed some of the enthusiasm from her tone. "Sure. I'd be honored."

The women turned, putting the Biomedical Engineering Associates building in the background. After Nicole heard the old-fashioned click from the totally modern device, she said, "Can you text me a copy of that shot?"

Greenwood glanced at the phone, then said, "Hmm, first no decent picture of that hawk and now this." Nicole leaned forward, looking at the phone's screen from the side. Even with the angle and the sun glinting off the surface, she could see the picture was off-center. Only about half of Greenwood's face was showing.

"Let me try again."

The women resumed the pose, with the result turning out much better the second time. Greenwood finished texting the picture by the time they reached the front door.

"So, tell me a little about the people you work with," said Greenwood. "Anyone particularly inspiring? Any good friends?"

"Both," said Nicole. "Those aren't questions I can finish before we get back to A27, but I can start." The women headed down the hall, Nicole lost in stories of her coworkers.

11:21 AM – The Evangelical Church of the Rock

The morning had been lost from the day, obliterated by a layer of dark clouds that promised rain but only delivered dreariness. Reverend Micah Eastin rose from his desk and parted the slats that covered his study's window. The spring flora beyond did nothing to lighten his mood. Their reds, yellows, and blues were but muted shades of themselves, the gray sky stealing their brilliance. Even the smell of the flowers some of the church women had placed in the nave earlier this morning failed to penetrate his sanctuary. All he could detect was the bitter odor of stale coffee and the lingering traces of the disinfectant used to clean their living quarters.

He moved to a corner of his study and turned on a floor lamp, determined that the darkness of the day not invade his soul. Last Sunday's sermon had disappointed. It had not been the call to action he had thought, a fact he gauged from the heft of the offering plate. True, his congregation's giving had increased but not enough to cover the need. His flock hadn't fully understood the threat from the slow infiltration of medical immorality, and that was a problem, lest his plans collapse of their own weight.

There was a knock, followed by the face of his wife as the door cracked open.

"Where'd you leave them?" he asked, surprised to see her in his doorway.

"They're in back. You can't see them from the parking lot or the road. I'll go back and keep an eye on them, but I was wondering if you wanted a cup of coffee."

Reverend Eastin released a long sigh. "Thanks, but no. I'm fine."

"Trouble finding divine inspiration?"

"You could say that," he replied.

"You'll find it. You always do."

"Thanks, Mary Jo," he said as she closed the door.

It was one of the ironies of his life that his wife bore the same name as his first love. But what made that coincidence even more significant to him was the fact that they wouldn't be where they were had it not been for the first Mary Jo. Of that, he felt certain. She had seen something in him that no one else had, least of all, himself. And when she revealed that insight—a mere sentence, a phrase really—his life's work had materialized from the fog of his doubts and uncertainties. And though some 21 years in his past, it still felt like yesterday.

* * *

A drop of sweat rolled down his forehead, stinging as it reached his eye. A sixteen-year-old Micah Eastin wiped it away with a hand, pushing the mop of brown hair from his face as he did. Although the sun had set nearly an hour earlier, he knew relief wasn't coming. The air refused to move, leaving the 40 or so worshippers in the one-room church to stew in the heat and humidity of a July night in northern Mississippi.

It was time for prayers and each member of the congregation raised their impassioned pleas. Micah couldn't make out the words, although "glory to God" and "hallelujah" reached his ears with regularity. He added a "praise the Lord" to his own mumblings.

Later, there would be time for the members of the church to share some of their victories—a birth, a marriage—as well as the setbacks that were always more numerous by comparison—an illness, time in prison, a death. Singing, piano and guitar playing, hand clapping, and more prayer would follow. Then, there would be a collection, hardly enough to keep the lights on, but more than these folks could afford. And eventually, some in the congregation would be overcome by the power of the Holy Spirit. At that point, dozens of twitching, twirling, and writhing bodies would nudge the mercury even higher.

It was a pattern seared into Micah's brain from the five years his mother had been bringing him here. For the last four, she hadn't stayed—at least, not for the Saturday night services when she needed to attend to "personal matters." He knew what she was doing. Hell, everyone in town knew. But he wasn't bitter; he wasn't ashamed. He felt sorry for her, but his pain was also mixed with a touch of pride, tempered to the consistency of steel by the whispers of the townsfolk. She was doing what was necessary for the two of them to survive, and that was more than could be said about several of the men sitting in the pews with him.

Micah took solace in the fact that this year would be the last his mother would be toiling alone. Next May, when he left school, he wouldn't look back because on the following twenty-fifth of August, he would turn seventeen. Had he been born a week later on the first of September, he would have to attend school a year longer. But he wasn't born later. As for the job he'd find? That worried him. There was always farm work, but he hoped for something better, something that would let him take more of the burden from his mom.

"Praise the Lord," said old Mr. Coonts, pounding Micah's shoulder as he sat beside him. "We be praying for your ma."

Micah glanced at the man, wispy gray hair around his ears turning to white stubble on his weathered cheeks. He had a first name, obviously, but "old mister" was all Micah had ever heard. "Thank you, sir. I'll tell her."

"I feel His spirit in the piano," said Coonts, pronouncing the word like the dessert and the girl's name—pie Annie. "Been feeling puny myself. Needs the power of the Lord." Coonts's head jerked a couple of times as if slapped by an unseen hand. He stood and walked to the front of the room.

Soon, one of the brothers was leading a prayer for him, one hand held in the air as the other squeezed Coonts's shoulder as he kneeled.

Micah had thought about skipping these meetings. His mother would never know, and he could be out running with his friends. He raised his bowed head slightly, peering through slits in his eyes. There he saw the reason he was still seated in the pew—Mary Jo Gentry. She had just turned eighteen, a woman, and was the most beautiful creature Micah had ever seen. Her pale skin and simple white dress gave her the look of an angel. Her silky, black hair and dark, brown eyes, however, hinted at something quite different, making Micah's heart thunder in his chest every time she was near.

Mary Jo knew something of what he felt, having caught him staring at her often enough. And twice, he had seen her looking back. He thought she might have been smiling, but whether the expression was from interest or amusement, he wasn't sure. And once, she had spoken to him, saying something about how she liked his green eyes. He now thought of them as his best feature. But that had been three months ago, and with the end of the school year, he saw her rarely now, maybe once or twice a week. He had to do something soon, lest her father share the good news of her impending marriage before he had even talked to her.

But when? These services were informal, the Holy Spirit moving people in different ways. Some confessed their sins; others spoke in tongues; still others spun until they dropped to the floor in dizzy exhaustion. But Micah didn't think Brother Gentry, Mary Jo's father, would believe he had been moved by the Lord to ask his daughter for a date. And besides, he didn't have the courage. It was a problem he needed to solve and quickly.

The din in the room hit new levels, and Micah pulled his thoughts back to the present. It didn't take long to spot the reason for the commotion. Brother Gentry and another man he didn't know had just removed two rattlesnakes from a wicker basket and placed them on the floor. These were followed by two more, then another pair, the group of six forming a tangle of twisting bodies, flicking tongues, and venomous fangs. Brother Gentry raised a hand. "Behold, I give unto you power to tread on serpents and scorpions and over all the power of the enemy. And nothing shall by any means hurt you."

Micah recognized the words from the Bible, as well as the ritual that was about to unfold. Some in the crowd would be moved to handle these reptiles, to take them up, to hold them over their head as they danced and sang. But while he had seen snake handling before, the practice wasn't common. It was opposed in the courts, and its practitioners were persecuted by their neighbors. There was no announcement in the church bulletin when it was to occur, only whispered rumors around the dinner table, out in the fields, or on backcountry lanes. And in this church at least, it was saved for special occasions. Micah, however, had no idea what that might be in mid-July.

After a few minutes during which four people took up the snakes, Brother Gentry raised his hand for quiet. "Most of you know, but Mary Jo here ...." He raised a hand to his daughter. "Well, she's full growed now. Time she witnessed. Time she followed in my footsteps." He held out a rattlesnake.

Micah's eyes darted around the room, searching for a face that reflected the shock he felt. He found none. Most of the congregation were nodding; some were perhaps praying for her safety, but no one opposed Brother Gentry. And while the church recognized every man as equal, children weren't men. No one would listen to him.

Micah took a breath, trying to slow his heart, quell the flutter in his gut. Rattlesnake bites, while painful, were seldom fatal. A reduction in a hand's dexterity or even the loss of a finger was more likely. Brother Gentry's missing digit on his right hand was evidence of that. But why would a man risk his only daughter? In fact, his only family. There was no Mrs. Gentry for as long as he had known them.

Mary Jo raised a trembling hand toward the snake. Micah squeezed his eyes closed. His thoughts in the dark, however, were worse; all he could see in his mind was her lying on the floor, writhing in agony. He opened his eyes a slit and dropped his head as if looking directly at the sight might burn his retinas.

As her hand came within inches of the snake, it struck, burying its fangs at the base of her thumb. Mary Jo jerked her hand back, crying out with pain, and dropped into one of the chairs lining the wall. The background noise of the room increased. The congregation was shifting uneasily, whispering concerns to their neighbors. Brother Gentry raised a hand. "The will of God," he said over the murmuring in the room. "It's His will." He turned to his daughter. "Let Him guide you in this hour of your need."

Micah watched, doubting his senses as Mary Jo reached out again and took the snake from her father. She raised it above her head. "Glory to Him who has made us all," she said, then handed the serpent back. She slumped, seeming to melt into her chair. A ragged chorus of hallelujahs and "praise be to God" swept through the church.

Even halfway across the room, Micah could see the pain on Mary Jo's face. And while no one would believe he had been moved by God to ask her out, none would question him comforting her. He stood and walked across the room. As he approached, he could see a drop of blood on the hand she cradled in her lap. Her thumb had swollen to the size of her father's. The sheen of sweat on her forehead magnified the pallor of her skin.

Micah pulled a handkerchief from his pocket, now glad his mom made him carry one. Mary Jo looked up and took the offering with a smile and a "thank you." After a few moments carefully dabbing at the wound, she held out the cloth.

"You can keep it," said Micah. He looked down at her, his eyes narrowing. She held his stare. "Why?" he asked after a moment.

"Like my pa said, to follow in his footsteps."

"But ...," Micah said softly, searching for the words. "You share his belief? In snake handling?"

She stood. He looked down into her deep, brown eyes.

"I share his belief in witnessing our faith—as should you, Micah." She paused, biting on her lip. She stepped closer, causing her to tip her head back even more. Her eyes were deep, dark pools of brown. Micah felt like he did when he stood on a cliff—like he might be pulled over the edge at any moment.

"If you let them," she said, her voice soft, "people will open their hearts and minds to you. I feel it. I feel it in you, Micah."

The drop of adrenaline that had given him the courage to walk across the room after the snake struck now became a flood. Was she saying she would open her heart to him? He couldn't think, the soft whispering of the voice in his head was drowned by the roar of his pounding heart. The room closed in around him. The temperature soared. He had to say something.

"Your hand ... thumb—I hope it's better soon," Micah stammered, turning almost before he finished the words. He retreated to the safety of his chair across the room, sat, and bowed his head. For once, he actually prayed. "Lord, give me the courage to tell this woman how I feel. And Lord, show me the way to take her from this life. She deserves better."

It was a prayer never to be answered. Two weeks later, Mary Jo Gentry and her father moved from the area, and Micah Eastin never saw her again. Her words, however, would live in his mind forever.

5:37 PM – A Downtown St. Louis Hotel

The night breeze felt cold, and Dr. James Conroy, Jr. pulled his jacket a little tighter around his shoulders. His hotel balcony had a single chair and a small table. He placed a glass of wine on the latter before approaching the rail. To his right, he could just make out a corner of Busch Stadium. The St. Louis arch was to his left.

"Probably spectacular from the top," he muttered to himself. But he'd never been that comfortable with heights; the third floor was fine.

Conroy turned from the view, took a sip of wine, and dropped into the chair. He was tired, bone tired. At least tomorrow, it would all be over. It was a comforting thought and at the same time, a terrifying one. Could he really end it all? But then, he had to.

Truth be told, six months ago might have been better for his finale. Conroy knew what it took to prop himself up for each performance. He was not the showman he once was, although he was still good. He still got their minds churning with memories, their eyes moist with pain, and their tongues belting out cheers. And it was important work. Since childhood, he'd had a personal stake in his message, and now, it was more important than ever. But tomorrow, his nights on stage and his days living out of a suitcase ended.

Through the open door to his room, Conroy caught the sound of his phone. He carried his wine inside to where his dinner sat, untouched, going cold. After a glance at the phone's screen, he answered. "Hi. I didn't expect to hear from you."

"How are you doing?" asked the woman, her voice soft, her tone sad.

Conroy released a long breath. "About like you'd expect. I wish you were here." There was no response save the soft sound of shallow breathing. "I know you can't be," said Conroy after a moment. "But I can still wish for it."

"No more than I," said the woman. "You know it's breaking my heart, not being there for you. Should we ...."

"No," said Conroy, not waiting to hear the rest. They had been through this, again and again. They had decided and to retread that same ground served no purpose except to increase the pain. "I shouldn't have said anything. I'm sorry." He paused a beat. "At least, I'm getting some great coverage. The crowds? Unbelievable. The group on Monday was hanging on every word."

The woman sighed. "I know. You make them feel the pain they've buried. You wake their minds to what is only common sense." Her voice trailed off, Conroy straining to hear the last of her words.

"And Monday will probably be nothing compared to tomorrow." Conroy tried to sound upbeat. "With the way Sister Constance has them worked up, they'll be eating out of my hand."

He obviously failed, the sound of soft sobs coming over the line. "I have to go," said the woman after a moment. "Can I call back? It will be late."

Conroy wanted to say no, save the woman additional pain. But he couldn't. He needed to hear her voice. "Please. I won't be sleeping anyway."

"I love you, Jimmy," came the voice on the phone. She disconnected without waiting for him to respond in kind.

Conroy looked around the empty room, his gaze coming to rest on his uneaten meal. The spicy smell of the curry, usually one of his favorite dinners now made him nauseous. He placed the cover back on the dish and set his tray in the hall. When he returned to his room, he pulled a new bottle of wine from a sack, opened it, and poured himself another glass.

It was going to be a long night, aided only by the alcohol that was starting to dull his senses.

6:58 PM – An Apartment in the Central West End

Nicole ran a hand across the small, mahogany dining table, adjusting the placement of a fork by a fraction of an inch. Then, she turned one of the plates slightly. Perhaps its decoration had been slightly misaligned, assuming there was a correct orientation. I wasn't certain, having seen this dinnerware only once in the last six months. She stepped back from the table, folded her arms across her chest, and nodded. A dishtowel was riding on her shoulder, ready to do battle against any speck of dust brave enough to show itself. None were. She removed the cloth and wrung it in her hands. "Have you opened the wine to breathe?"

Yes, for the third time.

What I said, however, was limited to, "I opened it about an hour ago. Should be ready when we are."

"Yeah, you already told me that, didn't you?" I just smiled in reply.

Obviously, Nicole was anxious for her dinner guest to arrive, and I wondered if a similar flurry preceded my visits when we first started dating. I doubted it, but then, I didn't have Dr. Laura Greenwood's reputation. And after studying the scientist's background a bit on my own, I fully understood

Nicole's butterflies. I even shared a few. Although working quietly to solidify her protocol, the woman was on the cusp of greatness.

"Want me to get that?" I asked when I heard a knock at the door.

"I will," replied Nicole, as she detoured to the kitchen to deposit the dishtowel on her way to the door. "Laura," she said, as she opened it. "Welcome."

"Thank you," said Greenwood, as she stepped inside.

She gave Nicole a quick hug, which admittedly, surprised me. It wasn't the closeness—I had clients who had become friends—but the rapidity with which it had developed. But then, they shared an interest in an extremely complex technology that few others would even understand. I knew I'd never keep up if they started talking about work.

"I didn't hear you pull up," said Nicole.

"I'm about a half-block away. I could have gotten closer, but I just took the first spot I saw after I reached your block." Greenwood handed Nicole a bottle of wine.

"Thanks. I know you said you were bringing wine, but I took the liberty of opening a bottle of Chianti we already had. Or actually, Sam did." Nicole took a half-step to the side and turned to me. "Laura, this is my fiancé, Sam Price. Or, if you want him to answer, you should call him Doc, like all his friends. Sam, this is Dr. Laura Greenwood."

"Dr. Greenwood," I said.

She shook the hand I extended. "We'll have none of this formality. If I'm a friend who calls you Doc, then it's Laura."

"Laura it is," I replied.

"Do you want a glass of wine before dinner?" asked Nicole. "Or we can eat now."

"If it's the same to you, let's eat. I'm famished."

Nicole turned into the area of her apartment that served as both living and dining room, the latter at the far end of the space. But before she reached the table, Greenwood took a detour to look at one of the pictures on the wall.

"This is interesting," she said. "All the layers and the different materials. Some text, paper with geometric designs, and even a few mechanical things like that small gear." Greenwood turned to look at Nicole. "It's like a photograph that's been double exposed. Except instead of just two or three exposures, it's dozens and in all different kinds of materials. Really interesting."

I too had studied that picture from time to time. And each time, something new jumped out at me. "I swear it changes as the light varies throughout the day. What you see now will look different tomorrow morning."

"I don't doubt that at all," responded Greenwood, as she turned back to the wall. "Oh, my, you're the artist, Nicole?"

"Art is sort of a love-hate thing with me. I love the creativity, but I have to battle my engineering side to get there. I'm always fighting the urge to pick up a ruler or a compass, to make every shape and angle perfect. To just let feelings guide my hand? That's tough."

"Well, the creative side won this time." Greenwood stepped back and let her gaze travel across the work again. She turned back to Nicole. "But I've made you stand there long enough with that bottle in your hands." Greenwood took the remaining half-dozen steps to the table. "Where would you like me to sit?"

"On the end," said Nicole, gesturing. She turned to me. "Sam, do you mind if I take the other end? It puts me closer to the kitchen."

"Sure." I took a position behind a chair between the women.

Greenwood pulled out her chair but then looked at Nicole, her eyes narrowing somewhat dramatically. "So, you call him Sam?" she said. "Does that mean you're not friends?"

A flicker of a frown crossed Nicole's face, and then she smirked. "Well, I thought about calling him Doc, but then, with my degree, wouldn't he have to call me master?"

Greenwood chuckled. "I see your point."

"I'll get the salad," Nicole said. "Sam, you want to grab the wine?"

I followed Nicole through the swinging door between the kitchen and dining area. She retrieved the salad and the dressing from the refrigerator and started toward a cabinet to get a bowl. She seemed to be floating around the room, her earlier nervousness only a memory. I grabbed her arm.

"Sam," she whispered in feigned impatience, leaning a shoulder against my chest.

I bent and kissed her lightly on the cheek. She turned toward me, perhaps to reciprocate, perhaps to continue my lesson on proper decorum during a dinner party. But she did neither. Rather, her eyes went wide, staring at the door. I turned to find Greenwood standing there.

"Sorry, just wanted to know if I could help."

Nicole was a bit flustered but quickly recovered. "If you want to get the rolls and butter, I think we'll have everything for the first course."

I grabbed the wine and glasses. After placing them on the table, I propped the swinging door open. "Less temptation for me to misbehave," I said, although preventing the inevitable collision was more the reason.

My admiration for Greenwood had been growing since her arrival. Had she been condescending, aloof, self-centered, or any of the other traits that might go with prestige and wealth, I wouldn't have been surprised. But the way she was making herself at home, kidding Nicole, complimenting her artwork? She felt like "real people." And when she winked at my quip, my appreciation of the woman grew again.

After we seated ourselves and started eating, Greenwood and Nicole shared a few moments talking about work. But before long, Greenwood declared an end to shop talk, saying, "Your engagement? I think you told me, Nicole, but it's recent, right?"

"Technically, three weeks ago today," replied Nicole. "We just got away to tell our folks this last weekend."

"Ah, the third anniversary," said Greenwood. Even though I was seated to her side, I could still see the twinkle in her eye. "Probably a bit soon for questions like where are you going to live."

"I'd love something like what you have," I said. "Nicole mentioned your place out of town, although it'll be quite a while before we could afford anything like that."

"Yeah, I love my little place in the country. It's not big. A little over twenty acres, but there's plenty of room for me." She paused a moment, looking into the distance. "I like the lady-farmer routine, but I have to admit, I miss Florida, too. I've been back here for nearly ten years, but I still think of my home there from time to time."

"The water?" asked Nicole. "My parents had a cabin at the Lake of the Ozarks when I was growing up. I still miss the way the lake looked in the evening, the fireflies in the sky, the sound of the frogs and birds in the woods."

"Yep," said Greenwood. "And with the ocean, it's the sound of the waves on the shore. Hard to beat that when you're dropping off to sleep. And I love the salty smell of the breeze coming off the water." Greenwood's eyes moved to my face. "You're a cognitive psychologist—not clinical, right?"

My forehead wrinkled in surprise at the reversal in the conversation. "That's right," I said slowly.

"Good, because what I'm about to say is too much of a window into my soul to say in front of a clinician." I grinned, now recognizing the conversational setup for what it was. "I have a small, swimming pool in my backyard. One side is your standard, wood deck. But on the other, I have beach chairs, sand, a volleyball net, umbrellas, the whole nine yards. It's an extravagance I allow myself—although I earn it with the upkeep. It's amazing how fast sand gets dirty around here."

"Anyone ready for lasagna?" asked Nicole, seeing our empty salad plates.

"I am," Greenwood said, as I nodded my concurrence.

Greenwood stood to help. "I've got it. It's just one dish," said Nicole. A moment later, she returned, and we passed the food around, each of us serving ourselves.

After a taste, Greenwood said, "Delicious. I've mentioned my time in Italy to Nicole. There, they've made pasta into its own food group, and this is every bit as good." Nicole smiled, some color coming to her face from the compliment.

"You mentioned that you're not traveling as much lately," said Nicole. "But when you do, if something comes up and you need someone to check on your place, I know Sam would love a drive in the country."

Greenwood hesitated, making me wonder if she thought Nicole had overstepped in volunteering my time. "Nicole's right," I said. "I was born and raised on a farm; it's in my blood. I'd be glad to tend to anything that needs it."

"It's kind of you to offer—both of you. But I have someone who looks after the place when I'm on the road." She paused, taking a bite of the pasta. "And frankly, I've been keeping the place locked up pretty tight. We've had some trouble with kids getting on the property. Nothing much, but I'd be liable if they got hurt."

"That's too bad," I said. "My dad had some of that same kind of trouble." An amusing story came to mind about a couple of teenagers who had decided one of our fields would be a good place for some privacy until they got their car stuck in the mud. Something about needing to get my dad to pull them out killed the mood. But by the time I had recalled the particulars, Greenwood had moved on.

"So, I know you're a psychologist working on learning and training but not much else. What is it that you do?"

"The work of my department at Ruger–Phillips is fairly evenly split between our own research and validating the work of other companies for the government. It's called ...."

"Independent verification and validation," said Greenwood.

"Right," I said. "So, you've worked with some IV&V contractors before?"

"I have," she replied. "Actually, it was pretty common early in my career. Funding agencies would want to make sure they were getting what they paid for. And unless they had their own, in-house experts, they'd find a third-party organization that could verify my methods and results." She paused. "That's got to be difficult work, what with the researchers on one side and the funding organization on the other?"

"It can be," I admitted. "The researchers, of course, will want to put their best foot forward, but pushing some technology out too soon can be costly. And when we're talking about training for military systems, which is about half our work, that cost can be measured in lives lost."

Greenwood nodded. "So, do I need to be especially nice to you?"

It took me a moment to catch on. "You mean because I might be evaluating your research someday?"

"Never hurts to have a friend on the other side of the table, so to speak," she replied, tilting her head slightly as if we were actually discussing a shady deal.

"I doubt we'll end up on opposite sides of a table. Ruger-Phillips doesn't do much work in the medical field."

"But it does some?" asked Greenwood, sounding somewhat more serious now.

"Only once that I know of," I said. "A couple of years ago. Actually, Nicole and I were both involved in that project. It was a medical device developed by a company called Worthington-Huston Technology, but they claimed it had uses in training. That's how Ruger-Phillips got involved."

Greenwood stared, her hand coming to her mouth, her eyes going wide. "I thought I had heard your name before. You were involved in that case where a madman stole some unfinished device, then went on a killing spree."

"Unfortunately, that's the one," said Nicole. "We didn't get to evaluate the device, but with the trouble it caused, everything was seized—the hardware, software, documentation."

"It doesn't take the skills you two have to know that was the right decision. Still, it's too bad you didn't get a closer look at it."

Nicole had given the public version of where things had ended, but I was worried that Greenwood might press for more. It would be hard to say no to someone with her credentials, but we would. Fortunately, her phone beeped, sparing us from that possibility. She glanced at the screen.

"Sorry, but I need to call about this text. Is there somewhere I could talk in private?"

"Sure," replied Nicole. "My office is down the hall, second door on the right."

Greenwood stood and left the room. After a moment, I heard the door to Nicole's office close.

"I'm going to put this salad back in the refrigerator before it starts wilting," said Nicole. She stood, picked up the bowl, and started toward the kitchen.

Thirty Minutes Earlier, Five Blocks Away

The soft beep from her watch told Sister Constance it was time. She carefully raised her head above the edge of the car window, checking the foot traffic in the fading rays of daylight. There were people, but none were close and no one was paying attention to the car.

She opened the car door quietly, the dome light already turned off. It was probably an unnecessary precaution since sunset was still a half-hour away, but disconnecting it removed even the slight chance a head would turn. Standing on the sidewalk, she straightened her knee-length, black dress. It felt odd; she wasn't used to such clothing, but the skirt was full and wouldn't hinder her mission. Reaching into the back seat, she pulled out a large handbag of matching color. A wide-brim, floppy hat, also black, completed the ensemble. So dressed, the stunning, black woman appeared ready for a night on the town, even if the area was residential.

Constance placed the straps of the bag over her shoulder and started walking down the sidewalk. Her arms swung loosely at her side, her casual gait belying the hypervigilance she maintained. But nothing in her surroundings threatened.

After ten minutes, she approached an alley running between two apartment buildings. She stepped into the deepening shadows and turned to check the landmarks. Climbing the wrong fire escape would end her evening in failure, and the mere thought made her shudder. But everything was correct. She turned and walked precisely twenty-three paces down the alley, knowing the distance from rote. Looking up, the fire escape was directly above her head.

Reaching into the bag, she removed a large metal hook attached to a short length of black rope. The hook was wrapped in dark gray foam rubber of the type used to insulate water pipes. In its current use, it would dull the sound of metal on metal. She checked in both directions. A car had stopped at the far end of the alley, so Constance stepped back into the shadow of the building. After a moment, the car discharged a passenger onto the sidewalk and drove away. Constance stepped back under the fire escape, and after rechecking the exits, she tossed the hook underhand to the bottom rung. It caught the first time.

After pulling the ladder down, climbing the steps, and letting it retract, Constance pressed her back against the warm brick wall. Again, she scanned the area for the expected landmarks and threats. Again, all was in order. She quickly scaled another flight of steps to a landing outside a frosted window. She checked it. It was locked, which is what she had hoped. The noise of unlocking it would warn her if someone was approaching from behind. Had it been unlocked, she had brought some duct tape.

Carefully, Constance pulled the parts of a rifle from her handbag and assembled it. After double-checking the fit and loading the weapon, she chambered a round. She sat, her legs crossed lightly at the ankle, her knees slightly raised from the landing. She placed her left elbow on her left leg and tucked it close to her body to cradle the gun. The right elbow went on her right knee. She peered through the rifle's scope. The edges of a darkened window on the other side of the alley appeared, the panes showing only an indistinct reflection of reds and pinks from the setting sun. She raised her head, waiting for the telltale sign of a light in the room.

Her wait wasn't long. After about ten minutes, the light came on, and Constance could see a figure between the partially closed slats of the window's shutters. It was her target. She clicked the safety off, took a deep breath, and slowly released it. She willed her body to relax. She willed her heart to slow. She squeezed the trigger.

7:51 PM – An Apartment in the Central West End

Nicole dropped the bowl of salad on the kitchen floor, the sound of it breaking joining the echoes from the crack of a rifle and the noise of a shattering window. I rushed into the kitchen.

"Was that ...?" started Nicole.

I didn't let her finish. I grabbed her wrist and pulled her back into the dining room. The shot had come from the alley, and since the kitchen windows were intact, the round must have hit one of the windows in her office or bedroom.

"Are you OK?" I asked, quickly looking her up and down. I didn't see anything except a few leaves of salad on her shoes.

"Just a bit freaked," she said.

I took my phone from a pocket and gave it to her. "Stay here and call the police. I'm going to check on Laura."

Nicole grabbed my arm, her fingers tightening like a vice. Her normally large, brown eyes looked immense as she studied my face. She opened her mouth to say something then closed it. Her eyes went to the door to the kitchen. "Sam, please be careful. Keep your head down and stay behind the island."

"I will."

I entered the kitchen in a crouch, taking the route she'd suggested. As I reached the hall, Greenwood came stumbling out of Nicole's office. A hand was raised to her forehead, blood seeping between her fingers and down across her face.

"Nicole, call an ambulance," I yelled down the hall. As I turned back to Greenwood, I saw her stumble, leaving a bloody handprint on the wall when she caught herself. I hurried to her, putting an arm around her waist to support some of her weight.

"Let's get into the bathroom," I said. It was on the opposite side of the hall, giving us protection against any further shots. We started walking, but Greenwood was unstable, staggering away from me one moment and stumbling into me the next. Eventually, we got inside, and she dropped down onto the toilet.

"Where are you hurt?"

"My forehead," she mumbled.

Greenwood hung her head, perhaps dizzy from the trauma. I stooped and looked up into her face. She appeared alert, although her breathing was shallow and rapid. I wondered if she was about to go into shock, which could turn this bad situation deadly in an instant.

Blood continued to ooze through her fingers, flowing down her hand until it reached the cuff of her white shirt. I got a washcloth, dampened it, and gently pulled her hand away while leaving her head bowed. The position should help, but if she became dizzier, I'd need to get her out of the bathroom. It was too small for her to lie down.

I found the injury—a long, jagged cut near her hairline. I knew nothing about wounds from gunfire, but as I dabbed away the blood, it seemed too thin to be from a bullet. Perhaps it was made by a shard of flying glass? In any case, my first aid did little to staunch the flow. I started to ask if she felt up to pressing the cloth against the wound when I noticed her hand was also bleeding. I cleaned away that blood, finding another thin cut. That done, I asked her to hold the washcloth to her head.

Nicole called from the dining room. I didn't catch her exact words, but I heard enough to know she wanted to come back.

"Stay there," I shouted. "And stay away from the windows."

The pressure Greenwood was applying to her forehead was working. The flow was easing. I got another washcloth and started gently wiping the blood from her cheek. I heard a gasp from behind me and turned to see Nicole in the doorway. Somehow, I wasn't surprised she was there.

"I hope you kept your head down."

Nicole didn't answer, turning to her guest instead. "Are you OK?"

"Stunned, mostly." Her voice was stronger.

We all paused, hearing the wail of sirens approaching. Nicole took over the cleanup. "Do you think it's safe to go back out front, be ready to open the door?"

"Yeah, should be," I said.

I turned to go, but Nicole caught my arm. "Sam, be careful." I nodded and left.

8:33 PM – An Apartment in the Central West End

The police arrived, followed closely by the emergency medical technicians, and Greenwood was taken to the hospital. Nicole and I sat helplessly in the living room watching and listening. One of the first patrolmen on the scene said something about "random gunfire." That could make sense, I decided, if Greenwood's injuries were from flying glass. And though still rattled by the incident, some of the tension drained from my body at the thought. It wasn't an attempt on Greenwood; it was just kids playing with a gun.

And that's better?

It was strange how careless gunfire had become a partial cure for my worries, but that's where my mind was. Nicole, on the other hand, seemed to be getting little relief from the patrolman's surmise. She was wringing a towel with a vigor that might soon turn it into a pulp of cotton fibers and lint.

One of the patrolmen wanted a statement, so I obliged. There wasn't much to tell. Neither of us had experienced anything beyond hearing the crack of the rifle and finding Greenwood dazed and bleeding. For her part, Nicole mostly sat fidgeting beside me, adding details or concurring when asked. Her constant motion was understandable; I was having a difficult time burning off the extra adrenaline dumped into my bloodstream as well.

As the officer was finishing his report, answering my unspoken plea to write faster so I could comfort Nicole, a detective entered the apartment. He nodded to the man taking our statement but continued to the back of the apartment without a word. When he returned to the kitchen, I could hear him through the open door. I couldn't make out every word, but the phrase "shooter on the fire escape" came through clearly enough. A chill ran through my body as if the temperature of the room had changed rather than only the implications of the shot.

Nicole must have heard too; she shuddered on the couch beside me. I placed a hand on hers, and she turned to me. Nicole had never been one for public displays of emotion, but her eyes were filled with so much pain and uncertainty that I pulled her close in an embrace. She returned the hug, pulling me tightly to her body. Either the patrolman heard the detective too, or he sensed the mood. He nodded to me quietly before standing and going into the kitchen.

The detective came into the living/dining room, introduced himself, and told us what we already knew—he believed the shot might have been an attempt on Greenwood's life. Then, he told us what was going to happen. A second detective was on his way. A crime scene investigation unit would arrive momentarily. They would need at least a couple of hours to process the area, with the worst case being that Nicole would have to leave her apartment for a day or two. And, they needed another statement from us, this time separately.

The second detective arrived. He and Nicole went into the kitchen. The first asked me to stay in the living room while he placed "a couple of phone calls."

I could see Nicole in the kitchen through the still-propped-open door, although I could hear little over the growing hubbub of people coming and going. Her discussion with the detective was going haltingly. Each time he was distracted by a question or call, I'd see her get up to clean the floor of the broken bowl and salad. And each time she was called back for more, she'd frown. Sure, the broken bowl was an unsightly mess, but it paled to insignificance when compared to the shattered window in her office, the pool of blood there and in the bathroom, and the bloody handprints everywhere in between. It was, however, something positive she could do while she was prevented from doing more.

The first detective returned from his calls. He started with much the same questions as the patrolman. When did Greenwood arrive? Did you talk before dinner? Where? How long? And so on. He spent more time recreating the timeline than it had taken to live it. And then, the questioning changed. Who knew Greenwood would be here? Had I seen anyone outside, either at the office or when I arrived? Did I have any enemies? That one caught me by surprise until I realized that with her hair color and height, mistaking Greenwood for me was more likely than mistaking her for Nicole.

Around 11:30, the police finished taking measurements, samples, and photographs. They'd strung crime scene tape in front of the wall where the bullet had lodged but had given us access to the rest of Nicole's apartment.

The door had hardly closed from the police departing when the building's superintendent knocked. I wasn't sure if I was impressed or concerned, but he was exceptionally well prepared for this eventuality. He had everything we needed: a piece of plywood the exact size of the broken window already pre-drilled, screws to attach it, disposable rubber gloves, and a bottle of disinfectant so strong that I was sure the fumes would kill germs in the next unit.

I cleaned up the worst of the broken glass and then gave way to the super so he could cover the window. Once done, Nicole grabbed two sets of gloves and the disinfectant and shooed him out of the apartment. I went back to work on her office. But after a few minutes, she came in and started cleaning there. I left for the bathroom, just to be chased back to her office a minute later.

Then, the pattern repeated, and I thought I understood. The loss of control, the violation of her personal space was weighing heavily on her mind, perhaps not consciously but certainly in the background. I had experienced an extremely small dose of the same feeling when my apartment had been burglarized in graduate school. But in my case, there was no violence. It hadn't even occurred in my presence. The violation of Nicole's sanctuary had to be much, much worse for her.

I asked her to sit for a moment in the living room, collect her thoughts, and she did, reluctantly. But none of her body would be still. Her eyes tracked across the walls, though there was nothing new to see. She wrung her hands in her lap. Her foot tapped the floor. After a moment, she got up and I followed. She slowly walked the affected areas, listing aloud what needed to be done and together, we decided responsibility. Finally, that worked. She tackled her office and the hall with focused energy, while I scrubbed the bathroom and cleaned up the shattered bowl in the kitchen.

When I finished, I sat at the island and laid my head down. Fatigue was starting to overtake me. I heard Nicole and looked up just in time to see her cross the hall to the bathroom. I considered calling down that it was done but knew she'd want her finishing touches on everything. I wasn't offended. Actually, I was pleased she'd let me stay to help, rather than chasing me out with the super. It felt like a small step toward sharing our lives, responsibility for her place now a tiny part of it.

After a few moments filled with the sounds and smells of more scrubbing, she joined me to inspect and finish cleaning the kitchen floor. When she was done, we moved to the living room and sat. "Are you going to be all right here by yourself?" I asked, her gaze coming to my face only after I spoke.

"No, I'm not," she replied simply.

"Do you want me to sleep on the couch?"

Nicole looked around the room for a moment. "No. I don't want to stay here at all tonight. Can I sleep at your place?"

"Of course," I said.

Normally, her question would have taken my breath away and brought wild images to my mind, but the reality of the situation overruled even my male libido. Nicole was old-fashioned, and in our 18 months of dating, we had yet to make love. I suspected she'd made a commitment to wait for the "perfect moment." And on a night when literally everything had gone wrong, this clearly wasn't it.

THURSDAY, MAY 9

8:12 AM – The St. Louis FBI Field Office

Special Agent Rebecca Marte pushed back from her desk, letting her head hang as she stared sightlessly at the floor. She shook her head and looked up at the computer screen again. The facts in the St. Louis Police Department incident report on the shooting were a mixed bag. Sister Constance's actions, if it was her, were all wrong. She preferred delivering her deadly packages in the middle of the night, often enabled by her athletic skills and facilitated by detailed planning. Taking a fire escape that could be negotiated by a 70-year-old grandmother in order to fire a rifle into a residence at sunset was totally out of character. But on the other hand, the target, a well-respected medical researcher, was spot on.

That last fact would have caught the FBI's attention eventually. But the act that took the incident from a possibility to a nearly certain Crusader attack was the flood of new social-media posts. They'd hit the Internet at 8:30, just in time for the channels that ran the news at 9:00, just in time to ruin everyone's evening. There was the possibility that Sister Constance saw the shot as an opportunity to take credit for someone else's handiwork, but Rebecca doubted it. The posts had too many details.

"So, what do you think?"

Rebecca didn't turn around; she'd recognize Clements's voice anywhere. "Does it make any difference?" she asked. "It's not my case."

"It is until one o'clock," replied Clements, coming into Rebecca's cubicle and dropping into a chair. Rebecca swung around to look at him. As he had predicted, Agent Bradley Hawkins was taking over, with the after-lunch briefing being the official handoff. "Hawkins called. He wants us to follow up on the shooting. We'll handle the coordination with the St. Louis PD and conduct the initial interviews."

"Why the hell did he call you?" Rebecca asked, mouthing the word "ass" before her question.

Clements held out a hand in a you-know-why gesture. "You really need a new pet name for Agent Hawkins. And the call itself is just good management. Better to make sure we have it covered than to assume we would."

"I guess," said Rebecca without any enthusiasm, although she knew he was right. She tapped a couple of fingers on her lips. "Coordination with the locals will take time. You want that or shall I?"

"I know the detective in charge," said Clements. "Good guy. I'll get that rolling. And I can swing by and talk to Veles, too, if you want. It's pretty much on my way."

"Sure. I'll take ...." She glanced at the computer screen, "Greenwood and Price. I saw an interview with Greenwood online—nice lady, well spoken. All I've found on Price so far is his resume on the Ruger-Phillips website. Or is that a curriculum vitae or whatever the academics call it?"

"In business, don't they call it a resume?" asked Clements.

"Beats me. And he may be in business, but he's an academic. His resume is loaded with papers that sound completely irrelevant to the real world. Get this." She picked up a notebook and flipped back a couple of pages. "How about 'The Spatial Visualization Aptitude as a Mediator of Learning from Immersive Environments.' I can't wait for that to be made into a movie."

Clements smiled. "I'm sure he'd be happy to explain the importance of his research if you ask."

"And I'm sure he'd either bore the crap out of me using nothing less than five-syllable words or he'd mumble while staring at his hands through coke-bottle glasses."

Clements grin became a laugh. "That's pretty harsh, but I guess you'll find out. Anyway, if either interview doesn't fit in this morning, you'll need to push it till tomorrow. Hawkins thinks Sister Constance won't be able to ignore the Conroy rally tonight. We're on the detail to check the security of the building after the one o'clock. But on the positive side, Hawkins said he has a full crew and won't need us tonight."

"Well, that's something," replied Rebecca. The security check, while not as glamorous in the public's eye as a protection detail, was no less crucial. And somehow, Rebecca liked the challenge of putting herself in a criminal's shoes. "At least Hawkins and I agree on one thing. Constance would love to make a statement at that rally. Hey, can I get the video feed from tonight's ops in here?"

"You can," said Clements. "In the Communications room. You're not coming in to watch, are you?"

"Why not? It's not like I have a life."

8:37 AM – The Offices of Ruger-Phillips

I closed my office door and did something I rarely do—I put my head down on my desk. I hadn't gotten much sleep and the three cups of coffee I had drunk weren't putting a dent in my fatigue. But still, I'd gotten a lot more rest than Nicole.

When we got to my place, I had told her to take the bedroom. She protested briefly but was so undone by the evening that I won that debate rather easily. But only an hour later, she came into the living room where I was sleeping on the couch. She wanted to talk, and we did until about 3:00. After that, she went back to the bedroom, but I don't think she slept even then. Every time I woke up, I heard her moving around. Even so, she was up at 6:00 so she could go home and get ready for work. My suggestion that she take the day off fell on deaf ears.

The sound of my phone broke into my thoughts, and I checked the display. It was Nicole.

"Hi. Is everything OK?"

"Yeah, fine," she said. "I was just wondering if the FBI has called you yet?"

"The FBI? No. They called you?"

"Yeah. About twenty minutes ago. Sister Constance is taking credit for trying to kill Laura. The person I talked to, Senior Special Agent Gus Clements, is coming by here. He said his partner would be calling you."

"He may be calling right now. The other line is ringing. Can I call you back?"

I heard Nicole's "sure" and disconnected. "Sam Price, Ruger-Phillips. How may I help you?"

"Hello," came a voice over the line, but it wasn't a "he" that was calling. "I'm Special Agent Rebecca Marte in the local FBI field office. I'd like to talk to you about the incident at the apartment of Ms. Nicole Veles last night. I believe you were there?"

I did a mental double take. It wasn't so much the gender of the caller, although I suspected women field agents in the FBI were still underrepresented. It was the energy in her voice. Or maybe she sounded full of life only because I wasn't. I was too tired to be sure of anything. "That's correct," I said. "I was there. How can I help you?"

"I'd like to talk to you about what happened. Sooner is better. I'm meeting with Dr. Greenwood shortly, but I should be done by 11:00 if that's acceptable."

It was, so I gave her my address and asked her to talk to the receptionist when she arrived. After we disconnected, I called Nicole back. It rolled through to her group's administrator, who said she was meeting with Agent Clements. The FBI wasn't wasting any time.

In the process of accepting the meeting with Agent Marte, I had noticed my calendar was open for the rest of the morning. And since we flexed our time, I set the alarm on my watch and laid my head back on the desk. I'd be of little use to anyone without a nap.

8:56 AM – A Hotel in Clayton, MO

FBI Special Agent Marte pulled to the far end of the hotel's circle drive. Looking up, she saw row after row of window, balcony, window in a simple elegance that repeated until the top two floors; on the last two, it was all balcony. A young valet hurried out to greet her, grinning as he approached.

"I'll be about an hour," said Rebecca, holding her FBI identification out through the open window. "I'd like to leave my car here if that's OK."

The grin disappeared. The man barely glanced at her badge before backing away as if it were radioactive. "Sure, no problem."

The morning was cool, and Rebecca closed the car window. She had a few minutes until her meeting with Greenwood, so she leaned back and released a long breath. The spring sun still hung somewhat low in the southern sky, and light flooded in from the side. She could feel its warmth soaking through her dark jacket, warming her shoulder and part of an arm.

Rebecca reached across the front seat and picked up a file folder on Dr. Laura Greenwood, then replaced it without looking. She knew what it said. The scientist was wealthy and well respected in her field. The former was the result of birth, the latter apparently due to years of dedication and a long track record of groundbreaking research.

Rebecca was as ready as she could be. She pulled a small notebook and pen from the file folder, opened the car door, walked across the drive, and entered the hotel's lobby.

"Bigger than my whole friggin' apartment," Rebecca muttered under her breath. Scattered around the space were several sets of overstuffed chairs and loveseats. One grouping even included a baby grand piano. A massive, marble reception counter sat to one side as if registering for the night was too pedestrian to be the focus of such a grand entryway.

Even though she was in profile, Rebecca recognized Greenwood standing across the lobby. The agent started forward, the click-clack of her shoes echoing in the nearly empty space. The woman turned, the corner of a bandage peeking out from under the hair combed down onto her forehead. "Dr. Greenwood?"

"Yes. You must be Special Agent Marte," replied Greenwood, a tired smile coming to her features.

"I am. Shall we have a seat?" Rebecca led the way to two armchairs sitting in a small, isolated alcove. A large, picture window overlooked a small garden. They sat and Rebecca opened her notebook. "How are you?" she asked when she looked up.

"I've been better," said Greenwood.

Wanting Greenwood to speak freely and knowing that these opening remarks were the best place to set that tone, Rebecca waited.

"Have you ever been shot at, Agent Marte?" Greenwood asked.

"Thankfully, no."

"It's terrifying," said Greenwood. "I didn't sleep at all last night. I can't remember hearing the gun go off, but the image of that window exploding in my face"—she squeezed her eyes closed, her head slowly shaking—"and the thud of the bullet hitting the wall behind me. It keeps running in loops in my head."

"Do you have someone you can talk to?"

Greenwood released a long breath. "I have no immediate family. Just a couple of cousins I never see. But one good thing about a career in medicine is that a few of my colleagues went on to careers in psychiatry. Two of them have already called offering their support. Long term, I'll be fine."

"Good." Rebecca looked at Greenwood a moment, considering whether there was any other small talk appropriate to the setting. She found none. She turned to her notebook and the questions she had prepared in advance. Over the next several minutes she had Greenwood recreate the evening from her arrival at Veles's apartment through dinner and ending with the attack. As she had expected, there was nothing new in the woman's account.

"Thanks," said Rebecca. "That couldn't have been easy, reliving last night." Greenwood gave an almost imperceptible nod in response.

"For a moment, I'd like to focus on the text message you received during dinner." It was of interest primarily due to its timing and possible criminal purpose—to lure Greenwood into an exposed area of the apartment. "You said you received it just before going into Ms. Veles's office, correct?"

"That's right."

"And it was from a neighbor, Mr. Joseph Holyfield, who was checking on your ... I guess you call it a farm?"

Greenwood smiled. "A very small and citified one, but yes, it's a farm to me."

"How did he happen to be at your farm?"

"He wasn't," Greenwood said. "I'm not even sure he drives at night."

Greenwood responded to the look of confusion on Rebecca's face without being asked. "Joe's old. In his 80s, I'd guess. But his house is the only one close enough to see my drive. He calls if he notices anyone hanging around there. That's not uncommon out in the country. We tend to look out for each other."

"Sounds like a nice guy. What was it this time?"

Greenwood massaged an eyebrow with the fingertips of one hand for a moment. "Truthfully, after the shot, I totally forgot about his text. I only talked to him this morning. It was just someone honking at my front gate."

Rebecca never liked it when someone started a sentence with "truthfully." Perhaps it was superstition, but it seemed that what followed was often pure fabrication. "Did anyone check your home, see if anyone got past the gate?"

"No one got in," replied Greenwood.

Rebecca was puzzled by the certainty in her tone, and although she didn't think her face showed the perplexity, Greenwood volunteered an explanation. "I guess I should say, no one did anything as blatant as driving or walking up my drive. I have several motion sensors and a couple of cameras on it. More in the house, plus an alarm system. While the medical equipment I have there is too specialized for nearly anyone else, I still have a lot of money invested in it."

"Seems a reasonable precaution," replied Rebecca. "So, Mr. Holyfield knew you were at dinner at Ms. Veles's apartment? That's why he called when he heard the honking?"

Greenwood's brow wrinkled in a frown. "If you're thinking Joe might be involved, I can't believe that. He's about the kindest, gentlest man you'll ever meet ... not to mention his age. But to answer your question, no, he didn't know my plans. He knew I was in the city this week but something like dinner? He wouldn't be interested unless I was dining with a Cardinals baseball player."

"Did you tell anyone about your plans?" asked Rebecca. "Maybe a co-worker?"

Greenwood paused, looking out the window onto the garden for a moment. "No, at this stage of my research, I'm pretty much a one-woman show. When I'm running clinical trials, I have an answering service that usually knows where I am. In case of emergencies, things like that. But I'm between studies now, so I'm not even using them."

Rebecca checked her notebook. The next questions dealt with the Crusaders. But for some reason she couldn't quite explain, she decided to go off-script for a moment.

"Immediately after the text from Mr. Holyfield, you went into Ms. Veles's office to call, correct?"

"That's right."

"And the shot came before you finished dialing?" Greenwood confirmed the timing. "Did you happen to move suddenly just before the shot? Maybe sneezed? Dropped something on the floor and stooped to pick it up?"

Rebecca was giving the doctor a chance to hatch some far-fetched miracle that had saved her life. Of course, on occasion, such things were true. But an individual who was being a bit too helpful might have something to hide.

"No, I can't say I remember anything like that."

No miracles here, thought Rebecca, although in this case, she would have been more prone to believe one. Exactly how Constance had missed from such a short distance was puzzling. Then again, they knew nothing about her prowess with a rifle.

"OK," said Rebecca, after she made a note. "You've probably heard, but Sister Constance has claimed responsibility for the attack. Are you familiar with her and the group called the Crusaders for Common Sense?"

"Those cowardly murderers," said Greenwood. "Yeah, I know who they are. Doesn't everyone?"

Greenwood's words were right, but the tone seemed a bit flat. Rebecca knew if their positions were reversed, and it was law enforcement that was being targeted, her words would be dripping venom. But then, it probably came down to upbringing. Greenwood had led a sheltered life, first by her family's wealth and now, by her status. Rebecca had grown up dealing with her problems in her own ways.

"Yes, unfortunately, they're making a name for themselves. Do you have any idea how many people there are in St. Louis with ... let's call it, visibility in the medical field that's similar to yours? People that might catch the Crusaders' attention?"

Greenwood's lips came together in a tight line as she slowly shook her head. "Sorry, but you'll probably need a different filter. How many medical researchers in St. Louis got patents in the last few years? Dozens? Hundreds? How many published important papers in their fields? Hundreds, maybe thousands? We may not have Johns Hopkins or the Mayo Clinic, but between the schools, the research hospitals, and the major commercial institutions involved in medical research, you're looking at a lot of people."

Rebecca nodded. "OK, thanks. You know a lot more about this community than I. Still, no particular lightning rods?"

Greenwood rested her chin on a hand, a single finger tapping her lips. "Dr. James Conroy," she replied after a moment.

Rebecca nodded. "Yeah, his stance is pretty much the opposite of theirs. Anyone else?"

"No, not that I can think of."

Rebecca again checked her notes. "As I understand it, you've mentioned a connection between your treatment and evolution. You think the Crusaders came after you because of that?"

Greenwood's head was shaking even before Rebecca finished the question. "You must have read some of the you're-calling-my-baby-a-monkey stories. Mentioning that possible connection has to be the biggest blunder of my professional career. And the funny part? It was the researchers at the Washington University School of Medicine who drew the parallel to evolution, not me. I even remember the title of one of their papers, 'Baby brain growth mirrors changes from apes to humans.' I just use their findings to explain some of what I see when I hold brain development steady while the body matures. Why didn't they get the bad press?"

"Wrong phrase at the wrong time, I guess," replied Rebecca, although she was finding it difficult to feel too sorry for the doctor. If that was the worst thing that had happened to her professionally, she had lived a charmed life.

"Must be," said Greenwood. "Anyway, as far as the Crusaders being particularly incensed by my research, I doubt it. You would know more about them than me, but that professor at St. Louis University? He was studying flu vaccines, right? I can't see any connection to evolution there."

"What about the other cases?" asked Rebecca.

"Sorry. I don't remember much about them."

"Besides SLU," said Rebecca, "Sister Constance placed bombs at the back door of a clinic that provided family planning services and under a car in the doctor's lot at a hospital. We don't see any connection between the car's owner and abortion—or evolution—but there's always the chance someone in the field, like you, would see a link we don't."

"This doctor whose car was bombed—what was his field?"

"Her field, actually," replied Rebecca. "Radiology."

Greenwood paused, looking out the window again. When her gaze returned to Rebecca, she said, "No, I don't see any connection ... other than medicine, of course."

Rebecca could see why Greenwood might not remember the first bombings. They had been covered in the media, of course. But those stories had none of the sensationalism that came after the death of the St. Louis University researcher. That later coverage mentioned the first two attacks, but the details tended to be buried at the end of an article or as an afterthought in a broadcast.

But she also suspected that Greenwood and St. Louis would soon be paying a lot more attention. Sister Constance was showing persistence and a willingness to adapt to the situation—whatever it took to kill another member of the medical community. The media wouldn't miss this fact, and soon everyone with an MD behind their name would be looking over their shoulder, jumping at every shadow. Then, the fear would spread to anyone needing medical treatment. If this continued, the Crusaders might prove even worse than the Unabomber. His attacks were horrendous, but they were scattered across the country and over time. Constance's hunting ground was a couple of hundred square miles with attempts spaced only about ten days apart. Panic would soon grip the city.

"Is there something wrong, Agent Marte?"

Rebecca left her thoughts to find a look of concern on Greenwood's face. "No, not really," she replied. She glanced at her notebook. The next three questions were the last of her prepared queries, and they were extremely long shots, at best.

"Did you notice anything suspicious from the time you left Biomedical Engineering Associates until you arrived at Veles's apartment? Maybe someone hanging around on the sidewalk or watching from a car?"

Greenwood smiled. "No. I didn't notice a tail if that's what you're asking. But then, checking for one's not a habit I have."

"Understandable," Rebecca replied, disappointed but not surprised. "We're also considering the possibility that someone other than Sister

Constance attacked you. The Crusaders might not have been involved but saw it as a chance to enhance their reputation without any risk. Can you think of anyone who would want to harm you?"

"Oh, lord, no," said Greenwood. "I have trouble believing I have any enemies. I'm not even the subject of any professional jealousy because my work is still immature."

Rebecca nodded. That left one question, and it was like the desperate, Hail-Mary pass a football team throws at the end of a game they're losing; occasionally it works, but no team can make a season counting on them.

"You said you knew of no personal enemies, but do you know anyone who thinks medicine, in general, has become too powerful? In other words, someone who would support the Crusader's agenda?"

Rebecca was surprised when the woman didn't immediately dismiss the question. In fact, she was troubled by the hesitation. Greenwood stood, moved to the picture window, and looked out for a moment. When she turned back, she said, "Walk with me."

Rebecca followed her outside. They rounded the corner of the hotel, reaching the same small garden they had seen outside the picture window. Two wood and wrought-iron benches sat at a right angle, forming one corner of the green space. Greenwood sat on one bench. Rebecca took the other.

"It's obvious that the Crusaders have some type of connection to medical science," said Greenwood. "They know too much. The words they use are too precise. And that makes it possible I've met that person, maybe even worked with him or her. But I hate to mention the name that's come to mind because ... well, because I hardly know him."

"I understand," said Rebecca. "But a name in this context would be held in strict confidence. And no action beyond a routine screening would occur until we know more."

"I'm trusting your word on this," replied Greenwood, holding eye contact until Rebecca nodded. "Last night, at dinner, a friend of Nicole Veles was present—Dr. Sam Price. Do you know what he does?"

"Not fully, no."

"His job is to verify every number and calculation in other people's research even when that work has been done by some of the brightest minds in the country. Sometimes he's called on to pass judgment on medical research, and at least once, the project he evaluated was terminated. Not paused until there was more information; it was ended and blacklisted, so it couldn't resurface in another lab. The research wasn't in cellular biology where I work, so I don't know the details, but that kind of action is unheard of in my field. He's the only person I know who's actively worked against medicine, and he's in a position to know a lot about the industry."

Rebecca nodded. "Thanks for confiding in me. We'll check, discreetly, of course."

Rebecca couldn't deny that the parallels between the Crusader's goal to throttle medicine and Price doing exactly that were setting off alarms in her head. Although it was possible that the organization that funded the work had been wrong, how often would such a group be so far off that banning the research was the only option? Most agencies were extremely careful with their money.

Wasn't it more likely that the rather extreme act of burying the project rested on Price's conviction that its goals were inconsistent with the common good, as he defined it? And if that was the case, it wasn't much of a leap to conclude he'd found others who shared his beliefs. Perhaps he had even started a group under that banner.

The interview with Price that she had expected to be equal parts routine and boring now looked anything but. She said her good-byes to Greenwood and went back to her car. With over an hour until the meeting at Ruger-Phillips, she had time to return to her office, see what else she could find on Price. Where she didn't have the luxury of time, however, was the interview with Veles; Clements might be finishing that talk at any moment. Fishing her phone from a pocket, she dialed her mentor. No answer. So, she composed a text.

Greenwood checks out, but she's suspicious of Price. Thinks he might use his job to hinder medical research and we know who else has that agenda.

If Clements was still talking to Veles and saw the text, he'd know what to ask.

9:36 AM – The Evangelical Church of the Rock

"Mary Jo." The Reverend Micah Eastin's tone reflected his disbelief as he looked through the doorway that framed his wife reclining on a sofa. He pushed the brown hair off his forehead revealing a furrowed brow.

His wife opened her blue eyes slowly and looked at him, her long, blonde hair fanned across the rose-colored pillow under her head. She stretched her legs and arched her back in her manner of waking—one that he still found seductive even after years of marriage.

"Just what are you thinking?" he asked.

She muted the soft music that was being piped into the large room and sat up. "I'm thinking it would be nice to have some natural light in here," she replied. "We don't always have to live like mushrooms."

"And what ...," he started.

"What would we do if one of the ladies of the church got a peek inside?" she finished for her husband, smiling. "None of them are around. And besides, there's nothing in here they shouldn't see. Unless you think my attire too revealing?"

She playfully pulled at the hem of her shorts, revealing another few inches of her long, lightly tanned legs.

The Reverend smiled despite himself. "The clothes are fine. I meant the accommodations." But as he stepped fully into the room, he realized his wife was much further along in her reorganization than he had thought. Most of the furniture had already been removed. What remained, save the sofa, had been pushed to a corner and covered with sheets.

"OK, it's emptier than I expected," he conceded. But he was still uneasy and rubbed at the tension in the back of his neck. "Even the room's proportions are incriminating. You can get this done fast; have you lined up all the bodies you need?"

"I do," she replied. "Six of them and we'll get it hammered out this afternoon. And when it's done, you'll see. We won't be tripping over each other anymore. Well, not so much, anyway." She rose from the sofa, walked to where he stood, and laid her arms lightly on his shoulders. "Not that I mind you tripping over me, time to time."

The Reverend chuckled, no longer able to even feign displeasure. "OK. Just make sure the drapes get closed before you start moving all the new stuff in."

"I will." She paused, now her face becoming the one that was serious. "Honey, what I'm doing in here will help, but it's not near what we have planned. How long are we going to have to live like this? And please, 'this is a marathon, not a sprint' isn't an answer."

The Reverend had come to think of their life's work in much the same terms that his first Mary Jo had said to him, and he used those words now. "Getting people to open their hearts and their minds takes time," he said. "Things will continue to accelerate, but still ... ten years, maybe five if everything goes perfectly?"

"Well, you know, for better or for worse, we're in this together. But let's aim for five."

Reverend Eastin smiled again. "I know. And I couldn't ask for a better partner."

He meant it. His diminutive, dark-haired, dark-eyed beauty in white had opened his eyes to the path he followed. But the statuesque, blue-eyed blonde before him in black shorts and a pink top was much better suited for that journey.

11:03 AM – The Offices of Ruger-Phillips

Special Agent Rebecca Marte pulled into the parking lot adjoining the Ruger-Phillips building and lowered the car's window. The structure didn't have the utilitarian look she expected from a company involved primarily in design, research, and engineering. A large water feature dominated the well-manicured lawn. Several, oddly-shaped pieces of metal extended from the pool, interspersed among small fountains. As she looked closer, recognizable objects materialized from the abstractions. One was an aircraft skimming above the water. Another was a submarine, its breach of the surface dramatized by the spray of water from a nearby fountain.

Behind the waterworks, steps led up to a set of glass, double doors on a simple, one-story brick building trimmed in white stone. Plantings of iris, roses, and peonies flanked the steps, several small birds finding food among their branches and blooms. The fragrance of the spring flowers drifted to Rebecca's nose, and she inhaled deeply, appreciating the setting.

It was all so idyllic, so welcoming—at least until her gaze traveled away from the building. To one side, a manned guard station sat at the edge of a concrete drive, its moveable gate now lowered. Across the road from the guard station, there was a 12-foot-tall, chain-link fence topped with barbed wire. It encircled the rest of the visible campus.

"At least it's not razor wire," she muttered through the open window. If it was, she thought, it would look exactly like a prison.

Rebecca was late, but still, she sat, mulling the upcoming meeting. After all, Price wouldn't be inconvenienced. He'd asked her to see the receptionist when she arrived; then, he'd come over to meet her. At the time of his suggestion, it seemed innocuous, but now she was irritated. Why was she supposed to wait while he wandered over from another building? He probably figured no woman could be on time—although now, perhaps she was furthering that prejudice. Whatever.

Rebecca raised the window and leaned back on the car seat. From the time she had scheduled the interview until now, she had reversed herself once and now sat at another, potential turning point. Initially, Price seemed an out-of-his-element scholar studying theoretical minutia in private industry. How else could you explain all those papers? Then, Greenwood's observations about him had kindled her suspicions. Maybe there was more to this misplaced academic than met the eye. How strong were his beliefs about subverting medical science? Was he just doing his job when he had one medical project terminated, or did his actions reflect something more nefarious?

The excitement she felt from unearthing a possible lead began to ebb, however, as she drove to her office between interviews. First, she had tried to recall the titles of his papers, a task complicated by the fact that concepts that don't have a lot of meaning don't tend to be memorable. But even so, she couldn't remember seeing the word "drug" or "pharmaceutical" or "clinical" or anything else remotely medical in them. Then, she started wondering—if Price was really involved with the Crusaders, would he draw attention to himself by planning a hit on Greenwood at his girlfriend's apartment? In his presence? It seemed unlikely.

Once back at her desk, Rebecca first checked his papers. Her memory was spot on. But maybe Price didn't publish in the medical field because of confidentiality. Weren't drug companies always worried about their proprietary formulas and treatments? So, she checked the online descriptions of Ruger-Phillips's business units, their current and past projects, and their current and past customer list. She found nothing about medicine or medical organizations, save one reference to a Veteran's Administration project. That was almost two years ago, and it hadn't recurred.

With those discoveries, Rebecca had just about put Price back in the innocent-bystander category. Just about, but she hadn't. It was better, she reasoned, to interview him as a person of interest than to assume he wasn't. And if she was careful in her questioning, he'd never know the difference.

She got out of the car and entered the building. A receptionist sat at a desk just to the left of the double doors. She was perhaps mid-40s in a dark blue jacket and white shirt. Her light brown hair was piled in a messy bun on top of her head. But something told Rebecca that there was nothing haphazard in its preparation; it was too randomly perfect. That precision was matched by her posture—ramrod straight as if poised to spring to action should the situation dictate. Prior military or perhaps law enforcement, thought Rebecca.

To the right of the doors, Rebecca saw several, upholstered chairs, comfortable but not lavish in appearance. A second set of glass, double doors sat straight ahead. Occasionally, people were visible, moving around the office space beyond them. She approached the receptionist, provided her particulars accompanied by her open badge holder, and asked to see Dr. Sam Price.

"Nice to meet you, Agent Marte. I didn't know Doc had any projects with the FBI."

If the woman assumed it was business, that wasn't a problem. But there was one thing that puzzled Rebecca. "Doc?"

The receptionist held up a finger of one hand while she dialed with the other. "Doc, Liz at the Building 1 desk. FBI Special Agent Rebecca Marte is here to see you." Then, she turned and said something into the phone that Rebecca couldn't hear. When she turned back, she laughed, followed with, "You got it."

"What was that about?" Rebecca asked, trying to sound only casually interested.

The woman—Liz apparently—grinned up at her. "Doc is just a nickname. And the laugh? He told me to be nice because you're probably armed."

Rebecca had hoped Liz would say something about the whispered comment, not Price's quip, but that was probably too much to ask. "Is that a problem? That I'm armed."

"Nope," replied Liz. "He won't take you any place where it would be an issue. Here's your temporary badge. You'll need to display it while on Ruger-Phillips property, and turn it into any receptionist or guard station when you leave. Doc will escort you wherever you go."

Rebecca nodded. "OK. Do I need to sign anything?"

"Doc verified your employment with the local office, and with the badge you showed me, you're good to go."

"So, you know him?"

She gave a half-shrug, half-nod with her hand extended, then said, "Just from people he meets up here. He's only about a minute away. Should be coming through those doors any moment now."

"Great. Say, what building is the medical research in?"

"Medical research?" The woman rubbed the back of her neck. "You mean like testing new drugs or medical devices?

"Yeah, that kind of thing," replied Rebecca.

The receptionist held out an empty hand while shaking her head. "Sorry, but I don't know of anything like that around here."

"Something I heard, but I probably have it wrong." She hadn't expected the woman to know about work that was excluded from the company's website, if there was any, but it never hurt to ask.

Rebecca retreated to a chair and sat. The fabric of the seat hadn't even warmed to her touch when a man about her age entered the lobby, obviously not Price. He was too young and much more the Midwest farm boy than the frustrated professor. A dark-haired, brown-eyed, somewhat lanky farm boy, she realized as she looked closer. And since Timmy Harris in third grade, males of that specific ilk had been her weakness. Too bad that wasn't Price. It could have made this talk easy on her eyes if nothing else.

Rebecca pulled her phone from a pocket. Who knew how long he might make her wait and solitaire would make the time go faster. But when she looked up, the man was approaching. She stood.

"Special Agent Marte?" he asked.

"Yes?"

She was thinking he would introduce himself as Price's assistant when he extended a hand and said, "I'm Sam Price. Nice to meet you."

Same Time, Same Place

Thank god Liz warned me.

Without her whispered, "she's a looker" over the phone, I probably would have spent ten minutes combing the nearly empty lobby seeking an FBI agent. Or maybe I'd just be stuttering my hellos to her because Liz wasn't wrong. The blue-eyed blonde with the spiky hair would stand out in any setting, her business suit only slowing my appreciation of her striking appearance, not stopping it.

Liz must not have given Agent Marte a similar heads up on me, as she merely glanced my direction, then turned away. Perhaps it was my imagination, but I thought I heard a soft harrumph as she glanced at the clock over Liz's head and started fishing for something in her pocket.

I walked across the lobby, getting to within a few feet of her before she looked up. Her eyes narrowed. Had we been in a bar, I'm certain she would have said, "What are you looking at?" But we weren't, and instead, she slowly stood. I extended my hand. "Special Agent Rebecca Marte?"

"Yes?"

"I'm Sam Price. Nice to meet you."

"Likewise," she replied. Her look of confusion disappeared so quickly I wondered if I had imagined it. "Are we meeting here?" she asked, dipping her head toward the chair she had just left.

"We can, or I've reserved a small meeting room that would give us some privacy."

"The room sounds fine."

I turned toward the doors, and she fell in beside me. "Have any trouble finding the place?" But as soon as the well-worn question had passed my lips, I wondered if she'd take offense. She was, after all, a few minutes late. I opened the door to the office area, letting her pass.

"Nope. The building's right where you said it would be."

I couldn't read any ire in her tone but decided a quick change in topic was in order. Marte, however, was already moving on. "So, this building's open to the public?"

"Not exactly," I replied, as we resumed our walk down the hall. "But the restrictions here are minor. With your position in the FBI, I could have gotten you a badge to the building where I work. But that requires that your security send your credentials to my security. I've seen that take a day or two, and I figured you wouldn't want to wait. After all, time's the enemy of memory."

"I guess you'd know."

I looked sideways at her, not certain what she meant. The questioning glance was enough to get an answer. "It's just that you have so many papers. Doesn't 'publish or perish' only apply to universities?"

"Yeah, here it's more like, publish and get a pat on the back, maybe a little bump in pay, but at least they don't stand in your way. I wrote a couple of papers before I got here—one from my master's thesis and one from my dissertation. That's fairly typical at most schools. And I've done two on my own since I started work. Truthfully, I would have been happy with that— two papers in two years—but I also had a few months of desk time working with one of our more senior scientists. He was nice enough to add my name to four other papers. It's a great start in my line of work. I'd be lucky to get another eight, even if I worked here 30 more years."

I stopped by a door, saying, "Well, this is it. There's a small break room just ahead. Would you like a cup of coffee? Maybe a bottle of water?"

"I'm fine," she replied, so I opened the door and she entered. The room was small and somewhat Spartan: just a table, four chairs, and a whiteboard. At least it had a window, although the view was the parking lot I'd crossed to get to this building.

Marte sat, and I took the chair across the table from her. She opened her notebook, studied it a moment. "You've been through the sequence of events at Ms. Veles's apartment on the evening of May 8 a couple of times now, and we'll cover it once more in a few minutes. But first, there are some other things I'd like to discuss. Things that fall outside the time period of the attack. First, did you mention your plans to dine with Dr. Greenwood to anyone else?"

"I did. My boss, Ken Waters. Unlike me, he's not that much into research, but it came up when we were talking."

"No one else? Not a colleague? Not a friend outside of work?"

"No."

Marte's head tilted to one side as if she was pondering my response. Or maybe she was waiting for me to fill in the silence. But I'd never been that uncomfortable with gaps in a conversation and found them preferable to rambling on about something that hadn't ever been the issue. After a moment, she clarified.

"You sound very sure."

"I thought you might ask because the Crusaders either followed Laura—Dr. Greenwood—from Biomedical Engineering Associates, or they knew she'd be at Nicole's apartment. So, I gave the question some thought. As for being sure, we occasionally use medically-related equipment at work—machines to monitor reactions like heart rate or brain waves when we're testing some new training technique. But no one I know gets into the kind of work Dr. Greenwood does, so it wouldn't have come up naturally. So, yeah, I'm pretty sure Ken was the only one, although, as we both know, memory isn't perfect."

"But it does sound like you've thought about it," said Marte. She spent a few moments jotting something in her notebook before going on. "Immediately after receiving a text, Dr. Greenwood excused herself to make a phone call. Did one of you walk Dr. Greenwood to the room where she called?"

My first thought was, that's not outside the timeframe of the incident. But if she wanted to change the ground rules, they were hers.

"No, Nicole just told her where the office was."

"And that's through a door into the kitchen, across it into a hall, and then the second door on the right?"

"Correct," I said, somewhat surprised. "Is that level of detail in the police reports?"

"It is," replied Marte. "It just seems that those directions are a bit involved for someone who's never been in Ms. Veles's apartment."

Her observation sounded odd to me, but perhaps it was leading up to something I hadn't considered. "Getting around Nicole's apartment is not as complex as that description makes it sound. It's small and Dr. Greenwood had already been in the kitchen, helping us set the table. So, she'd been most of the way there. And the first door on the right is a coat closet, so there's not much that could have gone wrong."

Marte looked away a moment, her brow wrinkled. She turned back to me. "Just before Dr. Greenwood's arrival at Ms. Veles's apartment, did you observe anyone or anything suspicious in the neighborhood?"

"No, nothing."

"No loud sounds, no one in the alley, nothing like that?"

"With respect, Agent Marte, it's the city. There are lots of noises at all hours of the day. Nicole's place isn't far from one of the big hospitals, so we hear sirens all the time. But something out of the ordinary that night? No, I don't remember anything like that."

"OK, how about in the days leading up to Dr. Greenwood's visit?"

Days?

My perplexity must have shown. "Something wrong?" Marte asked.

"I'd never thought of it that way," I said slowly. "I'd been thinking in terms of Tuesday, after Nicole extended the invitation, and Wednesday as the relevant time period—maybe 32 to 35 hours. But in the days leading up to the dinner? I'll have to give that some thought."

Marte paused a moment, studying me. "But you have thought about Tuesday and Wednesday?"

"Oh, yeah, sorry," I said, realizing my mind was already drifting back to the earlier time periods. "On Tuesday night it was raining. I remember because I had to shelter our takeout Chinese dinner under a raincoat. Hunched over that way, I didn't notice anything during the walk to Nicole's apartment. And nothing during dinner or as I left. And on Wednesday, I was at work."

She nodded and again took a note. "Is there anyone you know who might want to harm you or Ms. Veles? Or maybe just put the fear of God in you?"

"Enough to climb a fire escape and fire a rifle into Nicole's apartment? No, no one has that kind of grudge against me. Or Nicole, as far as I know."

"Perhaps this person took a potshot from the ground?"

Hadn't the police eliminated the possibility of a random shot after simply looking at the scene? I had, when I finally got into Nicole's office to clean. "Maybe," I said slowly. "But that would require that the bullet ricochet off something before entering the apartment."

"What makes you believe that?"

What's going on?

An FBI agent doesn't ask a private citizen to analyze bullet trajectory. Well, not to get an answer to that question anyway. So, what does she get if I describe what I think happened? Nothing. I'm almost positive it's the same thing the police concluded, unless ....

Damn!

Unless I start elaborating, making up stories that somehow implicate the Crusaders. And I might if I was involved and wanted to draw attention from myself. Maybe Constance opened the window in the building across the alley to take the shot, I'd say. And now that I thought about it, I remember hearing a squeaking sound. Soon, the rope from my lies would be enough to hang me.

I could always stop the interview and demand a lawyer. Even if Marte didn't consider me "in custody" and so, was required to read me my rights, I could ask for one anyway. That would increase her suspicion, of course, and probably drag this process out even more.

Let's play this out, see where it goes.

"Well, if you go into Nicole's office, stand in front of the wall where the bullet hit, and look out through the window, all you would see is the building across the alley and the fire escape. I cleaned up some of the glass before the superintendent boarded up the window, so I've done exactly that. For a shot from the ground to hit the wall where it did, the bullet would have had to change direction by almost 90 degrees. Maybe that's not impossible, but it's not likely, and it would have left a scar on whatever it hit before the window. That much of a deflection would have also robbed the slug of most of its power, and yet, I heard one of the crime scene investigators say it was buried pretty deep. Of course, your experts would be able to answer this question a lot better than me."

"We're still testing," Marte said simply, her expression unreadable. She looked down at her notebook.

Undoubtedly the FBI was still testing, but I doubted that a 90-degree deflection was among their hypotheses. Marte looked up, paused a moment. "So, let's assume it wasn't a ricochet. Constance has been getting deadlier, killing that professor at St. Louis University in her last attack. I'm sure you've heard about that?"

I nodded.

"So, why do you think she missed so badly at Ms. Veles's apartment? That alley must be, what, 15, 20 feet across?"

"Maybe she's unfamiliar with rifles."

Marte hadn't been slouching, but with my words she sat up even straighter, her eyes now locked on mine. "So, you don't think we could glean anything about her marksmanship from the previous attacks?"

Ah, a chance to either lie, ask for a lawyer, or incriminate myself by admitting I knew a lot about the Crusaders' attacks—even the early cases before Constance drew blood. But the reason I knew so much made sense to me, and it had nothing to do with being their ally. I just had to hope it would make sense to Marte, too.

"Rifle skills? From three bombings? Not really. I guess we learned that Sister Constance is pretty good at blending in with a crowd. How else did she get that bomb under the doctor's car in the middle of the day? And the bombs at the clinic and at SLU say a lot about her physical conditioning, although the fence around the clinic didn't appear that tall. But can she fire a rifle? Who knows?"

"You know a lot about the Crusaders' handiwork," Marte said. "You follow them closely?"

My answer to this question would either shift me away from her "persons of interest" spotlight or increase its illumination to the point where I'd end up sunburnt. "If you'd asked me two days ago, I could have given you a few vague details on the bombing at SLU and nothing about the earlier cases. But there's something about having one of your dinner guests used for target practice that grabs your attention and won't let it go. I've read a lot about Sister Constance and the Crusaders in the last day. And there's no lack of material."

Marte frowned, her ramrod posture slackening a bit. She looked off toward the corner of the room.

"Actually, I can't imagine not reading up after what Nicole and I went through," I added, hoping I wasn't going too far.

"Sure. Something like that would get my attention, too," she said after a moment. I released a mental sigh of relief. "So, you originally from St. Louis?" she asked.

"Nope. Born and raised on a farm near Kansas City. Came here after school." I wasn't sure what was significant in the statement, but Marte drew back, her eyebrows raising. "How about you?" I asked.

"Born and raised in St. Peters," she replied, mentioning a city just across the Missouri River from St. Louis. "There were some kids in my school from surrounding farms, but I was a city girl—or maybe, a small-town-near-a-city girl if you want to be technical." She released a long breath. "We didn't get a chance to review the incident itself, and I can't close out this interview until we do. Unfortunately, I have to leave for another meeting—probably should have left five minutes ago. And I'm tied up all afternoon. Can we schedule something for tomorrow, preferably in the morning?"

A Friday? Even in the best of times, a Friday would be difficult, and tomorrow was jammed with status meetings and customer calls. "Any chance we could meet tonight?"

Marte paused, appearing on the verge of agreeing, so I added, "I can come to your office if that helps?"

She looked at me a moment, then asked, "Are you sure that's not too much of an inconvenience?"

"No problem," I replied. "I'd like to get this finished, let you get on with your job—for obvious reasons."

We worked out the details of the meeting as I walked her back to the entrance of the building. As we neared the door, she said, "So, this paper about some aptitude affecting what you learn in an immersive environment?"

"Yeah, what do you want to know about it?"

She turned to me, a half smile on her lips. "Is it as dry as it sounds?"

I couldn't hold my laugh. "Unfortunately, yes. You might want to wait for the movie."

She found that more amusing than I anticipated, barely suppressing a laugh of her own. "I'll keep that in mind," she finally said. She turned and left.

4:33 PM – A Downtown St. Louis Hotel

Special Agent Marte sat in the break room for the hotel's kitchen. The din that had been increasing since 2:00 was now nearly deafening. Who knew cooking could be so noisy? She laced her fingers behind her head, leaned back in her chair, and stretched her legs in front of her. She wouldn't keep this pose if any of the help came by. It tended to emphasize her chest, and she'd already received her fill of ogles and catcalls for the day.

After talking to Price, she'd broken nearly every speed limit and run every stop sign to get back to the field office. She wanted as much time as possible to put the finishing touches on her notes for the handoff meeting with Agent Hawkins. Not that she gave a damn what he thought, but she wanted to do her job to the best of her abilities. And in her estimation, that meeting had gone well; she hadn't called Hawkins an ass once.

Hawkins always assigned individuals to specific parts of a case. In turn, they fed him and his inner circle their reports, which they integrated and examined for patterns. She'd never been part of his inner circle and didn't expect this case to be any different. And it wasn't. After her part of the proceedings, he had assigned her to the Greenwood follow-up. At least Clements was on the bombing at St. Louis University, so between them, she'd be able to keep up-to-date on nearly every aspect of the investigation.

After the meeting, Clements had only a moment to talk, but that was enough to make it clear that Veles hadn't implicated herself or Price in any way. About as close as she came, according to him, was describing a job they had both worked that involved some medical technology. It sounded like the same project that Greenwood had mentioned to her. But when she asked Clements why this hadn't made him suspicious, he just chuckled. Then, he said, "That's right. You would have been at Quantico when all this went down. Check out the stories on Worthington-Huston Technology from about two years ago."

She had. And after reading some of the online articles, she wondered how she had missed it, even during her training. Apparently, a new medical device originally developed by the Veteran's Administration had been blamed for a madman's killing spree. Testing, however, had proved it didn't work. But when she looked at who had given the technology the thumbs down, it wasn't Price. It wasn't even anyone from Ruger-Phillips. It had been ... the FBI. Rebecca would have laughed at the irony if she hadn't felt so frustrated.

After the meetings at the field office, she had spent the afternoon scouring her assigned areas of the hotel, which included the kitchen. Kitchens were always high-risk areas, given all their nooks and crannies, all the people coming and going, all the chaos—chaos, at least to the untrained eye. But she and two other agents had been over every square inch of it, most of it three times, and had found nothing. And in less than 30 minutes, no one would be entering or leaving unless they were on a list of cleared personnel.

She was pulled back to the present by hunger pangs, brought on partly by the aromas wafting through the door and partly from her stomach's protest. It wanted something a step above the fast food and coffee that had sustained her the last two days. Soon, she'd be off duty, able to find a nice quiet restaurant for a salad, maybe a glass of wine. Finishing the interview with Price, although technically work, would be much later, and the wine would have already run its course. And besides, the meeting with Price no longer held any suspense. He was about as innocuous as an accountant.

Where had that thought come from, she asked herself, knowing how often she used accounting as the prototypical occupation for the future Mr. Marte. Well, he is easy on the eyes. "And unavailable," she muttered to herself.

"You say something or was that just snoring?" Clements asked from the door to the break room.

"I've been working my rear off down here in the zoo," Rebecca replied, turning to Clements. "Where have you been, up checking the mattresses on the sixth floor?"

Clements just snorted. Rebecca sat up. "So, I didn't have a chance to ask. What's Veles like?"

"Smart as a whip, innocent as the driven snow, and cute as a button."

Rebecca guffawed. "I missed the memo that said the reports to Hawkins have to be written in clichés."

"Yep, that's my report," said Clements as he took a seat beside her. "Minus the cute as a button part. No need to draw his attention."

That was one of the many reasons Rebecca liked Clements. His opinion of Hawkins was little better than hers; he was just better at hiding it.

"And Price?" asked Clements. "Clichés are optional."

"A sharp farm boy who found himself in the wrong place at the wrong time. That good enough?"

"Sharp?"

"Yeah, intelligent. Maybe a bit prone to take things literally," Rebecca replied. "I asked him if he'd seen anything suspicious in the days before the incident." She put air quotes around the word, days. "He said there were only 32 hours between the time of the invitation and dinner, not days. I mean, who thinks that way?"

Clements chuckled. "He does, evidently. I assume you corrected him?"

Rebecca stared for a moment. "Corrected? Technically, he's right ... isn't he?"

"Except that we should look at anyone who knew Veles would be working with Greenwood even before the invitation was extended. Admittedly, it's a long shot, but that information alone might be enough for the Crusaders to stake out her apartment and wait for an opportunity."

"I knew there was a reason I phrased the question that way. In any case, Price only mentioned the plans to his boss and probably no one before the invitation, but I'll ask."

"Veles told two people about dinner. I'll get you those names." Clements paused, perhaps thinking of something funny Veles had said, given the smile on his face. "She's not sure who all knew she was going to be working with Greenwood. She's checking with her manager and will get back to us."

"OK," Rebecca replied. "Besides those interviews, I have Mr. Holyfield to talk to—the neighbor that sent the text message right before the shot?"

"Yeah, I remember the name. Anything on him yet?"

"Not really," replied Rebecca, "although Greenwood makes him sound harmless. Of course, that doesn't mean someone else didn't put him up to sending that text. I'm hoping to talk to him tomorrow."

"And since Hawkins gave you the Greenwood part of the investigation, that should make him happy."

"Don't try to talk me out of it," replied Rebecca, giving Clements a fake look of sincerity.

"I'm out of here. When are you getting relieved?"

"Any minute now."

Clements nodded, stood, and left. Rebecca was about to lean back in her chair again when motion near the door caught her eye. It was a woman. Rebecca blinked several times, her mind unable to move beyond the woman's hair. It was about as bright red as she had ever seen and looked a bit wild against her pale skin.

"Ma'am, this area is open only to the hotel's kitchen staff. May I help you?"

"Oh, no. Sorry. Guess I'm lost." Sheila Moore turned and walked away.

7:26 PM – The St. Louis FBI Field Office

I'd never been in the FBI Field Office before, but if you ignored the seal in the tile work on the floor and didn't read the nameplates below the pictures on the wall, it could have been the lobby of any government building. About the only indications it housed an organization involved in classified and occasionally violent work were the badge readers by every door and the glass wall in front of the receptionist. Of course, by the time I sat down in the lobby, I had already signed in with an armed guard and was admitted to the building only after showing my ID again. What I saw here was the second line of defense—or maybe the third, since there were probably other self-protection measures I couldn't see.

I placed a hand on my knee to stop the bouncing.

What the heck am I so nervous about?

It wasn't like I hadn't been in similar settings—no, make that ones that were even more tightly guarded. I'd spent days on grounds patrolled by heavily armed men in armored vehicles. I had worked behind blast doors capable of withstanding anything but a direct, nuclear hit. I'd accessed documents that never left the confines of their electronically shielded environs, examining them only after all the signatures and countersignatures had been verified. Nothing at this office came close. But that was my professional side and I was here as myself. Even the knowledge that the FBI had asked and I was trying to help did little to dry the palms of my hands. Of course, that's the problem with the ancient part of the brain; it doesn't listen to logic.

There was, of course, another possible source of my unease—the person I was here to see. Besides her appearance, which was evocative, Special Agent Marte had an aura of mystery, toughness, and perhaps a bit of recklessness. She was, what my college roommate used to call, a tri-dub or WWW—wild, worldly woman—although words like wicked, wanton, or others sometimes made it into his definition. And though that was a disparaging label when applied to a member of law enforcement, hundreds if not thousands of researchers had investigated the so-called "police personality," often finding profiles that showed resistance to society's usual norms. Of course, I reminded myself, almost as many had found nothing like that. What it meant to be in law enforcement wasn't a simple question, and apparently, researchers had developed nothing but simple answers so far.

But the real surprise for me came when Marte and I had started talking earlier in the day—all of those thoughts had vanished. The conversation had come easily, naturally, even though I was probably a "person of interest" at the time. Now, shed of that suspicion, could this talk be anything but amicable? Again, however, my lizard brain wasn't impressed by the reasoning. I'd just have to wait and see what this meeting held.

The wait wasn't long. Agent Marte came through a door on the other side of the lobby, a slight smile on her face. She nodded to me and started across. I stood and walked to meet her. "Dr. Price. Thanks for coming. I've been told that time's the enemy of memory, so it's good we can finish up tonight."

"If I'd known you were going to quote me, I would have come up with something catchier." And right on cue, my disquiet lifted like fog on a sunny morning. She turned toward the door she had just exited, and I dropped in beside her. "If it's not against your regulations, you can call me Sam."

"It's not," she said, glancing sideways at me. "But I thought people called you Doc?" She swiped her badge and entered a number on a keypad. We entered and started up a set of stairs.

"They do. And Doc is fine," I replied, realizing she must have heard Liz use my nickname.

"So, you're the expert," Marte said, as we climbed. "We're about to dig into your memory. Not that I'm saying I'll follow your advice, but how would you do it?" We stopped on the second-floor landing, and she badged us through another door into a long hallway.

"Seriously? You want to know how I'd do an interview?" She nodded to my question. "Well, we have the biggest concern covered," I said, as we started down the hall. "The longer you wait, the more the memory may fade or change to match your expectations. And the chance that other thoughts or sensations get mixed in with it also increases."

"That's it?" Marte asked. "All those years of schooling and all you have is, don't wait? Surely, there's more in your bag of memory tricks than that."

"I suppose if our places were switched, I'd be asking how much of what I see on TV is true. Something like that driving this question?"

"More or less," she replied, her expression denying me any further insight.

"OK, there are dozens of things you could try." I paused a moment, searching for a good example. "You probably know, but memories aren't complete recordings, like a movie, but bits and pieces of sensory experience that are stored in separate areas of the brain. Anything we do to trigger one of those elements might help in accessing other parts of the memory. In this case, we had lasagna for Dr. Greenwood. So, if we had some Italian food, the smell might help me remember more."

"Are you suggesting we go to an Italian restaurant just so I can get better information?" Marte raised her eyebrows suggestively as if I had asked her for a date.

I chuckled. "No, but your example will make the point even better. The smell of lasagna has little chance of helping me recall that night because I've smelled it dozens, if not hundreds of times before. It's overloaded with memories. And doing the interview at a restaurant would make the situation even worse. Now, we have an overloaded cue, the lasagna smell, competing with cues for hundreds of other, unrelated memories: of going to that restaurant before, of the guy at the next table who looks like my uncle, of the horn on the street that sounds like my first car. Best case, all these irrelevant thoughts don't get mixed into my memory of the night of the shooting. Otherwise, I'll be swearing my old car drove by while we were having dinner with Greenwood."

"A classic, false memory," she said.

"Exactly. What we recall is quite malleable; it tends to change every time we touch it. And someone's confidence about a particular memory is absolutely no guarantee it's accurate. That's what you get with a false memory. Near absolute certainty about something that's never happened because you've reconstructed the memory with the wrong parts."

Marte stopped in front of a door that said Communications but turned to me rather than opening it. "Thanks for indulging my curiosity. I guess I thought ...." She paused. "Never mind."

"What were you going to say?"

"It's not important," she said, as she turned and used her badge and a number to open the door. We entered a room with six large cubicles, although I could see nothing of what they contained.

"I'm going to be observing an operation we're running at the Conroy rally downtown. The FBI video and audio feeds will be off limits to you. Sorry, but I have a television tuned to a local cable company you can watch. We don't expect any trouble, so this should be a good time for us to discuss the incident involving Dr. Greenwood."

"Sure. A bit of multitasking."

We entered one of the cubicles. It held two chairs and a table, the latter supporting a laptop with a large external monitor, a small, flat screen television, a notebook, and an earpiece with a built-in microphone. There was a whiteboard on the wall. Marte gestured to one of the chairs, then walked around to the other side. The computer's monitor was turned toward her, while the TV was at the end of the table, visible to both of us. The TV's sound was off, but from the scrolling narration at the bottom of the screen, I could tell the rally was in its opening moments. Someone was introducing the governor, who I suspected would introduce Conroy.

Marte picked up the earpiece. "This is tuned to an alert frequency. We won't be interrupted unless there's an emergency. In that case, I'll find someone to escort you from the building." She was quite at ease with the uncertainty of the situation, as if it was just another day at the office. But then, for her, I suppose it was.

"Understood," I replied.

"OK, let's do the incident interview … by the book." The last phrase brought a slight smile to her face. "I'd like for you to tell me in as much detail as you recall, what happened from the time Dr. Laura Greenwood arrived at Ms. Veles's apartment until the arrival of the first responders after the shooting."

And by the book, it was, with Marte interrupting infrequently and then, only for clarification using my words. There was never a "didn't you hear anything from outside" or "how surprised did Greenwood look when the text came in." Of course, she had violated all those guidelines earlier in the day, but I suspected that was to see if I would lie my way into a contradiction.

"That's it," she said when I was finished. "And thanks again for coming in tonight. Not everyone would have made the effort."

"My pleasure. I'd like to see the Crusaders caught too."

"Anything you'd like to ask before I find someone to accompany you out of the building?" She dipped her head toward the television where Conroy was still speaking. "I want to stay until the rally is over."

"Of course." I paused. "There is one thing I was wondering. The question about how I'd interview someone—was that about me or the research?"

Marte laughed, but then her eyes narrowed. "I'll answer that question, but first, why do you ask?"

"Some *quid pro quo*, huh? OK. During the interview we just finished, you were too smooth to be using anything you heard 30 seconds earlier. You already knew what I told you, which makes sense. The FBI wouldn't be teaching techniques that are no longer admissible in court. And then, the question this morning about one of my papers? That wasn't to get me to explain it. These questions seem to be ... well, aimed at how I see myself or my field. Or am I imagining that?"

"Do you always analyze everything so methodically?"

I held up a single finger, wagging it back and forth. "Sorry. I answered your question. It's your turn."

Marte released a sigh. "It's been hectic. All I had a chance to find on you before the first meeting was your resume with the Ph.D. and that long list of papers. I admit I expected a guy in a tweed jacket with leather patches on the elbow, smoking a pipe. OK, maybe not that much of a cliché, but an academic anyway. I know better. We get trained to avoid jumping to conclusions like that, but it's tough."

"Maybe close to impossible," I said. "Even psychologists who've studied that tendency for years still fall prey to it. At least we got beyond me being a suspect."

My comment had just slipped out. Marte's head snapped back as if the words had hit her physically. "You were never a suspect."

"Yeah, I didn't mean that," I said quickly, searching my mind for a change of topic. But a look at her told me she wasn't going to be easily distracted.

Marte stared for several seconds before asking softly, "So, what gave me away?"

"An FBI agent asking a private citizen about bullet trajectories."

"I thought that might have been a bit over the top," she replied. "But that brings me back to my earlier question. Do you really slice and dice all these conversations as much as it seems?"

"So, we're entering round two, where I get another question?"

"We'll see," said Marte.

"Well, it's not just conversations," I replied. "It's everything from my research, where this kind of mindset is appropriate, to what toilet paper I buy. I've caught myself thinking about making a spreadsheet to decide how to spend two dollars. But I won't bore you with the details."

Marte chuckled, then glanced at the monitor. "Nothing's going to happen in the next five minutes, and I've got my earphone if it does. There's a galley just down the hall that always has coffee. Want to grab a cup? Since my life is so much seat-of-the-pants, I wouldn't mind hearing how the other half lives."

"I'll pass on the coffee at this hour, but I'll tag along."

"You're sure you don't mind?"

"Actually, I'd like to stretch my legs." She nodded and we left for the galley.

8:39 PM – The St. Louis FBI Field Office

The coffee trip and back was a welcome diversion. Marte said nothing about Constance and the Crusaders, deciding to spend her time talking about her youth. My impression? She was lucky she was never caught. Or died. There was the night she and a boyfriend "borrowed" her dad's car and went for a midnight joy ride. They were fourteen. Or the nights, plural, when she had broken into her family's liquor cabinet for a bottle to share with friends. Or the night she, at the ripe old age of sixteen, had snuck into a strip club with two other girls. That one baffled me, and I'd asked, "Why? You know what women look like."

She just grinned and said, "I wasn't there to see the women."

Of course not.

I noticed that all of her escapades, save the jaunt to the strip club, involved boys. She'd obviously been popular with the opposite sex in high school, and I wondered how much had transitioned to college and beyond. Just looking at her, I would have guessed a lot. But she didn't volunteer, and it wasn't the kind of thing you ask an FBI agent you hardly know. In any case, by the end of her stories, I was certain she'd earned the tri-dub label, with just about any combination of W's you preferred.

For my part of the breather, I stuck to my later years—college and beyond—where I had this marked tendency to get lost in the trees never realizing it was a forest. I told her about the month I'd spent researching a new car before realizing that the model I wanted had been discontinued. When Marte asked why I hadn't noticed the lack of data on the new model year, I replied, "Well, I wasn't expecting any real data until later, so I didn't miss it."

She stared at me so long I thought I was going to have to explain the difference between what I considered data—road-test results, maintenance records, all of which came later—and opinion, which could be generated at any time and didn't require more than a working tongue. Eventually, however, she broke into laughter.

The galley wasn't far, and soon we were back to the Communications room. We entered, Marte taking her position on one side of the table, me on the other. But while the positions were the same, the mood wasn't. The evening had started lighter than the first talk, but since then, it had become—I guess I'd have to say—friendly. For my part, I liked her laugh. I liked the twinkle in her eye when she talked about her misguided youth. I even wondered if she missed some part of it.

"Now that I know you analyze every word," Marte said, pausing for a sip of coffee. "You can't just sit there, looking off into space. I'll get self-conscious."

"You?" I said, feigning surprise. She smirked. "I was just thinking I should let you get back to work."

"Well, at least you're a lousy liar." She ran a hand through her hair. "It's early. You have someplace you need to be?"

"Not really."

"You want to share some of your thoughts about the Crusaders?"

If she was setting a trap with the request, I couldn't see how. "This has got to be as bizarre as asking me about bullet trajectories."

"Maybe," allowed Marte. "But when I was at Quantico, there was another NAT—new agent in training—who said he became interested in the Bureau after a psychic solved a big case in his hometown."

She must have picked up on my consternation about justifying a psychologist's remarks with a story about a psychic. She held up a hand. "I'm not saying you're clairvoyant or anything like that. Just bear with me a second."

"OK. I'll reserve judgment," I replied.

"Anyway, the NAT brings it up in class one day, and the instructor doesn't really defend or attack the practice. Says he's not familiar with the case. But he goes on to say that whether you believe others have a gift or not, he's certain a new perspective, a different set of eyes can help. So, how 'bout it? Help me with a new set of eyes? Even if they're not all-seeing and all-knowing?"

I chuckled, but my amusement was short-lived. I was having trouble believing what I was about to do. "You're very convincing, Special Agent Marte. Just don't blame me when you hear only hunches you discarded a month ago."

"Fair enough," she replied.

"Well, one thing that's puzzling. You have pictures of Constance, obviously. They're in the paper. You must have fingerprints, too. I've never seen her wearing gloves. And I'm guessing you have DNA as well. There was something about broken glass and blood in one article."

"Yeah, we're not sure how the reporters got that tidbit. Maybe the maintenance man."

Her comment was probably as close to a confirmation as I was likely to get, so I went on. "But even with all that, you don't have a name. And your database of fingerprints must include a big chunk of the adult population in the U.S."

"Over one-hundred million people," said Marte. "If you're thinking she might be foreign, we're looking into that."

"Or some subpopulation of the U.S. that's not well represented in your database. Maybe rural areas?"

"Maybe," said Marte.

My gaze drifted toward the television. "Looks like Conroy is wrapping up," I said, as the shot shifted between the man bowing on the stage and the audience standing and chanting something.

"It does," replied Marte. "Anything else on Constance before we wrap up?"

Anything else?

I expected her to hustle me out the door, not ask for more. In fact, I would have preferred it, as my hunches about the Crusaders got even less defensible from here. My security blanket of actual data was getting rather thin.

"To me anyway, it seems like her attacks have been shots across the bow. Warnings, rather than attempts to kill. The first two bombs were placed and timed so that it was unlikely anyone would get hurt. The third bomb, the one that killed the professor at St. Louis University? It sounded like a confluence of unlikely events. He came in unusually early, and apparently, he was holding the box when it went off. Or at least, that's the way it sounded in the news."

"So, you don't think she's just learning?" Marte tilted her head as she returned her coffee cup to the table.

"Maybe," I replied. "But I don't think so. Learning to make a bomb lethal would take time—figuring out the amount of explosive, what to pack around it, and so on? But knowing where it should go and when it should explode? That's not something she'd need to learn; it needs to explode near people. And the shot at Dr. Greenwood is just another example. It wasn't meant to kill unless we want to argue that Constance is learning rifles as well as bombs."

"I agree, the possibility makes sense," said Marte. "If the Crusaders can get people's support without bloodshed, so much the better. They avoid the possibility of a backlash. Of course, the million-dollar question, in that case, is, how much patience do they have? How long before they stop sending notices and start sending bodies?"

I really had no idea. Marte, on the other hand, had some thoughts. "With Constance shooting into Ms. Veles's apartment, I wonder if they're getting close now? I'm not saying the shot was more than a warning, but maybe the message is changing. With that shot, maybe she's telling people they're not safe even at home."

"Scary thought," I replied.

It now seemed more of a two-way street. Not that I expected Marte to reveal evidence known only to the FBI, but she appeared willing to discuss her thinking. That being the case, I said, "Something I've been wondering. Is rolling back the clock on medical science worth killing for? I mean, abortion has long been a lightning rod. And I've seen heated words over some experimental medical procedures like genetic editing or stem cell research. But across the board hatred of medicine?"

Marte responded almost immediately. "Maybe it's my job, but that's not hard for me to believe. Last survey, there were nearly 1,000 hate groups in the United States, their anger based on anything from sexual orientation to skin color. So, a group that hates how medicine is changing everything from our looks to the length of our lives?" Marte held out two empty hands. "Doesn't surprise me. Of course, in this case, it might be just one looney with a gun. Oops, that's the wrong word to use in front of a psychologist, right?"

"Yeah, I prefer rifle." Marte smirked. "But the idea it's one person seems unlikely," I said after a beat.

"Your reasons?" asked Marte.

"Ah, we're still in the 'new-set-of-eyes' mode. Well, the time requirements for one thing. Besides the obvious—the time spent learning and making bombs—someone has developed basic computer skills and has gained a great deal of medical expertise. And the athletic skills Constance has shown? Those don't come without a lot of long hours. Then, the time spent in checking out the targets. Other than the shot at Dr. Greenwood, the locations were scouted in advance. The first two bombings may not have required that much upfront planning, but apparently, Constance used one of the few windows in the SLU building that had not been replaced by a newer, stronger design. She never would have gotten in, if she hadn't known where the building was vulnerable."

Marte's jaw dropped. "Was that fact in the news?"

"Oops, I'm back to being a person of interest."

She rolled her eyes dramatically. Marte had obviously turned that expression into an art form.

"I happened to be on campus for a meeting, and it was in the school newspaper," I replied.

Marte nodded. "I didn't know that fact was out there. But you're right. Constance knows exactly where everything is, including the security cameras. She comes up to them, then winks or waves or some crap like that. And the media has plenty of those pictures."

I nodded, recalling several.

Marte picked up her coffee but set it back down without taking a sip. She frowned, a hand coming up to massage her forehead. I had the impression she was debating how much more she could say.

"The preplanning goes even deeper than weak windows and photo ops," she said after the pause. "Several times, we've seen her wait for something to happen, like a guard passing by on his rounds. And we think she wears something like a beeper that cues her when it's time to act. We have video where she's glancing at her wrist before she moves. That, too, suggests she's not working alone."

"Not unless she's beeping herself," I replied. "But that's interesting. It's like the Crusader mastermind is trying to pull a lot of the decision-making out of her hands. He or she rings the bell and Constance jumps."

"Seems that way," replied Marte. Then, she grinned. "Just don't go all psychologist on me and try to tell me Constance could be replaced by Pavlov's dog. Ring the bell and boom."

"Well, make the bombs small enough ...."

Pavlov wasn't the correct reference unless drooling was going to set off the bomb, but correcting this detail was obsessive, even in my view. Marte picked up her drink, the remnants of her early amusement still showing in her eyes. She took a sip and leaned back in the chair.

In the back of my mind, there was an earlier topic we hadn't completed, and with the break in the conversation, it was a good time to ask. "We've been putting a lot of emphasis on Constance's planning for these attacks. Does it bother you that there doesn't seem to be much, if any, for the shot at Greenwood?"

But Marte didn't respond, didn't even acknowledge that I was talking. She had moved forward in her chair, and her eyes were fixed on the computer monitor I couldn't see. After a moment, she said, "Dammit."

9:21 PM – The St. Louis FBI Field Office

My head snapped around toward the television. Apparently, in the 10 or 15 minutes since I had last looked, most of the crowd had departed. The hotel had cleared some of the chairs from the floor in front of the stage, creating a space where Conroy could mingle with a few of his well-wishers and patrons. But the individual I saw standing next to him was neither. It was Sister Constance.

I looked back at Marte, expecting her to find someone to escort me from the building. But as if reading my thoughts, she said, "They're fully manned, so I'm sticking here until I'm called. You can stay and watch the TV if you want."

"OK," I said simply, not wanting to talk over anything that might be coming through her earpiece.

I turned to the television. The camera was apparently positioned in the back of the ballroom. Dozens of rows of empty chairs appeared between it and the cleared area near the stage. The camera shot swept to the back of the room where I saw a set of double doors and several rally-goers. One of them looked a great deal like Greenwood, but if so, that was hardly surprising; she would be interested in Conroy's message. They were being hurried out by a police officer. He closed and positioned himself in front of the doors after the last one had left.

The shoulder of someone in a blue jacket appeared, and the television shot lurched. A hand flashed across the picture. It shifted to the floor in a series of jerky images of carpet and door threshold. The cable station cut to a female reporter standing in a hallway.

"End of my video," I muttered without thinking.

Marte glanced at the picture on the TV. Her gaze moved to my face, her lips pressing together tightly. She raised a hand, palm up, and with a single curl of her fingers, waved me to her side of the table without a word. Her hand went back to her earpiece as her attention apparently shifted to a communication.

As I positioned myself beside and slightly behind her, I was amazed by the quality of the picture on the computer monitor. It was not the dark, grainy video from a car or shoulder camera, but rather, a high-resolution, color image.

The shot zoomed in on Constance and Conroy, a lump rising in my throat as the details became clearer. Conroy was wearing a thick, black vest, his hands handcuffed in front of him. There was a small, blinking light on the vest near his right shoulder. Two wires—one white, one red—crisscrossed in front so that they would have to be cut to remove the garment. A thick, leather band, perhaps a dog collar, circled Conroy's neck. Constance's right wrist was handcuffed to the band. In that hand, she held a short, red cylinder, her thumb pressed down on its top.

"A dead man's switch," Marte said softly. "If the signal between the switch and the bomb is broken for any reason—released button, cut wires, dead battery—it's all over."

I nodded, feeling my body tense further, even though we were a couple of miles away. The camera zoomed in, the countenances of Conroy and Constance now taking up the entire screen. Conroy's face was red. His lips trembled as he gulped air. Sweat beaded on his forehead; a drop ran down to his cheek. I wondered if Constance's thumb might slip if he hyperventilated and passed out. He appeared to be on the brink.

Constance's demeanor, on the other hand, could hardly be more different. She was slowly canvassing the area, her gaze not lingering on any spot for long. Her breathing was slow and regular. Her hand was steady. And the look on her face? It wasn't exactly a smile, but rather, a look of .... My mind almost refused the thought. She looked contented.

"We're going to try to get some agents closer," Marte said. Her voice was soft, volume not needed in a room where all I could hear was my heart racing.

On the screen, I saw the house lights go down and a spotlight came on. Constance disappeared from the close-up. The collar tightened around Conroy's neck, then he too was pulled from the picture. I flinched from the sudden movement, instinctively ducking from the blast that didn't come. In a moment, the camera zoomed out to show the hostage and his taker in the middle of the cleared area. Conroy was bent over at the waist, coughing. Constance crouched slightly behind him, a hand shading her eyes. After a moment, Conroy caught his breath and started yelling something. The spotlight went out, and the room lights came back up.

Marte reached over to the computer and tapped a few keys. "Room mic," she said simply. I could hear Conroy's sporadic coughing, the muffled sounds of movement in the background. The camera zoomed in again but not as close this time. Still, the faces were large enough to see that Conroy had gone from red to purple. His eyes glistened with tears. Constance, however, still looked calm, as if she didn't have a care in the world.

How is that possible?

"Look at Constance," I whispered to Marte, hoping I wasn't talking over anything.

Marte said nothing for a moment, her stare fixed on the monitor. "That seems really bad to me," she finally replied. "Even the fanatics would be sweating bullets by now, but she doesn't appear fazed at all."

What was going on? Were we playing into the Crusaders' hands? And if so, where did their scenario lead? Ten million dollars in ransom to fight the medical community? An airplane to a foreign country? But I didn't need to wonder long. Constance held up her empty left hand, then slowly reached into a pocket and pulled out a digital recorder. She pushed a button, and an electronically altered voice came from the device.

It took me a moment to adjust to the strange changes in pitch and tempo, but soon, the sounds became words. "For much too long, the American people have let medicine prop up our physical bodies, letting our hearts and souls become cesspools of decaying morality. For much too long, we have taken our health out of the hands of nature and put it into the hands of men driven by greed and delusions of grandeur. Too long have we let medicine play God. And now, payment for our arrogance has come due. Medicine has started to pay, and today, one more of their immoral rank will forfeit his life toward relieving some small portion of that debt. With him, he'll take one of our innocent souls, Sister Constance, but such is the price we pay for our medical hubris."

I stepped back, reaching my hand out to the wall of the cubicle. Maybe I needed the support, but more likely, I just needed something that wasn't spinning out of control. My thoughts certainly were. And in the midst of them was the image of Constance releasing the switch and the two of them disappearing in a ball of flame.

Marte got up from her chair and walked to the whiteboard, brushing me as she passed. Her eyes never left the monitor. "Dammit," she said as she pounded the board with an open palm. She turned and walked back to her chair. "How the hell did she get in there?" She paced back to the whiteboard, pounding it again, this time with a closed fist.

"You need to go?" I asked.

Marte turned and stared at me a moment. "No. A bunch of unassigned agents milling around will just make things worse. I'll wait, be ready for the second wave."

Silence from the computer cut through the turmoil in my mind, and I looked back at the screen. Constance had stopped the recorder and had raised the dead man's switch as high as the collar and handcuff would allow. Marte moved back to the table. "Easy, Hawkins," she muttered under her breath as she slumped into her chair. She was holding a hand to her earpiece. At the same instant, the camera zoomed out.

"Who's the redhead?" I said, moving up beside Marte for a closer look. A woman had appeared at the edge of the picture. Although most at the rally were casually attired, she wore a long, black, sequined evening gown, each tiny disk strobing under the house lights.

"I saw her, earlier today, around the kitchen," Marte said, confusion clear in her tone. "Not dressed like that but definitely the same woman."

A man holding some type of shield rushed up behind the woman. Constance yelled, "Back." She thrust her hand with the switch even higher into the air. The man complied, but the woman actually took a step forward. Conroy began choking again. His head jerked toward the floor with each cough, Constance's hand being yanked behind. I watched through squinted eyes as the situation teetered on the edge, wondering which cough would finally dislodge her thumb from the dead man's switch.

Constance glanced down at the man and lowered her hand slightly. With the slack, Conroy caught his breath. He looked up at the redheaded woman, tears streaming down his face. "Sheila, get out of here." His voice was raw, but there was no mistaking his words or the pleading in his eyes. "This isn't your fight."

"I can't just leave you here," the woman said. All I could see now was her back, but I could hear the tears in her voice. "She'll listen to me." The woman slowly raised a hand. "I too have seen the sins of medicine."

Although the words were directed to Constance, they didn't get her attention. She was looking down at the floor as if studying the other woman's feet.

"I'm a living example of the evil of it," the woman said. "Together, you, Sister Constance, and I can slay this monster if you'll only let me." She took a step forward.

Without so much as a flinch, a bat of the eye, Constance released the switch.

FRIDAY, MAY 10

11:16 AM – The Evangelical Church of the Rock

Mary Jo Eastin hurried through their private living quarters, peering into silent rooms disturbed only by the echoes of her footfalls. Where was her husband? It wouldn't be like him to go outside and supervise the activities there. He usually let her crack that whip, although motivation wasn't really the issue. It was order. More than once, she'd had to separate some of them before their actions went beyond posturing. It wouldn't do to have a fatal riff among the troops.

Finally, she caught sight of his shoulder around the edge of a high-backed, wing chair—in the room she'd just redone. "Comfy, isn't it?" she asked, coming inside.

"Surprisingly so," he replied. "And I have to admit, I love the way you've organized everything in here. These little—what would you call them—conversation areas? Quite functional."

She came around his chair and sat in another facing him. He always featured utility in his appraisals of their quarters, but that didn't bother her. It was important to her as well. "Thanks, honey. You have plenty of places you can stand up in front of a crowd, but for the more intimate talks, hashing out plans and tactics, you can't beat something like this." She paused a moment. "And plans and tactics are why I came to find you. Everyone is talking about your last prediction."

"About Conroy?" he asked.

"Who else?"

"Well, it's not that difficult when you have—what did you call it before—divine inspiration?" He laughed once, softly. "But just who is everyone?"

"Everyone. Joe Gribbs, Debbie Wells, Marianna Heldman .... Oh, yeah, Layton Tyler. Saw him at the gas station. He said something about being surprised that judgment in this life would be so swift. And so final." She paused, now considering her words even more carefully. "I'm sure you've thought this through, but doesn't Conroy's death remove the most vocal supporter for this immoral advance of medicine?"

"Immoral advance of medicine?" he said. She shrugged.

"Nice turn of a phrase," the Reverend replied to her unspoken question. "It might just turn up in one of my sermons. But to answer your question, no. Conroy was symbolic of this immoral advance, not a perpetrator. I think the ten-dollar-off ad may have spoken to our congregation more than anything I said about Conroy. They need to hear about the real physical assault medical science is making on our souls."

"And I take it you're finding some of that?" she asked.

He smiled. "Plenty. I need to dig further, but there are all these new therapies that take the data from RNA and use it to stop what medicine considers genetic abnormalities. Some of the papers even use the phrase, interfering with genetic data. Basically, it's interfering with God's plan for our lives."

"A turn of a phrase you're considering?" she asked.

"It helps to hear these things out loud," he admitted. "And all the medicine we're turning over to machines? There's research on everything from artificial intelligences interpreting medical scans to robots doing surgery."

"Maybe," she said. "But that might be a bit sci-fi for our congregation."

"Perhaps," he admitted. "But I think you get the picture. How about I put together some ideas and we can go through them? Things that might stir the souls of our flock? And as long as everything is running smoothly outside, we can even put one of these conversation areas to good use."

"Yeah, I'd like that." She beamed at him. They really were a team in this journey. She got up from the chair and left the room, bending down to kiss her husband on the cheek on the way out.

SUNDAY, MAY 12

9:31 PM – The Central West End Neighborhood

I walked along the street between my apartment and Nicole's place, my mind where it had been for the last three days—in a downtown, hotel ballroom where Dr. James Conroy, a mysterious redhead, and Sister Constance had died. The scene haunted me, not only due to the death and destruction wrought by the bomb but also because of all the information that didn't add up. Since when did one plus one make three ... or in this case, since when did incinerating oneself in a fiery blast equal just another day at the office?

That was the crux of my disquiet. Constance had appeared completely indifferent to her impending death. And she had to know it was about to happen. She'd laced Conroy up in a lethal vest, she'd held the button that controlled their fate, and she'd released it when her script reached its end. And if there had been any glimmer of hope for survival in her mind, the recording she played would have dispelled that myth.

Faced with this contradiction, I'd first focused on the mysterious redhead—the woman Conroy called Sheila. It seemed unlikely, but perhaps she was the one in control of the bomb. And if Constance hadn't been privy to that fact, she might have remained calm ... or at least as calm as one could surrounded by armed local and federal law enforcement. But if Sheila was going to detonate the vest, why had she gotten close enough to kill herself? Could she have underestimated the effective radius of the bomb that much?

The day after the rally, the media made short work of my already flimsy theory that the redhead was in control. They identified the woman as Ms.

Sheila Moore, an avid Conroy fan. Or perhaps rabid was a better description. Her infatuation with him had reached the point where Conroy had placed a restraining order on her. Obviously, she was still sneaking into some of his talks. But her appearance in the aftermath of this one was apparently exactly what it seemed—an attempt to save his life.

So, I turned my thoughts back to Constance. I considered the possibility that she had been brainwashed, coming to believe she was doing right, saving the world. But even in the final moments, she was staring at the feet of Moore, not praying fervently for her passage to a better world. If it was brainwashing, someone had scrubbed her gray matter until it was white, and as far as I knew, no one had come up with a formula for that.

I'd also considered drugs, but again, Sister Constance's behavior didn't fit. She had moved quickly when the spotlight had hit her. She had surveyed her surroundings clinically, waiting patiently for her plan to unfold. It was Conroy who was unsteady on his feet while Constance held him up with a rock-solid hand. To my eye, she showed no dissociation from time or space; she was in the here and now, methodically working a storyline that had only one end—her demise.

About the only thing that supported the notion that Constance was under the influence of some type of drug was the single command she had yelled— "back." It had come out a bit garbled, sounding something like Bach, the German composer. But one slightly distorted word didn't outweigh all the evidence that her senses were sharp, her mind clear.

Perhaps Constance's pronunciation reflected a foreign accent; I didn't know, not being much of a linguist. But still, I knew of no foreign country whose citizens blithely went to their death. Being born outside the United States, if she was, said nothing about her sense of self-preservation. All it might explain was why the FBI was having trouble connecting their forensic evidence with a name.

Then, yesterday, I had hatched a variant of the Sheila Moore theory—that someone other than Sister Constance had controlled the bomb, leaving her oblivious to what awaited. If the switch she held was a distraction and the bomb was wired for remote control, all it would take to detonate it was a telephone. As for the killer? It could be anyone. It could be the psychopath watching the television across the street in a bar or in his penthouse in New York or on the beaches of Tahiti. OK, I suppose the cable company's reach didn't extend to New York, much less Tahiti, but there were still some 2.8 million suspects in the St. Louis metro area alone. For a numbers guy like me, that fact made my head hurt.

So, I tested my theory as best I could, hoping I could discard it. I found the video of the bombing online and watched it, over and over. If I could detect any discontinuity between the instant Constance raised her thumb and the explosion, it would be evidence that she hadn't caused it. But I found none. Her motion and the appearance of white noise were simultaneous. If she hadn't triggered the bomb, the phone connection had been made at precisely the same instant. That was too much of a coincidence for me to accept and given the inconsistencies in connection speed and delays in cell phone service, impossible for anyone to orchestrate.

So, the good news was that there probably weren't 2.8 million suspects but rather, just Sister Constance. The bad news was, that conclusion got me no closer to understanding what had happened. I was still wondering how one plus one made three.

I looked up, realizing I was standing in front of the door to Nicole's apartment. I had walked the familiar path from my place to hers noticing nothing, my thoughts some 5 days and 40 blocks away. I wondered if I'd stepped out in front of any oncoming traffic, but that was unlikely. With my tendency to be lost in thought, I'd had a lot of experience with being on automatic pilot, and dangerous events had always pulled me back. At least, as far as I knew they did. The same, of course, couldn't be said for the beauty of the flowers along my walk, the aroma from the bakery on the corner, the music floating from an open window—nothing like that would ever penetrate my mental space. Sometimes I consciously barred myself from that inner world, concerned with everything I was missing as I tread its unconscious pathways.

I fished the key from my pocket and let myself in. A couple of steps down the short hall and I found my intended sitting in the living room.

My intended.

I still found the thought exciting—and a bit unnerving. The woman I saw before me was such a perfect match to my ideals: intelligent, creative, and cute as hell. Second thoughts found no room in my mind. But what she saw in me? That was the more difficult question.

She was wearing a well-worn, long-sleeve Cardinals t-shirt and faded jeans. Her feet were bare, a fact I knew only because the heel of one poked out from under her. She was twirling a strand of her light brown hair around a finger, as she bent over some puzzle book—sudoku, crossword, jumbles? I could never guess, but she always had something occupying her hands and her mind.

"Hi, babe," I said.

She said something in reply that I didn't catch, as she turned a cheek for a kiss. I bent to place one there. The greeting was typical Nicole. When she was involved with something, it got her full and complete attention. No half measures. Thirsty from the walk, I headed toward the kitchen when her voice came from behind me.

"Sam, are you OK?"

I turned back to her. She had placed the book on a side table, and now, I had her attention, although I wondered if it was for the wrong reason. "Yeah, I'm fine. Why?"

"You texted twenty minutes ago that you'd just left your building. It's a ten-minute walk." She tilted her head slightly, looking up from the couch. "Are you still thinking about what happened at the Conroy rally?"

"At the moment I'm thinking, after a few more years together, I won't need to say anything."

There was a flicker of confusion on Nicole's face, quickly gone. "Can't forget about it, huh?"

"No, and I know it's stupid to keep replaying the attack in my head. The FBI has people much more qualified than me working on it."

"And you don't want to call because you have nothing new for them?"

I laughed. "You're just proving my point. And what am I thinking now?"

Nicole rested her chin on a hand, one finger across her lips. Her eyes were cast upward, forming the perfectly exaggerated, I'm-deep-in-thought pose. "You're thinking how lucky you are to know me because I've got something you can call about. And then, once I tell you, you can forget about all that for an evening."

"I'm always thinking about how lucky I am to know you. And I know it's crazy to believe I'd learn anything from the FBI, but …. Well, even hearing they were looking into Constance's strange behavior would be something. Anyway, what's this information that warrants a call?"

"Agent Clements was interested in who knew I'd be working with Laura Greenwood. So, I asked my boss, and he finally got back to me today. He said we didn't send out a press release. However, the decision to have me work with Laura was made over a month ago—April 8—when the contract was first signed, and that information went into the company's scheduling system. So, how many people knew? Anyone at Biomedical Engineering Associates could have found out."

I started to say that was worth the call when Nicole raised a finger. "Plus, we ordered a lot of components for the equipment suite Laura wanted. And evidently, every order went out with her signed specifications and my name as the responsible engineer. So, add everyone at six other companies—at a minimum."

"The FBI is going to love that," I said. "But it gets my foot in the door."

"And from there, maybe you can wangle what you want. Or maybe not, but at least you gave it a shot."

"Absolutely. I'll call Agent Marte tomorrow." I paused, thinking about how one-sided the conversation had been. "So, how have things been working out between you and Laura?"

"I'm not sure," said Nicole. "But come over here and sit beside me while I tell you."

I never needed to be asked twice. And when I did, Nicole snuggled her head under my chin, resting a hand in my lap. I put my arm around her shoulders.

"Mmm, that's better." She raised her head slightly, her eyelashes tickling my neck when she blinked. If this got any more intimate, I'd never be able to concentrate, but she went on with her story.

"Laura asked that I email my questions to her, rather than coming into the office. That, of course, got me concerned. And then, she answered a few of the issues on Thursday but nothing on Friday. I keep thinking that the attempt on her life got to her, but ...."

"But what?" I asked.

"I'm not sure why, but I keep thinking Conroy's death is weighing heavily on her, too."

"Could be," I replied. "You know, I thought I saw her at the rally, just before that Moore woman showed up. But she doesn't appear in any of the clips I've found on the Internet, so maybe I imagined it."

Nicole nodded; I could feel the motion. "Anyway, the material Laura sent on Thursday didn't make much sense. I'm going to give her a week or so, let things settle." Nicole paused a beat, again raising her head slightly against my neck. "So, with that plan, my mind's clear. How's yours, now that you're calling the FBI tomorrow?"

My throat tightened as I realized the possible implications of her question. "Have I been ignoring you?"

"Oh, no," Nicole replied, sitting forward to look back at me. "You've been a bit preoccupied, but I understand that entirely. And even in the midst of everything that's been happening, you've been very sweet, letting me crash at your place on Thursday. And now, staying here. Having you around has really helped get things back to normal. Better than normal actually. Thanks, Sam."

She leaned back toward me, placing her hands on my elbows. Then, we kissed, long and soft and tender. I wanted to take her into my arms, but her light touch held me fast. So, I did the only thing I could—melt into the sofa. Or at least it felt that way.

"It's been a long day. I'm going to take a quick bath and then, to bed."

I managed to catch enough of my breath to say, "OK." She got up, turned, and left.

I got my drink of water in the kitchen and then went to the half bath off the living room to brush my teeth. The brush and toothpaste were the only possessions I had brought for these sleepovers, necessities because I always got a kiss before going home to shower and dress for the day. I returned to the couch and sat, thinking Nicole was right. Just having a reason and deciding to call Agent Marte had stopped the endless cycling of concerns in my mind. That left me thinking of Nicole, something I already did most of the time I wasn't working or sleeping anyway. No, that's not right. She made it into a lot of my dreams as well.

But the problem with thinking about her now was the simple fact that she would be sleeping just down the hall. She would be curled up, soft and warm, under a blanket just fifteen, twenty steps away. It was a thought that not only took over my mind but my body as well. Sleep wouldn't be coming easily.

I stood and went to the corner of the living room where we had stashed an inflatable mattress, sheets, and a blanket. I heard the door to the main bathroom open; Nicole was apparently finished in there. I started spreading the sheet over the mattress when I heard light footfalls behind me. I turned.

Nicole stood in the doorway wearing a long, light blue T-shirt ... and maybe nothing else. She walked over, placed a hand on my cheek, and drew it down slowly until her palm rested against my chest. My skin tingled along the path of her touch. My heart drummed in my ears. She looked up at me, her eyes dark pools drawing me in. I could feel the warmth from the bath radiating from her body, the sweet, light fragrance of soap on her skin. We drew closer, but with her hand between us, a gap remained. She raised her other hand and took my wrist. Then, rising to her toes, her lips brushed mine, lightly, raising goose bumps along my arms. She turned, pulling me along by the hand toward the bedroom.

What on earth made this the perfect moment?

That thought, which would usually lead to a cycle of mental examination, re-examinations, and what-if's, didn't. Rather, I was drawn into the moment—one filled with passion I hoped would never end.

MONDAY, MAY 13

10:07 AM – The St. Louis FBI Field Office

The hallway on level two of the FBI building was filled with the din of an organization hard at work. In the rooms along its length, phones rang, copy machines whirred, voices were raised in laughter, in discussion, in argument. Agent Rebecca Marte, however, didn't notice as she walked slowly along the corridor. She paused midway in an open, common area. It boasted the only windows on this level that were not behind the walls of an office. She walked over and looked out, but nothing before her eyes registered in her thoughts. It had been an unusual morning, and her mind was filled with it.

First, Doc had called—Dr. Sam Price, she corrected herself in her mind. He had wanted to pass on some information; she had suggested lunch. At the time, she'd only been thinking it would be nice to get out of the office, talk to someone who knew the case but who also had a life outside of it. And given the breadth of topics, the casual setting was appropriate. But now she wondered what, if anything, was going on behind the curtain of her unconscious. Was there something percolating there, unbidden, in the silent reaches of her mind where Doc was more than just a witness to an attempted murder? If there was, the part of her mind she controlled needed to quash it.

But while her response to Doc had puzzled her in hindsight, it was the phone call to Dr. Greenwood that had tainted the morning fully with a feel of the surreal. Rebecca needed to talk to Clements about it. She turned from the windows and re-started her trek to his office. When she poked her head around the frame of his open door, he said, "I heard you coming down the hall five minutes ago. You could tap dance in those shoes."

Rebecca smirked. "It's just your ears trying to make up for your poor eyesight."

Clements pulled the glasses from his nose and placed them on the desk. "They're only for computer work. And if you doubt my eyes, we can decide this on the firing range."

"You know, one of these days I'm going to beat you."

"Yeah, promises, promises," replied Clements. "You headed for Hawkins's briefing?"

"I am, but we have 15 minutes. Thought I'd bring you up to date. But first, think Hawkins has anything new?" Rebecca came in and sat in a chair across the desk from him.

"Not that I've heard," replied Clements. "He's still got me and a couple of others working on how Constance got into the Conroy rally. We've gone through the security footage again and found nothing. So, now we're re-interviewing the hotel staff. So far, nothing there either. You're still working Greenwood, right?"

"Yeah, which is the reason I came by. Is it common for the stress of a near miss to catch up with someone?"

"Common?" said Clements. "I'm not sure about that, but it happens. What's she done?"

"Nothing really. She's just acting strange. I called her, thinking I'd touch bases and see how she was doing. But she kept pulling the conversation back to Conroy and what we were doing about his murder. She thought the FBI should be holding press conferences to laud the man and condemn his attackers."

"Hmm, us looking for the Crusaders isn't action enough," Clements said more than asked. "How'd you answer?"

"I agreed with her feelings—he was a great man and the Crusaders are evil, but we have no reason to be calling press conferences. And besides, the only known member of the group is dead. Part of the time, she was angry, but mostly, she seemed confused."

"Confused? In what way?" asked Clements, his eyes narrowing.

After a moment's reflection, Rebecca realized the question was more difficult to answer than she had expected. It wasn't so much what Greenwood had said as how she said it. "Well, she started a lot of statements that never got finished. Other times, it seemed like she couldn't remember. Like at one point, I asked if she'd talked to any of her colleagues, just to get things out of her mind. Last week, she said she might do that. Anyway, her first response was that they would have all heard about Conroy, so there wasn't any reason for her to call. And when I clarified, she got confused— almost like the shot at her had never happened."

Clements sat back in his office chair, his eyes closing as he raised a hand to massage his forehead. "That doesn't sound good."

"Tell me about it," replied Rebecca. "She got a little more lucid toward the end of the call. Like, I mentioned I'd met with Sam Price, just to change the topic. Him, she remembered and asked what I'd found. And when I said it was just a misunderstanding, she seemed relieved and the conversation became less strange. But I'm worried she'll revert. She's holed up on her farm with no one to talk to. That can't be healthy."

"And that's why you'll make a great agent," said Clements. "You never lose sight of the fact that we're dealing with people." He stood up from his desk and turned to the window behind him. He looked out a moment, then back at Rebecca. "I think you're probably right to be worried about Greenwood. Why don't you give her a couple of days? If she's out of it when you call back, we can contact next of kin."

"That's apparently a couple of cousins she rarely sees, but I can do that." After a few moments with no further comment from Clements, Rebecca glanced at her watch and said. "We should probably head over to Hawkins's briefing." Clements nodded, and they stood to leave.

"I don't think he's expecting much more out of the Greenwood incident," said Rebecca as they started down the hall.

"Why do you say that?" asked Clements, glancing sideways at her as they walked.

"The Council for the Right is meeting tonight, and apparently he offered me up for another catering gig so I can keep an eye on them. And that's not a criticism of Hawkins; I don't see much left to do on Greenwood either. I've interviewed the three people that knew about the dinner plans. They all check out. And I've got a meeting with Greenwood's neighbor, Mr. Holyfield, on Wednesday morning. After that, I can't think of anything else to check."

"OK, I'll give it some thought," said Clements. "Didn't you have Holyfield scheduled earlier?"

"I hoped to get to him earlier, until everything went sideways at the Conroy rally. Then, when I called, he'd gone to Springfield to visit a sister." Rebecca paused, smiling at the memory of contacting him. "I think he has one of those old answering machines that tapes incoming calls because it cut me off after about 30 seconds. I had to call a second time to leave the rest of the message. Anyway, when he phoned back, he sounded just like Greenwood described him—an older man just trying to be neighborly. If no one put him up to sending the text, I can't see him being involved."

"Good," replied Clements as they entered the briefing room.

Once settled into their seats near the middle of the room, Rebecca leaned over toward Clements so she could speak softly. "I almost forgot. Sam Price called saying he had information on who knew Ms. Veles would be assigned to Greenwood's project, so I'm meeting him for lunch. Apparently, you asked Veles about that?"

"I did, but why is he calling you?"

"You probably scared Veles," Rebecca said in mock seriousness.

That elicited a quiet chuckle from her partner, along with the comment, "I seriously doubt that, although I'm clearly not as chummy with her as you are with Dr. Price. Your first text made him sound like the Crusaders' handler. Then, he was just a guy in the wrong place. Now, it's Sam, and you're inviting him to lunch?"

Rebecca kicked herself mentally. While she had avoided his nickname, the camaraderie she felt had come through to Clements anyway. "Something about watching assassinations together on live TV, I suppose," she said. That was probably part of the answer, but she was still wondering if there was something else. Hawkins cleared his throat to start the meeting, breaking into her thoughts.

Over the next several minutes, Special Agent Bradley Hawkins framed all of their lack of progress as steps forward. Even with all the physical evidence they had, they couldn't identify Constance, but that eliminated everyone in the fingerprint, DNA, and facial recognition databases they had checked so far—and that was a lot of people. They didn't know how Constance got into the hotel but had eliminated most of the staff and the numerous places they had checked before the rally. The explosive devices were composed of commercial-grade, domestic parts, eliminating military and foreign sources. Gyms and recreation centers that provided climbing and parkour training had been contacted; none had trained Constance. And so on.

It was progress by negation, but was it fast enough to avoid further death? Somehow, in her bones, Rebecca doubted it was.

11:06 AM – Near Washington University in St. Louis

Sister Prudence exited the rear seat of the car, leaving the door open behind her. She wore a blue and white striped T-shirt over white pants and sneakers. Not accustomed to such attire, she smoothed the shirt with her hands. Closing her eyes, she turned toward the sun, feeling its warmth on her face and arms. A slight breeze was infused with the pungent odor of wood mulch, compliments of the well-manicured lawns in this residential area and last night's rain shower that brought out the scent. To the west, a brightly colored male robin used the water that had collected on the sidewalk for his daily grooming. After a moment, a female joined him.

Prudence looked across the top of the car as Brother Justice emerged on his side. He too adjusted his clothes: a dark, green T-shirt and jeans. Each of them bent into the back seat, retrieved a small pack, and put it on. Closing the car doors quietly, they scanned the residential area. It was still five days until the start of the summer session at the nearby university, so the area was nearly deserted.

They walked two blocks north, intersecting a major boulevard that ran beside the campus. There, they turned east, each of them reaching for the other's hand. His black hair and golden-brown skin complemented her pale complexion and light brown hair perfectly. From a distance, they appeared the quintessential student couple enjoying each other's company on a beautiful, spring day.

A careful inspection, however, would have detected some slight inconsistencies. For example, Justice appeared to be too young, looking more like a male in high school than college. They also weren't talking to each other, a discrepancy that didn't appear to be the result of an argument. Rather than angry, their expressions were perhaps best described as curious. The direction of their gaze was also wrong, their eyes searching their environs rather than the face of the other. The impression that they were maintaining a wary vigilance would have been further reinforced when a campus police car passed. Justice turned from the street as Prudence sheltered herself behind him as if sharing a secret.

There was, however, no attentive observer. In fact, no one gave them a second look. Why should they?

Soon, the couple reached their destination—a sprawling, three-story building across the boulevard from the main campus. Here, the couple split up. Justice walked to the front door, while Prudence circled around to the fire escape on the back of the building. He waited, his delay matching what they had practiced. Then, he opened the door and walked in.

A middle-aged woman looked up from a reception desk that sat in the middle of a wide, entry hall. As Justice started toward her, he looked up as if he had just noticed the surveillance camera mounted above and behind the desk. He waved and continued his slow walk. The receptionist smiled, recognizing the self-confidence she often found in these halls. Undoubtedly, he was seeking one of the advanced research groups that regularly met in this off-campus location. And while she knew the room numbers for most of them from rote, she pulled a sheet of paper from her desk to be sure.

But as the woman started to look up from the page, she realized the man wasn't standing across the desk from her; he was beside her. She started to turn toward him when a sharp, cold pain arrested her motion. Her hands flew to her throat, coming away soaked in blood. Her blood. She tried to scream but produced only a low, gurgling sound. She was dying. Her eyes searched for compassion in the face of the only person who could save her— her attacker. He, however, was already moving away. She tried to push herself up from the chair but lost her balance and fell across the desk. The sight of the man bounding up the stairs two at a time was the last thing she would ever see.

Brother Justice quickly found the door with the temporary placard he sought: Conference Room 2-C, Dr. Rajesh Agrawal. The name meant nothing to him nor would the faces he found beyond the door. But in the burgeoning field of synthetic biology, Agrawal was a renowned scientist, perhaps on the cusp of great things. And while the members of his graduate and post-graduate student team were less well known, the faculty at the school would recognize them as some of the best and brightest minds from disciplines as diverse as genetic engineering, systems biology, biophysics, and control engineering. Even the interim between semesters was no distraction for these seven men and three women. In fact, the break assured their attendance, as they were freed from their daily routines of teaching and grading papers.

The quest that had the power to bring together such a collection of talent was nothing less than the creation of synthetic life from non-living components. Should they succeed, the benefits were nearly unimaginable. Synthetic life forms could be used in environments unsafe or inaccessible to humans, such as the disposal of toxic materials or the manufacture of dangerous drugs. Or these manufactured life-forms might become the source of human body parts for those critically injured. They might even give humankind a window to the origins of life itself.

But with the immense potential for good came catastrophic risk. Through greed, intent, or accident, synthetic beings for high-risk work might become slaves and body parts for life-saving surgeries changed to designer components for a superior race. Mitigating those risks was a responsibility that Agrawal took seriously. So, for today's meeting, he had invited a young, Catholic priest from a nearby parish. Not only could the young priest speak to the crushing responsibility inherited by his research team, he could do so in a way that resonated with students. With the incredible pressure to take shortcuts, Agrawal wanted to make sure they understood that humanity trumped fame, wealth, and power.

Brother Justice pulled two Sig Sauer, P320s from his backpack, each loaded with 17 rounds. Prudence carried two Ruger LCPs to accommodate her smaller hands. While the latter handgun carried only seven shots, the 48 rounds between them were more than adequate. And should they encounter resistance afterward, each carried a half-dozen extra clips.

Justice pushed through the door. As expected, he was in the front of the room, left of the podium where Dr. Agrawal stood. "With us today ...." The scientist's words trailed off, replaced by a look of surprise and confusion as Justice shortened the distance between them from ten to three feet. "Excuse ...." Again, his statement was incomplete, cut short this time by a shot that hit him in the forehead. He slumped to the floor.

With the sound of gunfire, Sister Prudence came in from the back of the room and took a position in front of the door. Justice stepped forward and put a second bullet into Agrawal's brain, just as he had been trained to do. He quickly retraced the five steps to the door at the front of the room.

For a moment, the students sat in stunned disbelief; then, panic erupted. Two of the males charged the front of the room. Justice shot them. Perhaps driven by the gunfire, three other men and one of the women rushed toward the back. Prudence waited until the first man was only about four feet away, then dropped him. The woman stopped, but she was too late. She crumpled to the floor when the bullet hit her in the chest. The second man decided to rush Prudence as she felled two of his colleagues, but she snapped off a shot with her left hand. He spun to the floor as the bullet caught him in the shoulder. The last man in the group retreated to the center of the room, seeking whatever cover he could find under tables or behind chairs with those who had remained there.

Shrieks of agony, cries for help, and sobbing filled the room. The acrid smell of gunpowder hung in the air, mixing with the coppery odor of blood and the stench of urine and defecation. Justice looked at Prudence, the latter nodding slightly. He waded forward into the cowering mass. A woman broke from under a desk. Justice shot her in the back. He continued forward until his shadow fell on a man pleading for his life on the floor. If Justice heard, he showed no reaction as he squeezed the trigger.

Over the course of the next twenty seconds, Justice systematically executed each person in the room, all receiving the requisite insurance shot to the head, until only two remained—the woman he had shot in the back, who was still alive, and the priest who sat holding the woman's head in his lap. Brother Justice approached them. The priest raised his hand as if the power of his faith might stop bullets. Tears were streaming from his eyes, as two words escaped his lips. "Please, no." Justice's hand lashed out, hitting the priest on the head with the butt of his gun. The man slumped to the floor. One more crack of the pistol brought the end to the woman's life. Sister Prudence turned and exited through the fire escape door, with her partner following close behind.

The gunfire had produced pandemonium throughout the building and most of the occupants fled through the front door. Several, however, chose the fire escape. Justice and Prudence joined their ranks, leaving traces of blood from their shoes on its treads. Dropping from the fire escape to the ground, the two jogged to a wooden enclosure that held a large, trash dumpster. There, they shed their shirts and jeans, kicked off their shoes, and donned replacements that had been stashed there earlier. The guns went into the backpacks, everything else into the trash.

From there, the two matched the flow of the crowd, jogging at first but then slowing to a walk as they left the area. Soon, there were more people approaching the scene of the killing than fleeing it, drawn by the rumors that none quite believed.

The first sirens were just going quiet at the building when Brother Justice and Sister Prudence reached the car. They climbed into the back seat, deposited the backpacks at their feet, and closed the doors. After a moment, the car pulled from the curb.

11:53 AM – A Restaurant near Ruger-Phillips

I went over the basics again in my mind. One technician performed the diagnostic task on an elaborate power plant control console. Another role-played a second technician, as the job required two people. The training worked, but it wasn't efficient; it tied up two people and an expensive piece of equipment to train one.

The alternative I was studying was to represent the equipment as a three-dimensional model on a computer screen, eliminating the demand on actual equipment. Additionally, the second technician was replaced with a virtual human, reducing the manpower requirement. And because the computer-generated individual "knew" the underlying fault, it could report the correct symptoms and test results from its part of the task. The problem was that some trainees got better working with this system, while others hardly learned anything at all.

I leaned back in the booth, checking the wide, double doors leading out of the restaurant and into the hotel's atrium. I could just make out travelers stopping by the front desk. I was too far away to read their faces, but their postures said it all. A man dropped his bag to the floor and stretched in a yawn. A woman raised a wrist in front of her face, holding the pose for too long to just be reading her watch. She was probably trying to make a statement about how long she had been standing there. Two children, a boy and a girl, raced across the scene, followed a moment later by a woman with a phone pressed to her ear and a hand raised in the air.

My phone was sitting on the table. I tapped the power button, bringing the screen to life so I could check the time. It was still early for my meeting with Agent Marte, so I went back to my work question. The company that had developed the virtual technician and computer model had run the first study, producing the inconsistent results. But when they couldn't determine why, they brought the question to us. Unfortunately, there were at least two major changes from the old to the new training: a virtual model replaced physical equipment and an artificial intelligence was used instead of a role-playing human. Given that, it was tough to know what was causing the breakdown—the model, the AI, or both.

Perhaps the company could make variants of their training. One variation could be two humans using the computer model, while a second possibility was a human and the AI working on the physical equipment. Those variants would help in isolating the issue. Otherwise, I'd be looking for factors that correlated with learning. And that could take a while.

"Hi, Doc," I jumped at the sound of Marte's voice. "Sorry," she said. "Didn't mean to startle you. And yeah, I remember. You tend to get lost in thought."

I stood, smiling. "I did that just in case you needed proof." She smirked as I extended a hand. We had barely seated ourselves when a waitress swooped in to take our drink orders.

"So, you have information about who knew Ms. Veles would be working with Dr. Greenwood?" Marte asked, peering over the top of her menu as she studied her options for lunch.

I told her how just about anyone in St. Louis could have known. Somehow, she didn't seem surprised. Having taken care of the "official" purpose for the call, I wondered how I could change topics, get to the real reason. Marte, however, made it easy; she asked why else I had phoned.

Was I really that transparent?

I filed that question for later and launched into an explanation of why I believed Constance must have been oblivious to her fate. Marte listened as my monologue lasted through ordering lunch and being served. As soon as the waitress had deposited her salad and my burger, Marte picked up her fork. But she didn't take a bite; she just held the utensil aloft like a conductor holding the baton before the start of a concert. Her gaze was focused on the wall behind me or perhaps something even farther away. But I was hungry and not feeling like part of the orchestra. I took a bite from my sandwich.

"So, you don't believe Constance could have been so blinded by the Crusaders' rhetoric that she wouldn't show stress?" Marte asked. But when her eyes came back to the single finger I had raised in the air in the universal, just-a-moment gesture, she smiled. "Sorry. Waiters are always coming by, asking me how everything is, just as I take a bite."

"Yeah, it's like a sixth sense with them, isn't it?" I remarked after swallowing. "I think it's unlikely she could be that cool about her own death. But let's say it's true, that the Crusaders can do that to a person. Then, the next attack, if there is one, should tell you a lot. If they have another brother or sister ready, willing, and able to take up their cause ... well, that suggests a production line, a compound where they're churning out their disciples. And if it's big enough, it'll leave a paper trail—bills for shelter, food, services. On the other hand, if there's a delay or a change in tactics so they're not so visible, then they don't have a lot of followers or they can't create soldiers like Constance easily."

Then, remembering that Marte was the one with training in criminal behavior, I felt my face warm. "Sorry, I'm sure you've been over all of this already."

Marte shook her head. "Different set of eyes, remember?" she said. "And what you said about the paper trail? We've started looking at groups that might be supporting them financially or giving them quarter. After all, if we turn off the money spigot, we stop the group—or at least, slow them down a lot. But as for getting some insight from the next attack?" She paused, her lips pressed together tightly, her head slowly shaking. "I'm hoping Sister Constance was the one and only and that the Crusaders are done. But we've had that discussion."

"Right," I said. "And neither of us really believes she's working alone."

Halfway through the sentence, however, I realized Marte was no longer listening. Her full attention had been drawn to the television hanging over the bar behind me. She rose and walked toward it. I turned to watch, immediately seeing the headline that had caught her attention: "Crusaders

Attack Again." Marte sat down on an empty stool at the bar. I thought about joining her but decided she'd want to focus on the report.

From my vantage point at the table, I wasn't picking up every word from the TV, but I heard enough to know that the attack had occurred near Washington University and had left either ten or eleven well-respected medical researchers dead—there was some confusion about the number. One person, a local Catholic priest, was injured but was expected to survive. Many of the previous statements released by the Crusaders had hinted at a fundamental, religious orientation, but sparing the priest was the clearest declaration of their leanings so far. Or, it was clever misdirection, made even more convincing because it fit the stereotype. But misdirection for what? I had no answer.

Some additional details of the killings made it to my ears. The shooters had sealed off the room, then systematically executed all except the priest. The cold-blooded nature of the murders sent chills down my spine.

This is getting too damn close to Nicole.

The thought flooded my mind, changing my shock to anger mixed with worry. So far, the Crusaders had only targeted leaders in their respective medical fields, and Nicole wasn't one. Not yet, anyway, although her company was well known. Was she in danger?

While I was turning that thought over in my head, the picture on the television pushed my emotions even further. It was a short video clip of a young couple walking hand-in-hand. But just as they were about to pass from the field of view, they stopped and gave this mock salute—one finger touching the forehead, then flipped forward as they stared directly at the camera. Even the gesture was perfectly choreographed, each using their outer hand so they wouldn't interfere with the other. And the look on their faces? I'd never seen a grin that looked so emotionless, so empty.

In one massive attack, the Crusaders had crushed all hope that Sister Constance's death was the end of their reign of terror. They were still among us, just as brazen as before, but now, even more ruthless.

I slumped in my chair, a hand coming to my forehead to massage the tension I felt there. I took a long breath, telling myself my worry was unnecessary and largely irrational. But I knew even before the self-talk started, my gut would never listen.

"Are you OK?"

I looked up to find Marte rejoining me at the table. "Yeah, getting there."

"Your fiancé?" she asked as she sat down.

I nodded. "I know there are thousands of people involved with medicine in St. Louis. Even more when you start counting all the companies that support it, which is where Nicole is. It's just difficult, being so helpless." Marte nodded, picked up her fork, but then set it back down.

I released a long sigh. "You headed to the University?"

"No," she replied. "By now, the place is swarming with agents and forensic teams, not to mention the local police." She placed a hand on the back of her neck, her eyes closing as she twisted her head to the side. I didn't hear a pop, but if it had been me, there would have been one.

"This can't be easy for you, either," I said. "They're taunting law enforcement with that jaunty-salute crap."

"Yeah, it's a slap in the face when they do stuff like that. Not that we need the extra motivation." She paused a moment. "But it doesn't seem like it's just law enforcement they want to hack off. When you kill students who have done nothing but promise a brighter future, that's brutal. It's like they don't give a damn if they alienate the whole country."

"It does seem that way, doesn't it," I replied.

"We also got an answer to one of your earlier questions. The Crusaders definitely have people ready, willing, and able to step in for Sister Constance."

"And probably people they don't think you can identify," I said. "With the way they stared into the camera and left a witness, I wouldn't be surprised if you find their fingerprints all over the bullets and in the room where they killed everyone."

Marte's phone beeped, and she pulled it out. "I need to get going," she said, after apparently reading a lengthy text. "As soon as I get the rest of this salad to go." She flagged down our waitress and asked for a to-go box.

"I've pretty much lost my appetite for now, but in a couple of hours ...." She let her words trail off. "My boss is pulling people to work the attack at Washington University, so I'm backfilling on Conroy. I need to go in for a briefing on it, get up to speed. And then later, there's another coordination meeting. Not sure what that's about, but it sounds big."

She scraped her salad into the box and started to pull some bills from a wallet. I waved her off, saying it was my thanks for her listening when it wasn't part of her job description. She accepted with a smile, the only one in the last several minutes, then left.

My gaze went back to the television. It was showing a block of quoted text with the caption, "Latest Crusader Post." The font was too small for me to read, so I pulled out my phone. A few taps later and their declaration was on the screen.

This post is dedicated to our beloved Sister Constance, gone but never to be forgotten. She made the ultimate sacrifice in order to stem the tide of drugs that kill our senses and treatments that mock our Creator. She gave her life so we could be free of the tyranny of all who say they know best when all they know is how to enslave us in false dreams and an artificial existence.

Sister Constance has fallen, but our cause will never fail. In her stead, Brother Justice and Sister Prudence have taken up our banner. Strike them down, and more will follow until the decision-makers of this great but decaying land recognize medicine as the scourge it is on the bodies and minds of all peoples.

I placed an elbow on the table, my forehead resting in my hand. Were the Crusaders trying to force the government to the negotiating table? Some of the words sounded like it. If you stop the mandatory vaccination of children, we'll stop blowing up hospitals? Clamp down on the excesses of the drug companies and we'll spare the neighborhood clinics? End abortion and the med schools can hold classes in peace? But if that was their aim, where were their demands? Who represented them? Perhaps all of that was coming, but in the six weeks since their emergence, there hadn't been a word on these fronts.

Or maybe the Crusaders believed their actions would embolden a large, silent faction that shared their worldview. That avenging force would rise up, circumventing the slow grind of government. That strategy, however, appeared deluded. Only the most extreme detractors of medicine would endorse the Crusaders after what they had done today.

What objective makes sense in light of these tactics?

I had only confusion in my head where the answer to that question should have been. I looked down at my half-eaten sandwich, realizing I had lost my appetite, too. I waved at the waitress. "Another to-go box, please."

3:03 PM – The St. Louis FBI Field Office

Agent Rebecca Marte slipped into the back of the small auditorium, relieved that Hawkins hadn't started the meeting on time while being perturbed for much the same reason. There were a lot of people here, talking, texting, or just worrying about what lay ahead while he shuffled his notes.

She spotted Clements seated on the aisle, about a third of the way to the front. And although she had no right to, she had come to expect that her friend and mentor would save her a seat. He had. When she reached his row, Clements slid over. After mentioning her preference for the aisle once and then, only as an off-hand remark, it had become his routine. Clements was thoughtful that way.

As she sat, he threw a sideways glance at her, then turned for a longer look. "You look nice. New hairstyle?"

"Aw, crap," she whispered. She ran both hands through her short hair, returning it to its spiky look. "Not styled, just combed," she explained. "Trying the look on for my catering gig tonight, when depraved leers are part of the job."

Actually, she had wanted to look a bit more "put together" for lunch, which, she told herself, wasn't unusual. It was less common, however, for her to forget to return to her office look; in fact, she wasn't sure it had ever happened before. But with the attack at the school, it was understandable.

"There, that's much worse," said Clements, smiling with the non-compliment.

"So, is the rumor true? Are we about to raid the Crusaders' hideout?"

"With Hawkins running the brief and all the agents here?" said Clements, his gaze slowly moving across the crowd. "I'm not sure what else it could be. But we'll know soon enough. So, who knew Veles would be working for Dr. Greenwood?"

"Just about everyone and his brother," Rebecca replied. "Her office plus anyone at the medical supply houses they used for the equipment could have found out. Sorry, but short of a half-page ad in the newspaper, I'm not sure how it could have been kept less quiet. The other thing Price wanted to talk about was how to make sense of Constance's complete lack of fear."

"And he doesn't think it was drugs or brainwashing?" asked Clements. "Her strange calm doesn't come up in the news often, but when it does, they blame one of those two."

"He doesn't buy either. And since Forensics has just about ruled out drugs, all we have left is the possibility she's one in a billion—someone who could buy into the Crusaders' myth so fully that she would go to her death without a care. That one bothers me."

"That one bothers everyone," Clements responded. "And now, with the rather cavalier behavior of Brother Justice and Sister Prudence immediately before they commit mass murder, we'll be working that issue even harder."

"He also thinks we're not going to find a match to Justice and Prudence in our databases."

"I'm not taking that bet," said Clements. "They certainly acted like we can't touch them, but we'll find out. Word is, we've got lots of bloody handprints and footprints from the site. A lot of them will be from the victims, but probably not all of them."

Rebecca's eyes were drawn to the front of the room when she heard the sound of Hawkins's chair being pushed back from the table. "Showtime," she said quietly.

Hawkins walked over to the podium and cleared his throat. "We all know what happened this morning," he said. His voice was soft, but his naturally deep tone would have carried even without the microphone before him. "The Crusaders executed some of the best and brightest in cold blood. Systematically. Without mercy. But Thursday morning, first light," he said, his voice rising, "we may have our chance to stop these bastards."

These were the words the assembled group had waited for, and a soft murmur of affirmations spread through the room. Hawkins waited for quiet to return. "Given the nature of this raid, absolute secrecy is a necessity. I don't care if you tell your significant other everything, he or she can wait until Friday to hear about this. And if even a hint of this op makes it to the media, I'll have the person with the loose tongue checking parking meters on Cardinals' game days for the rest of his or her miserable career. You got that?"

A few in the crowd responded with "got it," but most chuckled at the contrived threat.

"Seriously, people. Not a damn word," Hawkins said and stared for a moment as if wanting someone to laugh or make a joke now. When no one did, he tapped a button on the laptop sitting on the podium. A picture appeared on the screen behind him. "This is where we're going on Thursday—the Evangelical Church of the Rock." Rebecca would have guessed airplane hangar, had it not been for the stained-glass windows and a cross rising above the front door.

"It's a large, nondenominational church sitting out ... well, basically, in the middle of nowhere about 55 miles to our west and south. The front three-quarters or so is the church itself. The back part is living quarters for the

Reverend Micah Eastin and his wife." Hawkins tapped the computer again, and a picture of a couple replaced the building.

"And here they are, direct from the church's Facebook page. They're big in the southeastern part of the state—not quite televangelists yet but moving that direction. During the drive on Thursday, you'll see this same picture on billboards along I-44 as we get closer."

The background, props, and pose in the image said professional photographer—and a good one at that. But it was the figures in the foreground that made Rebecca do a double take. These two were clearly a couple of the beautiful people, with dazzling smiles and perfectly coiffed hair. Their attire was simple and sensual, the man's black knit shirt just tight enough to suggest he worked out regularly. The wife was in white, her blouse also suggestive of her well-developed anatomy. And somehow, the photographer had caught the light just right, making the man's green eyes appear to twinkle. Regardless of what they had paid, it was a million-dollar shot.

"When I got the case last Thursday, this church was way down on the list of possible sources of money or shelter for the Crusaders. But by Friday afternoon, we'd accumulated enough intel to paint a very different picture. They are supporters, no doubt, but we don't know how far it goes. We started surveillance on Saturday, hoping to catch a glimpse of someone we could later connect to the terrorists. Sunday, as you might expect, was pure chaos, with hundreds coming and going. But even so, we have tentative identifications for both Justice and Prudence from those tapes. We're working to get the surveillance images enhanced, firm up these IDs."

"How good are they?" came a voice from the back of the room. Rebecca turned but couldn't pick out the speaker.

"Think the 70 to 80 percent level," said Hawkins smoothly.

"Did the fact that the Crusaders spared the priest at their latest attack have anything to do with getting the go-ahead on this church?" Rebecca recognized the voice as belonging to Agent Dorothy Williamson. The ten-year, black veteran was something of a role model to her.

"Good question, but no, the timing was wrong. The search was approved before the attack. Anything else?"

No one responded, so Hawkins continued. "We'll be looking for the obvious: weapons, bomb parts, any computer equipment that might be used to post their propaganda."

"And we're looking for Justice and Prudence, too," came another voice from up front.

Hawkins chuckled. "Yeah, them too. And the whole gang, if there are others. The warrant also calls out financial records specifically. Since a lot of the church's money comes in the form of cash, every scrap of paper could be important. Those working the inside, keep your eyes open."

Hawkins paused, taking a long breath. "Other than the tentative IDs on Justice and Prudence—and by the way, those came when the two people were leaving on Sunday, not going in. But other than those possible sightings, we don't know that the Crusaders use this location. Who or what or even how many we will find inside is unknown. We're trying to get a count on people arriving and leaving, but even if we come up with a number, I wouldn't give it much weight."

Hawkins brought up a floor plan. Even before he spoke, however, another voice came from the side of the auditorium. "Is that scale right?"

"Should be," replied Hawkins. "It's the architect's drawings."

"Then the living quarters are something like ...." The man behind the voice was obviously crunching some fairly large numbers.

"Just less than 9,000 square feet," said Hawkins. "Clearly enough to hide a small army. But what I wanted to show you are these double doors on the south side of the building. They're closed before the service, but at the end, they open them along with the main church entrance on the east. The missus takes one of these, the Reverend the other. And frankly, we weren't as well prepared for that as we should have been."

"What about the door to the living area on the south?" It was the same voice as the first question, Rebecca not bothering to turn this time.

"They mainly use the one on the east end of the building," said Hawkins. "The other one may be for emergencies. Anyway, because of the unknown and the size of the space, we're going in with overwhelming force. In addition to those present, we're bringing in a bomb squad from Chicago. Supposed to be one of the best in the country. We'll also be joined by a few agents from other federal organizations that are based here. And finally, we'll be backed up by local law enforcement during the raid itself."

Rebecca glanced at Clements, as a low rumble of discontent rolled through the room.

"I know. I just read you the Riot Act on keeping quiet, but involving the locals is necessary; we simply don't have the manpower. To help keep this quiet, only command at the local agencies know anything other than the time of the operation. Yeah, it's a risk, but it's the best we can do. OK, let's get to the details."

Hawkins tapped the computer again and a map of the grounds with a list of personnel assignments appeared. Rebecca didn't bother looking at the teams breaching the building at the main church entrance or the main door to the living quarters. She skimmed the names of the agents covering the south side—the secondary door for the church and the living quarters emergency exit. Then, her gaze went to the north side of the building where there was nothing except windows. There she was, paired with another, relatively new agent, Randy Blewitt.

She wasn't surprised that Clements wasn't with her. If it were her call, she'd put him on the west, the door to the living quarters. It was, in her mind, the high-risk, high-reward entry point. Someone with Gus Clements's training and experience would be invaluable in that role. And sure enough, that's where she found him. Hawkins might be an ass, but he wasn't stupid.

"OK, everyone find their name and team lead?" asked Hawkins. After a moment of silence indicating they had, he said, "OK, leads breaching the doors—front, back, or either of the side entrances—find someplace to meet with your teams and review the tactics we've discussed. We'll meet back in my office at 4:30 to review status. One final chart."

This time, the picture changed to a local area map showing the church, the surrounding grounds, and a road that wound through a wooded area to the north before spilling into the church's massive parking lots.

"The good and the bad of our situation is that there's only one road to the church—good because there are few escape routes, bad because it's a potential bottleneck for our ingress. So, to reduce the possibility of a traffic jam, the north perimeter team, Blewitt, Marte, and local personnel, will assemble along the road here." Hawkins ran the light from a laser pointer along the stretch of road that paralleled the north side of the building. "From there, they'll move as a unit, maintaining line-of-sight spacing through this brushy area. I understand it's a bit muddy in there, so dress accordingly."

"Are we talking a little damp or a mud wrestling pit?" asked Blewitt.

"No one's been through it, but looking in, the guess is it could be up to your ankles. So, like I said, come prepared. Once you radio that the perimeter is secure, Agent Blewitt, the other teams come in by car. The living quarter's team will be first. They'll drive through the south lot and park outside the west entrance. Then, the teams for the side entrances and finally, the team that will be breaching the front door on the east. To keep the element of surprise, we'll need to move quickly, but let's avoid the fender-benders on the church steps." That got a few chuckles.

"So, unless there are questions?" No one spoke. "OK, breach teams to your breakout areas and get ready to kick some Crusader butt. Blewitt and Marte, give me ten, and then I'd like to see you up here for a moment."

3:17 PM – The Offices of Ruger-Phillips

I placed the receiver back on the hook and stared at my office wall a moment. The company with the new maintenance training application had balked at a study using the actual equipment. It was pricey and heavily used, so taking a console out of service for this research was a last resort. I wasn't really surprised. But the option of using the computer model of the equipment and a human in place of the computer-generated, artificially-intelligent technician? To them, that was a no brainer, and they readily agreed. They'd provide the application with the virtual technician muted, routing its dialog to a tablet seen only by the role-playing human. They'd even offered one of their experts as the role-player and I'd accepted.

Now, I needed to think about the instructions to this person, because the last thing I needed was for him or her to go off script, doing something the AI couldn't. Even in my limited experience, I'd seen people in this kind of situation do things unconsciously. If the next step for the trainee was to remove a screw, their wrist would twist. Their eyes would accidentally move to the next component to be tested. Their head would jerk when the trainee reached for the wrong tool. And even with the best instructions, I'd probably need to videotape each session and review them later. On the other hand, the positive side of using experts was that they'd notice any incomplete or inaccurate information provided by the AI. The company said that was impossible, but it was worth a double check.

My ringing phone interrupted my thoughts. I glanced down and smiled at the name on the display. "Hi, beautiful."

"Hi, Sam," Nicole responded after a soft titter. "I wanted to know if you were free for lunch on Wednesday? Say, come by here at 11:30?"

"Sure. Now let's see. It's not an anniversary for the first time we ...."

"Sam Price," she replied, trying to sound cross. "Not on the phone."

"I was just going to say, the first time we told your parents we're engaged, but I guess that will be a first and only time, huh?"

"Better be," she said. "Anyway, Laura called, wanted to know if you and I would like to go to lunch with her on Wednesday."

"Laura? You're talking about Dr. Laura Greenwood? The one who can't get her head straight enough to answer a few, simple questions?" Mostly, I was joking, but I was somewhat surprised, too. It was a rapid turnaround.

"One and the same." There was a pause, and when Nicole continued, it was in a more serious tone. "I have to admit, I'd started wondering if her problem was something more than what happened at my apartment, the way she had been so preoccupied, like she was mad at the world. But she was in a totally different mood today. She was all apologies for the delays. She even made the lunch reservation for us."

"Great. So, it's a date. You, me, and the new and improved Dr. Greenwood on Wednesday."

"Perfect. I'll see you after work."

"Nicole, wait. You have a second?"

"Yeah, why?"

"You've heard about the latest Crusader attack, right?"

"Yes," she said, the excitement in her tone replaced by resignation. She released a long sigh. "In fact, it's about all I've heard this morning—about how we're such an obvious target. But if you search for biomedical engineering online, you'll get dozens of hits in St. Louis. And that's just one of the many industries that support medicine. The Crusaders aren't after small fish like us. They want to knock off the big names, get a reputation no one can forget."

She'd obviously used these arguments before, probably with her officemates. "True, but you add the word 'research' to the biomedical engineering search," I replied, "and the hits shrink to two or three. I'm just saying, you and everyone there needs to stay vigilant until they're caught."

Nicole sighed again. "Yeah, I know. And we are. Building management has put the facility improvements on hold, so that'll get the unfamiliar workmen out of the halls and roaming around the outside. And they're adding a security service starting next week. That meet your approval?"

Nicole was about as stubborn as anyone I had ever met, so her refusal to be chased from her place of employment by a hate group came as no surprise. "Well, if I can't get you to hire a bodyguard and wear a Kevlar vest to work each day ...."

A quiet laugh came through the phone. "Are you applying for the bodyguard job?"

"I would, but I'd be ogling the client rather than watching for threats," I replied, then turned serious. "It's just that I don't want to lose my new roommate, now that I've found her."

"You won't," she said. "I'll be careful."

"All I can ask." Actually, it wasn't, but it was all I was likely to get. "See you at home tonight." We disconnected.

3:37 PM – The St. Louis FBI Field Office

It took most of the ten minutes Hawkins had given himself for the raid teams to get organized. But eventually, they left the auditorium to discuss tactics and to assign individual roles and responsibilities. Hawkins reviewed a few papers and then waved for Rebecca and Agent Blewitt to join him.

"This won't take long," said Hawkins. "There are two main things you need to worry about: first, getting into position without giving away our presence and second, holding the northern border of the church grounds for the duration of the operation. Since the bulk of your team is local law enforcement, you'll be working with unknown quantities. You'll need to impress upon them the importance of steady but quiet movement, maintaining their spacing while in the woods, and holding the perimeter until the all clear is given."

"How much help can we expect?" asked Blewitt.

"We've asked for nine people," replied Hawkins. "So, with you two, we can keep the spacing under ten yards. I want you two on the ends of the line, Marte on the east, Blewitt on the west. The brush is thick enough that you won't be able to see more than a couple of people, but that should be enough if everyone watches their neighbor. The other thing you need to stress to the locals are the rules of engagement. There's to be no use of deadly force except in self-defense or in the defense of another agent or officer. You hear any grumbling from them, you see any rolls of the eye, you sense any hotheads, then that person sits it out. I don't care if the whole line is just you two, I don't want any innocents getting shot. That clear?"

"It is," said Rebecca, while Blewitt followed with a "Yeah, got it."

"Good. Last thing I have is navigating the woods. Either or both of you miss your mark and the line gets pinched or spread. So, from your starting point on the road, you'll need to walk at a heading of 215 degrees until you reach the church grounds. That will place Marte at the northeast corner of the grounds and Blewitt at the northwest."

"Two-hundred, fifteen degrees?" said Rebecca. "Not GPS coordinates?"

"We considered GPS," said Hawkins. "The heavy foliage would cut down on the update rate and accuracy. Then, there's the weather forecast—heavy cloud cover with light rain. Should be good for stealth but another negative for GPS. Since the woods are only about 50 yards across, we thought we'd go with a lower-tech approach."

With those words, Hawkins pulled two compasses from his pocket. "If you don't remember how to use these, go read up and practice. That's it unless you have questions?"

Neither agent did, so the group broke up. Rebecca had taken a couple of steps, when she felt a hand on her shoulder. She jumped and turned to find Hawkins.

"Easy there, Becca." He smirked, looking around. "You know, if you're a bit tense, I could help with that."

Rebecca glared at him, her stance unconsciously widening. "That bullshit ever work, Agent Hawkins?" She bit off the words.

"Oh, sorry. I forgot you hate that nickname," Hawkins said in a way that seemed as genuine as the cheesy grin on his face.

Actually, his words weren't true. Becca was the nickname she reserved for her closest friends. Even Clements hadn't made it into this circle, although that was mostly because theirs was a working relationship. But she wasn't about to tell Hawkins. If he knew she liked the name, he'd never call her anything else.

Rebecca continued to glare in silence, and after a few moments, Hawkins apparently abandoned hope for more. "I just wanted to say, you probably think I gave you a crap assignment. Sure, the chance you see any kind of action is pretty slim. But if anyone catches wind of the raid, there's a good chance they'd try to sneak out through the woods. Keep your eyes open and your guys in line."

Rebecca opened her mouth to say she would when Hawkins raised a hand. "And, yes, I'll be giving Blewitt the same pep talk."

Rebecca believed him. When Hawkins wasn't being a jerk, he was an excellent tactician and he wanted this raid to go well. It would be another feather in his cap. But still, it amazed her how well he could compartmentalize these disparate personalities—the leader who wanted them to succeed and the jerk who wanted her in bed.

"Thanks. I'll do my best." She turned and left before he could revert to the degenerate.

She was about halfway back to her work area when she spotted Clements and a couple of other agents walking her way. When they were close, Clements said his good–byes and dropped from the group. "Mind if I walk along?" he asked.

"Course not," replied Rebecca. "You're done fast."

"We got through basic assignments, then broke for homework," he said, waving a small stack of papers at her. "So, what'd you think about the plan?"

She glanced sideways as they walked, wondering if this was a test of her tactical knowledge, an attitude check, or just small talk. "I think I'm going to need new boots after this ditch crossing."

When her comment failed to generate a chuckle, Rebecca crossed small talk off her mental list. "It seems solid to me. Hawkins adapted to the setting, took what it gave him and worked around the rest. What did you think?"

Clements didn't answer. "What about going in without much intel on the place?"

If that was to make her scratch her head, she didn't see it. "I'm more than OK with it. True, delaying would improve our intel, let us know what we're facing. But the Crusaders could find out and dig in further. And even if they didn't, it might give them time to kill again. Nope, now is the right choice in my opinion."

Clements nodded. "And your assignment?"

OK, this was mostly an attitude check. "I'm fine with it." Clements started to say something else when Rebecca cut him off. "And no, you don't need to tell me about the time you thought you'd pulled some make-work surveillance at a drug lab, only to have a Hummer come barreling through the back wall of the building. What did you say he missed you by, two feet?"

"Less than a foot," said Clements, frowning.

"I swear he gets closer every time you tell that story." Clements opened his mouth to say something, but Rebecca never gave him the chance. "Sorry, gotta run. Can't keep the boys in the Council for the Right waiting for their beer."

TUESDAY, MAY 14

12:17 AM – The Seven Hills Baptist Church

In another 43 minutes, Agent Rebecca Marte, acting member of the Just Desserts caterers, could start to pack up. She still wondered about the name of the company they used for her cover; they served a lot more than sweets. Catchy, she figured, if not especially accurate.

Her eyes were drawn from the wall clock by a wisp of blue smoke. A local sitting at a nearby table had lit up, the sickly, sweet smell of the cigar now reaching her nose. She started toward the man but stopped when she saw Wanda Jennings moving his way. Wanda was their crew lead and not a woman to be treated lightly. Rebecca had seen her deal with problems like this before and had no doubt the man was seriously overmatched.

Wanda stopped at the table and stood silently looking down. After a moment, he looked up, a guilty grin coming to his face. "Can't a man have an after-dinner smoke around here?"

Rebecca concealed a smile behind a hand at the man's plaintive tone and Wanda's scowl.

"Beer and buffalo wings don't make a dinner," replied Wanda as she waved a hand at the table full of empties and red-stained, paper plates. "Now get that dirty stogie out of here."

"Ah, Wanda, have a heart."

"Ain't got one. And besides, we're making the trek clear out here to this church basement because you and your cronies got us kicked out of the last place in town. Now, take it outside before I call Sally Ann."

The man glared at his friends who were now chuckling at his plight. He stood without another word and headed for the door.

"Thanks, Wanda," said Rebecca when the woman walked over. "I don't think he would have left so easily if I had asked."

"No asking with these boys," Wanda replied. "And it helps if you've known their wives for the last 30 years. I like this place. Don't want to get booted again, 'cause you never know where this bunch will land."

Rebecca looked around the dark, somewhat dank basement. The floor was battleship gray. The ceiling was suspended panels, water-stained brown in places, yellow everywhere else. An industrial shade of green paint covered the concrete block walls; it reminded Rebecca of pictures of hospitals from the 1950s. But while not luxurious by any standard, Rebecca understood Wanda's sentiment. The kitchen was clean and spacious. Setup was simple, with the tables and chairs stored just off the main room. They even had separate men's and women's restrooms; the last place had required a guard at the door of the communal facilities whenever a woman needed them.

"Say, what's wrong with Connie?" asked Wanda. "You just filled in for her—what was it? A week or so ago?"

Connie Tischner had agreed to take a night off with pay when the FBI wanted Rebecca on the scene. It was an arrangement known only to the owner of the catering company, Connie, and the Bureau. "Just a touch of a stomach problem," replied Rebecca, using the agreed-upon excuse. She was supposed to add something about a 24-hour bug going around, but some heated words at a nearby table caught both women's attention.

So far tonight, none of the discussion had been even vaguely anti-Islamic—or about any religion or nationality for that matter. Rather, the Council for the Right had focused on automation. Their misconceptions about technology ranged from appalling to amusing in Rebecca's view, but whatever their notions were, they were always passionately held. The consensus was that in five years, the only work that would be left would be servicing the robots who stole their jobs. But what drew Rebecca's attention now was the mention of another despise-worthy group—doctors.

"He's a damned, cut-first hack," said a balding man, the veins starting to show on a neck that was already beet-red. "And now Janey's in the hospital 'cause of him."

"That's all they know, Bobby," said another. "I was getting tired jumping off the tractor every half-hour to relieve myself, so I went to see my doc. He wants to put me on some pill, but I took care of it myself. I quit climbing down."

"You won't even bother stopping the tractor before long," said a third man over the chuckles at the table. But if they were trying to calm Bobby, it wasn't working. If anything, he appeared angrier than ever.

"I'm not lettin' that bastard kill my niece," he said. "No one does that to my kin and gets away with it."

A fourth man joined the talk. "I know something you can do about it, Bobby. Something permanent, so that quack won't ever bother you or yours again." He held Bobby in a hard stare.

"What are you gonna do?"

"Not here," replied the man, shaking his head. "Call me when you have time. But I will tell you one thing. What I'm thinking is nothing some damn robot can do." That brought another round of laughter to everyone except Bobby. "How about another round?" asked the man. He left to a chorus of thanks and slaps on the back.

"Bobby's niece having some trouble with surgery?" asked Rebecca, as she and Wanda started back toward the kitchen.

"Surgery?" Wanda gave Rebecca a sideways glance, her forehead wrinkled.

"He said something about a cut-first doctor."

Wanda took Rebecca's elbow and guided her to a quiet corner. "That has more to do with Bobby's wife than his niece." Wanda released a long breath.

"She had some sort of growth around her heart. The way I understand it, he prayed on it for months. When he finally brought her to the hospital, they tried surgery but couldn't save her. As for his niece, I'm not sure. They live a ways down south, and I don't see her much. But she's been in and out of the hospital for meth. You need to keep quiet about that, though. Bobby's a proud man."

"Of course," said Rebecca quickly. "And the man who just got the round of drinks? He's familiar, even said hi earlier, but I don't remember his name."

"Handsome, isn't he?" said Wanda, her elbow poking Rebecca in the ribs. "Well, if he's flirting, you should know—he's married. Keeps someone on the side happy, too, if you know what I mean." Wanda winked suggestively. "You might want to wait for someone with a bit more lead in his pencil."

"Oh, no, I didn't ...." Rebecca only got that far before realizing that Wanda wasn't listening, having drifted off to some imaginary world of her own. But the problem was, she was afraid Wanda had forgotten the question. And if she had, should she ask again? Being too curious could be a bad thing if this 'fixer of problems with doctors' was somehow connected to the Crusaders. Fortunately, the woman was only sidetracked for a moment.

"I'm surprised you don't know him. That's Walter Bledsoe, treasurer for the Council and a dirt pimp in real life. Has his office up north a bit, off the interstate. Lives up that way, too."

"Dirt pimp?"

Wanda drew back and looked at Rebecca. "Real estate agent."

"Oh, OK. At least I can say hi in return. Say, has the company changed the recipe on the wings? I swear they're better tonight." Actually, she had no opinion, hadn't even tasted them, but knew she needed to change the topic.

"Nah, you're just hungry, girl. You should eat more, put some meat on those bones." Wanda looked away for a moment. "Looks like that table in the far corner needs something. I'll go check."

Seeing that Walter Bledsoe had taken a chair there, Rebecca replied, "No, let me get it. You could probably use some time off your feet."

"I could. Thanks."

Rebecca spent the rest of the evening trying to eavesdrop on Bledsoe's conversations but to no avail. The man was always leaning over to whisper in someone's ear or pulling a fellow council member to a corner for a private talk. About the only words she ever caught were something about a will and later, a strip shopping mall. But she did see him accept some money—all in cash.

After the cleanup and drive, Rebecca got home at 2:30. She didn't even debate going to bed; she knew she couldn't sleep without words on paper. By 3:30, her report on the evening was done, and she sent it as an encrypted email to her supervisor and Clements. She also added Hawkins to the distribution at the last moment, figuring he should know about the possible connection to the Crusaders, even if it was extremely tenuous.

Rebecca went to bed, wondering if she'd get a call in a few hours with news of the latest Crusaders' massacre, but the thought lasted mere moments before exhaustion overtook her.

8:03 AM – The Offices of Ruger-Phillips

I got up from my desk, walked to the door, and peered into the hallway. It wasn't like my boss to be late, but he was nowhere in sight.

I'd finished a design for the virtual maintenance technician study, as I had taken to calling it. The next step was to present it to the customer, get their concurrence. That would happen right before lunch. This meeting with my boss, on the other hand, was *pro forma*. He had never changed any of my designs and, frankly, didn't have the background to do so. He just wanted to hear about them in advance, which was only logical. But the lockstep process left me with little to do for the next ... well, two hours if he was a complete no-show.

I wandered over to my window, stuffed my hands in my pockets, and looked out at the traffic on the freeway just beyond the Ruger-Phillips fence. Rush hour was still in full force. The traffic exiting a quarter of a mile up the road was at a near standstill in front of me.

My thoughts returned to the early morning. I could almost feel Nicole snuggled up against my back, the warmth of her body coming through my T-shirt. Her soft, slow breathing caressed my neck. Her hand twitched on my arm, perhaps a meaningful gesture in her dream. After a while, she stirred and stretched. I rolled over, placed a hand on her cheek, and kissed her softly.

I turned from the window, smiling with the memory, but knowing it was pointless, perhaps even frustrating to follow it further. I sat down at my desk, another thought popping into my head unbidden. And with certainty, I knew this one would drag my mood down because the same issue had been cycling in my mind for the last two days.

Just what the heck are the Crusaders trying to accomplish?

The question had surfaced as I watched the news of the mass shooting near Washington University, and nothing had happened since to resolve it. The problem was, they couldn't kill everyone in medicine or even all of those pushing state-of-the-art. There were just too many people involved and the need for their services too strong. It was equally unlikely that they could obtain concessions from the government on public policy. Conceding to terrorists was considered a lose-lose proposition—give them what they want now and it only emboldens them to demand more in the future.

The Crusaders might be able to slow the demand for treatment if people became fearful enough. But given the choice between the certainty of a fatal illness or the slight risk of being caught in the crossfire of a Crusader attack, wasn't the choice obvious? In fact, if anything, the attacks were having the opposite effect on the masses. People were starting to circle the wagons around medicine, rather than turning from it.

Damn, is that what the Crusaders want?

Were they using reverse psychology? Were the attacks designed to increase support from public backlash rather than stall medicine's advance? Despite how convoluted it first appeared, it was an explanation that fit what I knew. Public outrage was increasing by the day. The state legislature had passed a resolution condemning the Crusaders and pledging support for the embattled schools and clinics. The mayor of St. Louis had declared May 19 a day of solidarity with the medical community. She'd also identified emergency funding to increase police presence on and around medical facilities. Even commercial businesses were doing their part. Two local security companies were offering alarm system upgrades to medical facilities at cost, presumably hoping the goodwill would impact their bottom line later. And one well-known, local businessman had donated a million dollars to both the Washington University and the St. Louis University Schools of Medicine.

But when I ran this line of reasoning to its logical conclusion, it too made little sense. As a result of the attacks, the medical community had received several million dollars in donations and a bump in public support, but at the same time, they had paid with ten lives. Even I didn't need to turn those deaths into dollars of lost productivity to know that medicine had come out on the short end of this exchange—the very short end. And if you added the reduction in quality of life due to missed and delayed scientific breakthroughs, the gulf between medicine's gain and its loss was enormous. They couldn't be trying to help medicine by attacking it.

I rose from my desk, recognizing that pacing my office was my only option for dealing with my frustration. But no sooner had I stood than my phone rang. It was the administrator for my group, telling me my boss was tied up in another meeting. He'd come by later for the call to the customer. After I hung up, I sat back down and opened the briefing I'd prepared, thinking I would review it one more time. But each time I started rehearsing the pitch in my mind, my earlier concerns pushed it aside. Finally, I gave up and went to walk the halls.

I couldn't see a flaw in my reasoning, but maybe if I considered the implications of using reverse psychology, I find the error in my arguments. Or perhaps, I'd show that the notion wasn't quite as crazy as it sounded. But nothing affected the idea until I considered it in light of James Conroy. Unless his entire life was a lie, he represented a movement to increase access to medicine and reduce its cost. And the Crusaders? Under the assumption they were trying to create a public backlash, they wanted the same.

Ergo, Conroy and the Crusaders were working together.

When the thought struck, I was walking in a short hall between two buildings, the bottom half of its walls a solid panel, the top, large windows. I moved to the side and placed a hand on a pane of glass as if needing its stability. I stared sightlessly at the strip of green lawn and the gray of the parking lot beyond. Two people walked behind me. I hardly registered their presence.

If this was true, James Conroy had allowed himself to be martyred for the Crusader's cause. It seemed an unbelievably high price to pay, but I'd heard his story. In his mind, medical policy had condemned his sister to death, and he had been powerless to stop it. He had suffered from these thoughts every day. So, perhaps dying to make sure this never happened again wasn't that farfetched.

I pulled my phone from a pocket and stared at it. Should I call Agent Marte? To some degree, this deduction fell into the new-set-of-eyes category. And it certainly helped explain how Constance had gotten into the rally—something that had clearly bothered Marte. The problem was, nothing in this hypothesis came from my eyes. Rather, it was the product of a chain of logic that rested on a highly improbable assumption—that the Crusaders could inflict so much death and destruction that long-held beliefs about medical science would shift. And I still couldn't accept that premise.

There had to be more, something I had overlooked. But I had no idea what it might be. Perhaps with time, the predispositions that kept channeling my thoughts to the same flawed conclusion would fade. Then, an insight could emerge—if there was one to be found.

With no other option, I turned back toward my office.

2:06 PM – The St. Louis FBI Field Office

"Morning, sunshine," said Clements, peering over the top of her cubicle wall rather than coming around to the opening. She'd come to think of this particular choice of locations as a buffer between some disappointing news he was about to deliver and her reaction. But since the Bureau wasn't a place where a woman succeeded by being meek, he'd just need to take whatever precautions he deemed necessary.

"I got my sunshine before I ever went to bed," Rebecca replied, knowing it was an exaggeration but only a slight one. "What's up?"

Clements looked around, which struck Rebecca as odd. From his vantage point, all he would be able to see was the tops of other cubes. "Walk with me," he said after a moment.

Rebecca mumbled "crap" under her breath, the request virtually confirming that bad news was on the way. She got up from her desk and followed Clements into the hallway.

"I saw your email on last night's surveillance," said Clements as they walked. "Good work."

"Thanks."

"Hawkins took note, too. He thought we should take a closer look at the realtor."

"OK, I did my job. So, why all the drama?" asked Rebecca, tiring of the suspense.

Clements took a breath. "He wants someone to meet with Bledsoe. But not you."

Rebecca stopped; Clements turned to face her. "Is that all?" she asked.

Clements's eyes narrowed as if trying to see through a calm façade that hid a smoldering anger. But after a moment, he apparently gave up. "Yeah, that's it," he said. "The Council is used to seeing you around, and it looks like their tongues are loosening. If you go interview Bledsoe, that cover's blown. So, Hawkins asked me to handle it."

They started walking again. "The only thing that surprises me," said Rebecca after a few steps, "is that we're not trying to get something firmer before you go see him. For all we know, Bledsoe has some swampland in Florida he plans to sell to the doctor, and that's his idea of getting even."

Clements chuckled, then turned serious. "That's possible, but there's a hell of a lot of pressure on Hawkins. The mayor calls daily—the governor, almost as often. Even the president is talking about the moral decay in St. Louis, to use his words." Clements glanced back as they continued down the hall. "And don't spread this around, but Hawkins's intel on the church we're raiding Thursday may not be all he claims. So, yeah, the Bledsoe interview may be something of a ready, fire, aim exercise, but can you blame him?"

"What's wrong with the intel on the church?"

"Nothing's wrong," replied Clements. "It's just not that deep. The preacher has voiced support for tighter reins on medicine, and there may be some discrepancies in their finances, which, by the way, are the same two things that got him interested in the Council and your realtor, Bledsoe."

"I was told the Council had some members with deep pockets, but jeez, you'd never know it if you met them," said Rebecca. "Half of them show up at these meetings in jeans and a baseball cap that looks like they were born with it."

"Trust me, they've got money. And as treasurer, Bledsoe would be in the middle of it if some is getting to the Crusaders. So, have you had a chance to check on the guy at all?"

"A start, but nothing much so far. No arrests or warrants. He's on social media, but I think his wife does most of the posting. It's all family—vacation pictures, birthdays, stuff like that. The reason I think it's her is that there's a link to some family history. It's mostly about the Walkers, which is her maiden name. But both families have been in the area for several generations, mostly in farming although there was one in law enforcement in the late 1800s."

Clements nodded his head slowly. "The law was different in those days. Lawmen, too."

"So I've heard," replied Rebecca. "Bledsoe's business also has a web page. He appears to handle just about everything: commercial, residential, farmland, even dabbled in some of the legal issues. That's about it, so far. When are you planning to see him?"

"Thursday, we're searching that church, so I thought I'd talk to him tomorrow. I don't want to be caught waiting for a raid when in the end, it produces zilch."

"Sure," Rebecca replied. "I've got that interview with Holyfield tomorrow. I mentioned it before?" Clements nodded. "What do you think about going together? I can stay out of sight during the Bledsoe interview. I can even drive."

Clements had his concerns about her behavior behind the wheel, using phrases like "beating the road into submission" to describe it, so she had made the offer as a distraction. If he was thinking about her gesture, perhaps he wouldn't consider the pros of combining the trips too closely because there weren't many. She just wanted to be nearby as the Bledsoe lead was being explored.

"OK, sure, but I'll drive," he replied after a moment.

"You know, sooner or later, you're going to have to let me behind the wheel."

"Let's go with later ... for now."

Rebecca was certain he wanted to end that sentence with "forever."

WEDNESDAY, MAY 15

7:51 AM – Outside the Office of Walter Bledsoe

Agent Gus Clements drove past Walter Bledsoe's storefront real estate office, his head casually turning to look as he did. His motion was all Rebecca could see from her vantage point. She was leaning over in the front seat beside him, protection against Bledsoe looking out through his dirty windows and recognizing her. Of course, she didn't know his windows were dirty, but if they looked anything like those farther up the street, they'd have the transparency of dense fog on a cool summer morning in the Mississippi river valley.

"With all the pretty, quaint towns around here, why does this one look like they unplugged life support five years ago?" Rebecca asked. She sat up now that Clements was turning onto a side street, two blocks past Bledsoe's office.

"Supply and demand," Clements replied. "The main occupation around here is farming, and farms are bigger nowadays. They get everything they need in bulk, leaving little for the two-pump gas stations and the mom-and-pop stores. If a town doesn't have a history or a spectacular view to bring in some tourist money, they end up like this one—fighting over the crumbs."

Clements turned the car around and parked it on the side street facing the main road through town. "Best be going," he said. "Don't want to be late."

"Yeah, you don't want to risk that he's run out of information on retirement homes before you get there."

Clements grumbled something she didn't quite catch but figured he wanted it that way. They both exited the car. Clements stared over the roof at her. "Where are you going?"

"Thought I'd stretch my legs. There was a garage sale back on the main street, just past where we turned. I'll be at it or walking on this block."

Clements hesitated but eventually agreed. The two of them walked to the intersection, Clements turning right toward the real estate office, Rebecca to the left.

By the time she had walked ten paces, she realized the feel of the town had changed dramatically. Here, the houses were neatly painted and the lawns carefully trimmed. Each yard boasted flower gardens, all bursting with life. There was lawn art, ranging from religious statues to abstractions that twirled in the wind. Some seemed a bit tacky to Rebecca, but all suggested pride of ownership and stubborn defiance against the commercial death and decay just a few blocks away.

Arriving at her destination, Rebecca found the driveway lined with everything from used clothes to drink glasses from Bourbon Street bars to hunks of a black, shiny stone identified as "obsidian from Yellowstone National Park." She smiled to herself, wondering what Clements would say if he came back and found someone cuffed in the back seat. Taking rocks from national parks was against the law, after all.

"Lordy, girl. What are you doing in my neck of the woods?" The voice was familiar, but Rebecca couldn't place it until she turned to find Wanda Jennings staring at her. "And all duded up, too," the woman added. Wanda had never seen her in anything but the short, pink uniform she wore to catering jobs. The tailored, black suit over pale blue shirt she wore now were quite the contrast.

"Wanda." Rebecca stepped over and gave the large woman a hug. They weren't really that close, but Rebecca needed a minute to think and Wanda took the gesture in stride. "Just headed to a funeral."

"Here?" her tone a bit incredulous.

"No, up north at Hawk Point," Rebecca replied, recalling the name of one of the towns they would pass through on their way to see Holyfield. "Find anything good here?" Rebecca was hoping for a change in topic.

"Naw, just the usual. How'd you come to be going through here, anyway? You overshot the exit to Hawk Point by at least 10 miles, besides turning south, not north off the Interstate." She chuckled at her own words.

Rebecca, however, didn't see the humor. In fact, what she saw in her mind's eye was anything but funny. Less than 36 hours ago, she had asked Wanda about Walter Bledsoe, finding out not only his name and occupation but that they might be romantically involved. At least, that was one interpretation of Wanda's suggestive wink. And now, to discover Wanda lived in the town where Bledsoe had his office? Was everything she said to Wanda later whispered in Bledsoe's ear? She straightened her jacket, suddenly aware of the slight bulge caused by her service revolver.

"I couldn't sleep, so I headed out early—just for a drive. But I should get going."

"Oh, OK," Wanda replied, shrugging. "Guess I'll see you next time we're short-handed."

Rebecca walked down the block, turning when she reached the side street. Wanda was still visible, perhaps looking at the wares at the end of the drive. Or maybe she was watching her? If Rebecca continued, she'd be only a block from Bledsoe's office. If she turned down the side street, Wanda would know where they had parked, maybe even get a look at the car. And with the government plates on it, she'd need a good cover story lest Wanda was left to her own imagination.

Rebecca raised her phone, pretending to take a call while watching the woman from the corner of her eye. Eventually, Wanda moved farther down the driveway and out of sight.

Rebecca hurried down the side street, got in the car, and closed the door. She watched the intersection in front of her. Occasionally, a car or truck would pass, but no one was on the sidewalk. No one turned down her street.

She continued to watch as seconds became minutes. She moved forward on the car seat so that she could check the passenger-side, rearview mirror. And there was Wanda, approaching from the rear. She must have circled around the block.

"Crap," Rebecca muttered to herself. She slid down in the seat, keeping her eyes just above the edge of the window so she could watch the woman's approach in the mirror. There was something in Wanda's hands. It was a small purse but definitely large enough for a gun. Rebecca was certain the woman's hands had been empty when she returned the hug. Wanda had either purchased the bag at the sale or had retrieved it from somewhere. When she was three houses away, she brought the bag up to her face and started reaching into it.

Rebecca focused all her attention on the possible threat, wanting every split-second advantage she could get if things went sideways. The driver's side door opened. Rebecca's hand flew to her revolver, her mind now screaming that she should have removed the safety strap earlier.

"Easy there, partner. It's just me." Clements had jumped back from the door when Rebecca's motions registered in his brain. Now, he crouched in the street two feet away, peering cautiously into the car's interior.

"Get in and close the door," Rebecca hissed.

Clements looked around quickly and complied. "What the hell's wrong?" he asked.

Rebecca checked the rearview mirror but saw nothing. "That woman who was on the sidewalk behind the car—you saw her?"

"Yeah, she went in a house a couple of doors down. Saw her turn in just before that warm welcome you gave me. Who is she?"

"Wanda Jennings, our catering lead," replied Rebecca. "And I think it's possible I blew my cover. Not today, but yesterday, when I asked about Bledsoe."

Clements started the car and drove away. After putting several blocks between them and Wanda, he pulled over. "So, what happened?" he asked.

Rebecca proceeded to fill in the details that had seemed too insignificant for her report earlier but which now felt crucial. Wanda hadn't merely known Bledsoe's name, his role in the Council, and his business, but also his philandering ways. And she apparently lived less than three blocks from his office.

When she finished, Clements released a long breath. "Funny. When I was walking back to the car, I was thinking I'd say something like, I'm either losing my touch or Bledsoe is one of the smoother characters I've met. I guess I have to add a third possibility. He was waiting for me."

"Damn. I'm sorry."

"No need to be," Clements replied. "I think there's a good chance this is just a coincidence. She knows everyone, so it makes sense she'd know him. And an affair, if there is one, doesn't mean she'd say anything about you. But you made a possible connection, so we need to check it out before you take any more catering gigs. OK?" Rebecca nodded.

"Say, you recall Bledsoe's wife's name?" asked Clements.

"Yeah, Sarah. Maiden name, Walker. Why?"

"He had a picture on his desk. The woman in it seemed familiar, but that name doesn't ring a bell. I'm going to call this in."

Once the call was connected, Clements requested "... the collection and coordination of all existing information on one Walter Bledsoe and his wife, Sarah Walker Bledsoe, with the intent of initiating a preliminary investigation."

The smooth way these words rolled off Clements's tongue made Rebecca think he had used them before, perhaps often. Or maybe they were the prescribed phrase in some regulatory manual Rebecca had yet to study. If so, she would do so eventually because the transition from assessment to preliminary investigation was significant. Achieving the latter status would greatly increase the information they could access, including logs of incoming and outgoing phone calls and emails, bank and credit card records, even the content of public conversations obtained with high-power microphones.

Before Clements disconnected, he added two caveats to his request. First, he asked that special attention be paid to any references to a Ms. Wanda Jennings. And second, the subjects of this pending investigation, Bledsoe and his wife, might be aware of the FBI's interest.

"So, what happened in there?" asked Rebecca when he disconnected.

Clements started the car and pulled away from the curb. "He took a visit from the FBI awfully casually, like he gets agents coming in all the time. Even when I got to the Council, he didn't react. He just said it was a private, by-invitation group—in other words, none of my business—and he refused further comment. So, that plus the strange feeling I got from the picture of his wife—it was enough to peg my suspicion meter."

"Peg?"

Clements chuckled, glancing sideways for a moment, then back to the road. "I forget you kids have no experience with gauges. I'll let you figure it out, but in the meantime, think about how you want to handle Holyfield. That's your call and you have about an hour."

How to handle Holyfield? That sounded like a setup by a mentor who thought every minute on the job was another teaching moment. There was no need to plan for that interview; all she had to do was ask him one or two, simple questions. So, Rebecca pulled her phone and started tapping on the screen. After a moment, she said, "To peg a meter means to make it hit its top possible reading. It's derived from a physical post or peg, used to keep the needle of an analog gauge from rotating too far and being damaged."

Clements snorted softly. She put the phone away and turned to watch the countryside roll by outside her window.

8:23 AM – The Offices of Ruger-Phillips

"Ruger-Phillips, Dr. Sam Price. How may I help you?"

It was the standard greeting for unknown numbers, so I was a bit surprised to hear Nicole's voice on the other end of the phone call. "Hi, Sam. Got a minute?"

"Sure, but where are you calling from? My phone's not recognizing the number."

"I'm in the lab. I left my cell phone at my desk. Anyway, I wanted to tell you, Laura can't make lunch. Something came up."

"Nothing bad, I hope."

"I don't think so. She didn't explain but apologized over and over. I'm just disappointed we missed the opportunity. I even suggested we try dinner again, but she declined."

"With bullets for dessert, one time in your apartment is probably enough," I said.

"Sam." She tried to sound irritated, but I could hear a touch of amusement in her voice. "Besides, that was the second time. We dropped by before dinner so she'd know how to get there. I even gave her a quick tour."

That was an interesting tidbit—one I wish I had known when Agent Marte asked how Greenwood had found Nicole's office so easily. Oh, well, it was irrelevant now.

"Anyway, you still want to go to lunch, don't you?" asked Nicole. "Laura offered to cancel the reservation, but I said no."

"Sure. Lunch sounds great. And you said around 11:50?"

"Right," she replied. "Park in the visitor lot, and come in when you get here. We can walk over. It's less than two blocks."

"Got it," I replied. "This thing that came up with Laura? It's not going to be a problem for your project, is it?"

"Just the opposite. We went over all my questions, and I think we have it wrapped up."

"That's outstanding," I replied, seeing an opening for a somewhat corny quip. "After all, you need to do everything you can to hurry her along."

There was a pause, followed by a tentative, "I'm not sure I want to know, but why's that?"

"Because I want her to freeze my brain now. My life can't get any better."

Nicole groaned. "That's incredibly sappy ... but really sweet. Thanks. And to think what you'd be sacrificing for me."

"Sacrificing?"

"Yeah. Stopping your brain development for a month probably takes six months off your life."

"Really?" I said, amazed by the statistic. "Her treatment is that hard on the body?"

"No, it's not that," Nicole said quickly. "It's not stress from the treatment reducing life span. It's just rapid growth of the body while brain development is paused. The body matures at about six times its regular rate, or at least, that's Laura's estimate for preemies."

"Interesting," I said slowly. "I wonder if the age when the treatment is applied determines the speed of growth. After all, babies are developing fast. Maybe the treatment just lets that pattern continue. So, if she applied it to me, maybe my body would age at its current rate."

Nicole laughed. I suppose some might be offended by her reaction, but I wasn't. In fact, it was comforting that in her eyes, my obsessive ruminations about scientific phenomena were amusing or ideally, endearing. I'd dated a few women who held a very different opinion. One even told me I'd never have a serious girlfriend until I got "... my f'ing head out of the books".

"That's why I was hoping the three of us could get together over lunch," Nicole said after a moment. "Laura and the researcher in you could have finished the talk we started over dinner. But I guess I better get back to work. See you a bit before noon."

"I'll be there," I said.

As I hung up the phone, an uneasy feeling started creeping into the corners of my mind. Something wasn't right. I replayed the conversation, coming back to the fact that Greenwood had been in Nicole's apartment before the dinner. Besides Agent Marte wanting to know how Greenwood had found her way around, Agent Clements had also asked who knew about the dinner invitation. Obviously, Greenwood knew. And with knowledge of Nicole's apartment, she could have even orchestrated the shot if she was working with the Crusaders. But if Conroy working with them rested on an untenable premise—that the Crusaders could facilitate medical advancement through murder—then this reasoning failed for the same reason. In fact, if that premise wasn't bogus, anyone in medicine might be working with the Crusaders ... even Nicole.

Suddenly, the whole logic seemed absurd, and I told myself to push it from my thoughts. But as is often the case, my gut didn't listen. The nagging doubt remained, waiting for an insight that would give it meaning.

8:52 AM – The Holyfield Farm

"Mr. Holyfield?" Rebecca asked when a grizzled, elderly man in overalls, house slippers, and blue work shirt answered her knock. She was standing on the porch of a white, frame farmhouse along with Clements.

"Whatever you're selling, I got one. Probably two."

"I'm not selling anything. I'm FBI Special Agent Rebecca Marte, and this is my partner, Senior Special Agent Gus Clements. I called about meeting you this morning."

"Yeah, OK, sure," Holyfield said slowly. "I'm Joe, it's just ...." The man's voice trailed off, one bushy, white eyebrow rising. "Girls in the FBI?"

"The first female agent was hired in 1922," replied Rebecca, knowing the date by heart.

Holyfield rubbed a hand over the gray stubble on his chin, his head slowly shaking. "Pretty little thing like you, missy? Thought sure you were one of those door-to-door sales ladies. Don't see 'em much anymore. Course, at four bits for a plastic, sandwich box? What dang fool would pay that?" He harrumphed, his hand back at his chin.

Rebecca glanced at Clements, wondering when there had been door-to-door salespeople in this area and when a sandwich container was just 50 cents. The 1970s? Earlier? She wasn't even certain four bits was 50 cents, but that seemed right.

"That kind of business was never very efficient, Mr. Holyfield. A lot of it probably gets conducted over the Internet these days." With the reply, she realized she'd strayed far from the topic of her interview. Perhaps Clements had been right. Maybe she should have planned her questions.

"It's Joe," said Holyfield. "Like I said."

"Right, sorry, Joe," replied Rebecca.

"Anyway, missy, don't know about that Internet," continued Holyfield. "Never had much use for it. But where's my manners. Come in, take a load off."

The interview wouldn't take long, and Rebecca considered declining the man's offer. But Holyfield, although apparently fit for his age, looked like he needed to "take a load off" as well. "Thanks," she said.

There were two doors into the house from the front porch. Rebecca had knocked at the one that appeared to be the main entry, and Holyfield had appeared there. But now, he closed the door behind him and walked to the second door. The trio entered a mudroom, which for once, served a purpose that fit the name. Two pairs of dirty boots lined a wall, a light jacket hanging above them. To their side was a bench, another pair of shoes peeking out from under it.

Holyfield led the way through another door into a cramped, dark kitchen. He turned on the lights, revealing a décor that had seen a woman's touch long ago and a man's inattention since. But though old and faded, the space was clean and tidy. The smell of bleach with an overtone of bacon floated in the air.

"Coffee?" Holyfield asked, waving a hand at a pot sitting on the stove.

"None for me, thanks," replied Rebecca.

Clements paused before saying, "Since it's already made, I'll take a cup. Thank you."

Holyfield walked to a cabinet and removed two cups. "Sit," he said, waving his hand at a small, oak table and two chairs. He went to the stove, poured, and handed one of the cups to Clements.

"I'll stand," said Clements.

"I got more chairs," said Holyfield. Without asking if that fact affected the agent's decision, he retrieved a wooden, folding chair from a closet. Opened, it effectively blocked the only path through the room to the living space beyond. When Holyfield turned his back to close the closet door, Clements shrugged and sat.

"I want to ask you a few questions about the text message you sent Dr. Laura Greenwood a week ago," Rebecca said when everyone was settled. "You remember that message?"

"Reckon I do," the old man replied, taking a sip from his cup.

Rebecca paused until she realized he was finished. "What did you text her about?"

"Some dang fool sittin' at her gate, blarin' his car horn. Thought about callin' the Sheriff, but the doc said I should let her know if something's goin' on at her place." A sound that was a cross between a chuckle and a snort came from his throat. "Bet you think I was surprised by a lady doctor next door, but I had me one of them ... well, been a long time now. Not like a lady FBI agent." He still sounded a bit skeptical.

"What happened then?" asked Rebecca. "After you sent the message?"

"The honkin' stopped."

"How long after you sent it?" asked Rebecca.

Holyfield looked off to the corner of the kitchen, his hand rubbing the back of his neck. "Couple of minutes, I reckon, missy."

"And then the car drove off?"

"Nope. Left the dang car right there in the drive. Saw it there the next morning."

"What did it look like?" asked Clements. He sipped his coffee as the old man thought.

"Gray ... maybe light blue. Too far to be sure. Later, it disappeared. Never saw who took it. Maybe the doc had it hauled off."

"So, you text Dr. Greenwood often about problems at her place?" asked Rebecca.

Holyfield fished a chunky-looking cell phone with large keys from a pocket. "Got me ... this here ... phone ... three years ago," he said, each break in his statement corresponding to another hunt and peck on the built-in keyboard. "Texted her four times," he said, holding the device toward Rebecca.

"It looks like there are a few more than four texts there."

Holyfield turned the phone back around to stare at it, then handed it to the agent. "Them other three is to my sis. She never answered, but she's old. Probably never figured it out."

"I see," Rebecca said, after studying the display and realizing that she was looking at his texts for the last three years—all seven of them. "Did you see anyone around the house that evening, before dark?"

"Nope. Wouldn't. There's trees all round it."

"Did you see anyone around the car before it disappeared the next morning?"

Holyfield looked at the FBI agent for a moment. "See these ears?" He waved a hand at one side of his head. "Pert near as big as Obama's. Can't say I voted for the man but got his ears. I hear everything. But as for seeing anything smaller than a car at the doc's drive?" He shook his head. "Can't say I would."

"So, ever hear anything over that way?" asked Clements.

Holyfield shrugged. "Not much. Bit of shoutin' once in a while."

"Like someone's angry?" asked Clements.

"Naw, not like that. More like kids playin'. But mostly, it's quiet."

"Children?" said Rebecca. "You can hear children over a half-mile away?"

"Didn't say that, missy. Said it was something like that. And, yeah, get out here away from the city, you hear a lot at night. Hell, I had a cousin in from Chicago once. Said she couldn't sleep 'cause of the bullfrogs. And that pond's a further piece than the doc's. More coffee?"

Clements stared at his cup. "If you have enough to top it off?" Holyfield nodded and retrieved the pot.

"Your coffee's really good, Joe. What's the secret?"

"Don't know it's a secret." Holyfield returned the pot to the stove. "Just don't let it boil hard, and I add eggshells. Learned that in the Navy."

"Eggshells? In with the grounds?" Holyfield nodded. "Well, it's good. Strong, but not bitter."

The agents spent a few more minutes repeating some of their questions, both to make sure they had understood and that Holyfield would give the same account twice. He did, and without fail, he ended or started each statement with "like I said." Satisfied they had gleaned all they could, Clements and Rebecca thanked the man and returned to their car.

"So, Agent Missy. What do you think?"

Rebecca scowled, more for effect than for feeling. "Not my favorite nickname, so let's not bring it back to the office." Clements chuckled.

"I think this makes Joe's message seem even fishier," continued Rebecca. "Someone is laying on the horn until he texts? And then, it stops almost immediately? That's quite the coincidence. But I've got no idea why the car would sit there all night."

"Me either," said Clements. He started his car and pulled back onto the road. "So, you're thinking Greenwood might be involved?"

"Well," Rebecca replied slowly, "the text sounds like it could be some sort of signal. Add that to the possibility that the shot at Veles's apartment was staged, and the whole thing looks pretty suspicious. Still, if the murder attempt is a distraction, it bothers me that Greenwood made it so complex. I mean, she could have just excused herself at dinner to return a call and not rely on Joe to message her."

"Maybe that was the backup," replied Clements. "It's pretty common for people to elaborate on their lies. The detail makes them seem more real, more believable, but it also increases the chance we find an inconsistency. And on that front, we need to get a list of the calls Greenwood made around the time of the shot. She would have texted the driver or the honking would have continued. Of course, she could have had a prepaid cellphone that's long gone now, but you should check."

"I'll get it started as soon as we get back. So, we're really thinking that Greenwood, a medical researcher, might be attacking medicine with her Crusader friends?"

"I'm entertaining that possibility." After a pause, he added. "With others, and before you ask, I don't know why she'd do that. But if we can verify her involvement, we'll find the motive."

They had completed the half-mile drive to Greenwood's farm, and Clements pulled over. Across the road, a metal pipe extended from the ground next to her driveway. A speaker and keypad were mounted on top. Beyond them, a massive, black metal gate hung between two limestone columns. There was a camera perched conspicuously on top of one of them. A dense growth of evergreen trees flanked the gate and lined the driveway beyond. Looking through the bars of the gate, the road turned after about twenty yards, creating the impression that the entrance protected a vast forest beyond.

Even though it was warm, and warmer still since the car had stopped, Clements rolled up his window, turned to Rebecca, and spoke softly. "Notice anything unusual about the camera?"

Rebecca leaned over so she could see out of Clements's window better. "The way it's aimed?"

"That and the shields around the lens," said Clements. "They're used to cut down on glare, but they make it obvious that the camera's focused on the drive. So, if you wanted to avoid it, you'd just come in low, from either side. You could get to the gate without ever being seen. But when you get there, the other camera, down the drive a bit, gets you."

"Where?" Rebecca asked, bending over again. "Oh, I see it—on the left, almost in the trees."

"Right," said Clements. "There're probably some motion detectors, too, but I have to admit, I don't see them."

A tone came from Clements's phone indicating he had received an encrypted email. It was followed closely by the same sound from Rebecca's. She read the subject line. "Your message about new data on Conroy?" she asked.

"Yep," replied Clements. The two agents read in silence. After a while, Clements mumbled, "Didn't see this coming."

"I suppose Hawkins broadcasting this to everyone means he thinks it's true," said Rebecca. "I mean, a doctor's report from ten years ago saying Conroy was diagnosed as terminally ill and then nothing? I guess he could have treated himself. And if this is right ...." Rebecca paused, trying to check all the connections among the facts and conjectures running through her mind. She glanced at Clements, but he was waiting, probably to give her a chance to run everything to ground.

"Then, Conroy may have participated in his own execution, which implies the Crusaders support his agenda or he supports theirs. And since Conroy's record goes back dozens of years, it's probably the former. Basically, the Crusader attacks are pro-medicine at heart. And if that's the case, then the chances that Greenwood is playing the same game are also better."

Rebecca looked at Clements, waiting for his reaction. "It's a brutal way to get sympathy for medical research, but yeah, I'd have to agree."

"Are all cases like this?" asked Rebecca.

"Like what?"

"Like the way the number of leads is exploding. What was it, three days ago and we had virtually nothing?" Rebecca replied. "Now, we have a preacher and his wife who may be housing, feeding, maybe even funding the Crusaders. We have a realtor and possibly his catering girlfriend who may be handling them or just throwing cash their way. Then, there's a researcher who may have disguised her involvement by faking an attack. And now, the martyr, Conroy." She massaged her forehead with a hand, her brow knitted despite the effort to the contrary.

"It'll come together," replied Clements. "And somehow, I have a feeling we're getting close to that breakthrough on this one. Shall we see if we can drop in on Dr. Greenwood for a friendly chat?"

"You don't need to get back to St. Louis?" asked Rebecca. "If Conroy was a Crusader, then it should be easier to find out how Constance got into his rally. He's got to be the guy on the inside."

"There'll be people all over that lead already. No, let's check this out while we're here."

"I'm with you, partner," replied Rebecca.

Clements crossed the road, pulled up next to the keypad/speaker, and rolled down his window. He pressed a button, producing a tone. No response. He tried again with the same result. "Hello," he called loudly toward the box. Nothing. He backed out of the drive and closed his window again. "Well, dang, as Joe would put it. No one's home. Back to St. Louis?"

"Yeah, guess so," said Rebecca. "I'll start on Greenwood's calls as soon as we get back. But who knows, maybe we'll round up the Crusaders tomorrow when we raid the Church of the Rock."

"Wouldn't that be nice," said Clements, as he put the car in gear.

9:31 AM – The Crusaders' Compound

The woman raised her head from the prayer for their mid-morning snack. Every eye around the table—all eight pairs of them—studied her face with anticipation, eager for food after a full morning of physical training. "Well, go ahead, children. Eat up," she said. It was all the encouragement they needed as they tore into the muffin and banana on their plates. That was, all except Prudence. The woman looked at her charge, sadness coming to her eyes.

After a moment, she took the banana from her own plate and started peeling it. "It's a great day, children," she said. The eight pairs of eyes came to her face again, although the motion of their hands to their mouths never paused. "We have the nation's attention. And yet, I know their memory is fleeting, so today, we strike again. Nothing as dramatic as Monday but a reminder of our resolve."

Grief overtook the woman's face as she thought of the events yet to unfold. She stared down at the half-peeled fruit, her hands shaking. A soft grunting came from one of the figures around the table. She looked up, wiping the moistness from her eyes. "It's OK, Sister Charity," the woman said, smiling sadly. "Everything will be fine."

The woman took a long breath, composing herself. "In fact, children, it will be better than fine. It will be glorious because today we start the second part of our plan. A plan that breaks the stranglehold of big pharma. A plan that yields an America where life-giving treatments aren't withheld by greedy bureaucrats until they've extracted their thirty pieces of silver from the lobbies."

Brother Justice swallowed his last bite of muffin, then issued a string of grunts and gurgles. The woman smiled at him. "Couldn't have said it better myself, little one. And you're right, the country is ready for that change. What they lack, however, is direction. They need leaders. People with vision to show them the way."

The woman paused, the earlier pain returning to her face. "Jimmy was one such person." All around the table looked up, recognition of the name showing in their eyes. "He was a man whose passions nearly matched my own. Passion for a new order, one where medicine transforms the impossible into reality. No one will ever replace Jimmy."

The woman slowly shook her head, as if trying to gently dislodge a ghost from her mind's eye. "We won't replace him. Not with one person. But we can recruit others. Individuals who will find a reason to rail against the inhumanity that is our public policy. Together, these ambassadors for medical justice will finish what Jimmy started."

As if the assemblage sensed the woman had reached the finale, a chorus of murmurs spread through the room. The woman sighed deeply, her eyes traveling back to Sister Prudence and the untouched food sitting on her plate. "Justice," she said, nodding toward the plate. Justice reached over slowly, carefully watching Prudence's face, but his sister showed no reaction. He took the food and started eating.

"That's good, little one," said the woman. "Today's a big day, and you'll need your strength."

The woman got up and walked to the other side of the table. She pulled an empty chair from along the wall and sat beside Prudence. Raising her hand, she gently stroked Prudence's hair. "You're so beautiful, child. The first real generation of my family. The first to be born and raised here. Everyone else?" The woman slowly shook her head. "They came from outside, but you're mine. You're all mine."

Everyone except Brother Justice was finished eating. The woman rose and pulled a deck of picture cards from a pocket. She walked around the table, handing several cards to each person. As they shuffled through them, their verbalizations became more animated. They didn't dread the demanding physical activities denoted on the paper; they reveled in them. They opened doors to relaxation, to additional food, to games with their siblings. And for the older ones, they provided an opportunity to explore their sexuality.

Prudence had reached that age, but the woman had stopped her journey. She had missed the early warning signs of juvenile idiopathic arthritis, thinking the child's pain was just part of her training. And now, the damage was done.

Justice reached out and touched the woman's hand as she passed behind him. "No, no cards for you today. Today, you have a mission." He smiled. "Yes, you know that word, mission, don't you?"

The woman sat again beside Prudence. "And you, too, my child. I'm so sorry I didn't figure out what was going on with you earlier. And now, even the methotrexate isn't helping much, is it? Just killing your appetite."

The woman turned away, tears starting to roll down her cheeks. "Oh, how I wish you could be the mother to the next generation of warriors. You have the soul of a tigress. But your affliction ...." The woman stopped, the words catching in her throat, mixing with the sobs she tried to swallow. "It's just too likely to follow in your sons and daughters. I can't let that happen."

The woman looked into Prudence's eyes, steeling herself for what had to be done. "Today, child, I promise you an end to your pain. Today, you'll send a reminder to a forgetful city and nation. But more importantly, today you will recruit the first of our spokespeople, individuals who will kill for our cause. It's your legacy. It's what I will remember when I think of you."

The woman got up. She pointed at Justice and Prudence. "Stay." Then, sweeping her finger across the rest, she said, "training." When the six had left, the woman spoke. "OK, let's get ready. We've got a lot to do before I see Nicole Veles and Sam Price one last time."

Dr. Laura Greenwood stood and led her two charges from the room.

9:57 AM – The Offices of Ruger-Phillips

Warmth rose from the sun-drenched concrete as I walked across the parking lot and got into my car. Glancing at the clock, I confirmed what I already knew; I had an hour to pick up an anniversary card. It had been one month since I had proposed to Nicole. I expected another "sweet, but incredibly sappy" remark from my fiancé when I gave it to her, but she liked the attention. I could tell. After the errand, I'd need to get back for a call on the virtual maintenance technician study. The 60 minutes I had, however, would be more than enough with a drug store only about ten minutes away.

Funny or romantic?

The question struck me as I pulled onto the road. But with it came the realization that I had no idea what was available. Did they even make funny anniversary cards? For the first month? Were the funny ones mostly about sex? We had become intimate—had we ever—but that didn't mean Nicole would appreciate quips about our lovemaking. Or maybe I wasn't ready, not knowing exactly what they said?

Even my somewhat compulsive mental simulations sputtered when I had no data and I was quickly realizing I had none. But this mystery was easily solved. It just required a short drive.

I knew the route well, often coming this way for lunch or a tank of gas. It would be easy to negotiate it without paying attention, but I did that too often. I pushed my thoughts out to the world around me, intent on enjoying the day. And that wouldn't be difficult, because it was beautiful. A rain shower had moved through overnight, and the air was clean and fresh. There were residences just a block to the north, adding the scent of freshly mowed lawns to the aromas of coffee and bread escaping from the small eateries and a bakery lining the street. I put my arm out the window, letting the rays of the sun warm my skin. The shouts and screams of playing children reached my ears from the elementary school across the street.

As I passed, a boy was pushing a small girl of maybe eight or nine in a swing. At the peak of the outward arch, she slipped from the seat. I tensed, wondering if she would get hurt, but she landed lightly on a foot. Then, she spun around and curtsied to the boy. With a move like that, someday she could be a Crusader.

That's it!

I swerved to the side of the road, eliciting a few honks of irritation, a couple of raised middle fingers. I apologized, although no one paused to hear, and reviewed the sudden insight. It was, in a word, horrendous. I didn't want to believe it. And if I was wrong, saying it aloud would brand me as a crackpot. But the inference fit the facts too well to ignore. I pulled my phone from a pocket and dialed Marte. She answered on the second ring.

"Hi, Doc. What's up?"

Same Time – I-70 Eastbound, outside of St. Louis

Rebecca glanced at her ringing phone, then at Clements behind the wheel. "Sam Price is calling."

She was surprised—pleasantly so, but still surprised. She could think of nothing in the ongoing Crusader saga that would have affected him. But then, that wouldn't stop him from turning it over in his head, again and again. She smiled at the memory of some of his stories and raised the phone to her ear. "Hi, Doc. What's up?"

"It's Greenwood," Doc said. "I think she may be growing her own army of Crusaders."

Rebecca pulled the phone down and stared at it for a long moment. She raised it back to her ear. "What are you talking about?"

"Let me start at the beginning."

"Just give me the condensed version," interrupted Rebecca. Then, realizing how that sounded, she said. "Sorry, Doc, your greeting caught me off guard. Let's start with a summary, so I know where we need to go."

The oddity of Rebecca's side of the conversation caught Clements's attention, and he glanced sideways at her. She held up a single finger in a wait-a-moment sign.

"No, it's my fault," said Doc. "I shouldn't have blurted that out. Anyway, Greenwood's treatment has an unusual side effect. As all the news stories say, it pauses brain development in newborns, but at the same time, the baby's body continues to grow and it matures quickly. If she used it on a newborn, in three or four years, she'd have a full-grown Crusader. And yeah, I know that sounds crazy, but it fits what we know. And maybe most important for the FBI—well, for me too, really—you can test this idea quietly."

"Hold on a moment," Rebecca said into her phone and pressed mute. She turned to Clements. "Doc has either had an insight into a totally heinous crime or ... well, he's completely lost it. Can I bring you in?"

"Doc?"

"You can give me grief later," said Rebecca. "Right now, I need you to hear this."

"OK. What's he said so far?"

Rebecca summarized quickly. As she was finishing, Clements pulled off at an exit from the freeway. "I want to be able to concentrate on this."

Rebecca nodded and unmuted the phone. "Doc, I'm in a car with Special Agent Clements. Mind if I put you on speaker so both of us can listen?"

There was a long pause. "I was sort of hoping you'd play devil's advocate before anyone else heard this because what I'm suggesting she's done ... well, it's atrocious, completely devoid of humanity. Even saying it out loud makes my skin crawl."

"I understand," replied Rebecca. "But Agent Clements will treat anything you say as confidential, just as I would."

There was another pause but shorter this time. "OK, put me on speaker."

Rebecca tapped her phone. "Doc, say hi to Senior Special Agent Clements."

After introductions and Doc's disclaimers—this is nearly impossible to believe and there's no definite proof—he summarized his thoughts, ending with how Constance could have been an adult in body and a newborn in mind. Rebecca felt his reasoning was logical, although approaching unbelievable. As for Clements, she couldn't tell. He just sat there, tapping two fingers on his chin, looking out the windshield.

"I looked up Dr. Greenwood online," said Doc, after covering the fundamentals. "Just curiosity, before we had dinner, but I noticed she had worked on a project at St. Louis University. In her line of work, she'd know the buildings where the bombs were planted and the routines of the people who worked there. I also told you that dozens of people could have known that Nicole was working for Greenwood, and any one of them could have located a floor plan for Nicole's apartment. But I found out just this morning that Greenwood already knew the layout. She was in Nicole's unit earlier on the day of the attack. Add that to the fact that the whole assassination looked staged ...."

Doc paused. When he restarted, he said, "I just realized something. Did you get a report on Greenwood's injuries?"

Rebecca glanced at Clements. "I'm not sure we asked, but we can. Why?"

"Well, the cut on her forehead was long and jagged, but thin. I thought, flying glass. But I just remembered. She had another one on the palm of her hand."

"Like an accident she might have had when cutting her forehead?" asked Clements.

"Damn," said Rebecca. "I remember a Band-Aid on her palm the morning I interviewed her. I didn't think anything about it."

"Neither did I," said Doc on the phone, "until just now."

"Can you give us a minute?" asked Clements. But almost immediately, he said, "No, forget that. You've been upfront with us. There's been a lot of speculation about how Constance was controlled, but nothing's ever appeared on the medical screens stronger than ibuprofen in her system. Not even the telltale signs psychological stress might leave on someone's body. But if we knew what drugs Greenwood uses in her treatments? Well, that could be very enlightening. Is that what you meant when you told Agent Marte there was a simple test of your ideas?"

"Actually, no," replied Doc. "Not to sound crude, but I wasn't sure you could run tests on what remained of Constance. I was thinking you could compare the DNA you got earlier to the databases for missing children, say newborns who disappeared three to five years ago. In that amount of time, they'd be fully grown."

"OK, we can do that," said Clements. "Between that information and any residual drugs in Constance's system, we'll have more than enough to bring her in."

"I can't believe I'm going to say this, but there's another possibility," said Rebecca. The line to Doc stayed silent as Clements stared at her. "We could be looking at second-generation Crusaders, meaning they're the sons and daughters of babies stolen six or more years ago."

"You're right," said Clements. "Or for that matter, the fathers could be sperm donors rather than stolen newborns. That'll add another complication to the DNA search." Clements paused. "Sorry, Doc. It's not like we're trying to shoot holes in your plan. It just might not be as straightforward as you thought."

A single laugh came through the phone. "No worries. I'm just relieved you're not asking where I am."

Clements and Rebecca exchanged a confused glance. "Why would we do that?" she asked.

"To send the men in the white coats with a straitjacket."

Clements snorted. When Doc's voice came through the phone again, his amused tone had been replaced with seriousness. "The thing I still can't figure is why Greenwood would be doing this. I mean, she's delusional if she's growing an army, but could she be so far out of it that she thinks people will rally around medicine if she hurts it enough?"

Unsure how much she should say, Rebecca glanced at Clements. He seemed to read her mind and took the lead. "We're in the same place," he said. "But we have enough to go back to our Behavioral Analysis Unit, see what they think."

"Thanks," said Doc.

"The place I'm stuck," said Clements, "is how a person with a newborn's mental ability could break into a building. OK, maybe it's not rocket science, but a newborn doesn't even know what a window is, much less that you can break one."

"I got this," said Rebecca toward the phone, then turned to Clements. "Doc explained it to me. A human with the brain of a newborn could be trained to perform simple things, like hiding in a spot until a beeper went off. With each new signal, the person would take the next step—scaling a wall to get to the top of a passageway."

"Behavioral chains," said Clements softly.

It was probably a comment to himself, but it elicited a somewhat animated response from the phone. "Exactly," said Doc. "If we're right, Constance was trained to respond when a stimulus occurred, then another action with the next stimulus, and so on. When the sequence was complete, she would receive reinforcement—food, water, warmth, sex, whatever Greenwood used. After that kind of training, her mind would be trapped during a mission, performing these chains with no concept of right and wrong to stop her."

"Doc, I'm convinced," said Clements. "At least enough to take the next step, so we need to get going. Agent Marte will be in touch."

After a quick round of goodbyes, Clements drove up the exit ramp. But rather than continuing through the intersection to St. Louis, he turned onto the overpass, then onto the ramp going west.

"I was afraid you'd want to go back to the office," said Rebecca, "even though in my mind, checking out Greenwood is a lot more important."

"Ditto," said Clements. "It's time for a closer look at her farm."

As Clements accelerated onto the freeway, Rebecca leaned back in her seat, wondering about the bizarre conclusion they had just reached. "Who would have thought," she said aloud, although mostly to herself. "A mind in chains."

11:17 AM – The Greenwood Farm

Clements pulled off the road about a quarter mile from the gate to the Greenwood farm. "The place is too heavily monitored for me to feel comfortable walking up to the front door—assuming we could get past the gate. Maybe we can ...." He stopped, since Rebecca was already bringing up a satellite map on his in-car display.

When she located the address, he said, "I'm thinking this long, narrow plot is Greenwood's, since the fields on either side are large and look like they're used for crops."

Inside the rectangle that defined her farm, the driveway ran straight from the road for a short distance, turned sharply to the right and then, immediately back. Finally, it resumed its original path toward the farmhouse. "That bend in the road is probably to block direct, line-of-sight between the gate and the residence," said Clements. "But we should be able to see the house if we come up to her property from the fields on either side or from the back."

"Ah, maybe," said Rebecca, as she zoomed into a section of the driveway. "The evergreens are in a double row, but is that a glint off metal between them?" she asked, pointing at the display. "Maybe a fence?"

"I think you're right. But when we get past the first row, we'll be able to find gaps between the branches in the second. Even a small opening can tell us a lot about what's going on."

"And the fence placed between the rows of trees? Is that to disguise the fact you're inside a secured compound?" asked Rebecca.

"Yeah, makes the cable guy a lot less suspicious. I'll take some wire cutters with me, just in case we need to get inside."

Rebecca panned along the driveway. As it approached the farmhouse, the lines of trees left the road to encircle a large yard with the farmhouse at the center. The drive continued to the right of the house, leading to several small structures and three, larger outbuildings. Left of the house was green space, which gave way to a fenced pool.

"These small, fuzzy areas around the pool and the outbuildings—is that camouflage netting?" asked Rebecca.

"Camouflage, if you're suspicious. A patio shade screen, if not. But either way, along with the mature trees, I can't make much sense of the grounds. Is that a swing or part of an obstacle course?" He asked, pointing at the map. He released a long breath. "OK, how about you go into the field on the left side of her farm. I'll walk past her gate and enter on the right. I have a better chance of staying out of any camera shot if I go on foot. We'll check out the house from each side of her property, then meet up in back."

"Sounds like a plan," said Rebecca, as they exited the car.

The land on the left of Greenwood's farm was surrounded by a fence typical of the area—four strands of barbed wire nailed to posts spaced about 15 feet apart. Rebecca had negotiated plenty of these in her misbegotten youth and was soon inside, walking along the edge of a recently planted field.

It was only a matter of minutes before she reached the point where the evergreens came out to the edge of the property. Just beyond them would be the yard. She climbed the barbed-wire fence, then pushed through a row of evergreens—a fragrant but sticky task. There, as they had guessed, stood a ten-foot-tall, chain-link fence topped with barbed wire. Rebecca was glad that scaling it wasn't part of the plan. The foliage on the second row of trees was thick, but it only took her moments to find a natural break in it. And when she did, the aerial shot hadn't done justice to what she found.

The lawn was dark green and neatly mowed. Flowers sprung from beds carefully weeded and mulched. Each garden was lined with bricks set into the ground at an angle, like a row of dominos that had been tipped halfway over. A wrought iron bench circled a tree, and through her narrow window between branches, it looked freshly painted. A brass sundial on a short, limestone column appeared to wink at her as it caught light one moment and then blinked out as a wispy cloud passed in front of the sun.

She could also see the front of the farmhouse—a large, white, two-story building. Steps led up to a porch that stretched its full length. A door painted dark green sat in the middle with two sets of curtained windows on each side. One end of the porch boasted a wooden swing; the other held two rocking chairs with a small table between them. It was the quintessential setting for sipping lemonade on a hot, summer afternoon.

She looked toward the back of the property, trying to see the pool area, but the gaps between the branches were too small, the viewing angles too sharp. So, she retraced her steps through the outer row of evergreens, walked along the fence toward the back of the property, and then pushed back through the growth to find a viewpoint. If her surveil of the front part of the yard was surprising, this perspective was little short of breathtaking.

The designers of the pool had eschewed straight lines and sharp angles in favor of gentle bends and sweeping curves. On the far end, a wooden deck glistened in the sun. Its mellow warmth gave way to a brick patio that ran to the back of the house. But it was the closer end of the pool that left Rebecca speechless. It looked exactly like a beach. Wooden, reclining chairs with seats and backs of colorful material were scattered over a surface of white sand. A volleyball net was strung along a side. Umbrellas protruded from the ground, shading small, wooden tables. Beach balls in bright, primary colors stood out against their white background.

A 12- to 15-foot-tall, brick wall rose behind the pool area. Rebecca suspected this was the back edge of Greenwood's property. The wall turned at the far end of the pool area and ran up to the house to enclose the patio. There was a single, arched door painted black on that end; otherwise, there were no breaks in the wall.

Rebecca scanned the area one more time, committing the details to memory before leaving to meet with Clements. She made her way through the evergreens and was about to climb the barbed-wire fence when she heard a thump—just one and then, silence. She turned back toward the trees, controlling her breathing, asking her heart to be still in her ears. She reached down and felt the familiar bulk of her revolver. For a moment, she felt a bit self-conscious about the action, knowing that so far, she had risked nothing more severe than sticky, pine residue on her hands, maybe a tick bite. But surrounded by the unknown, its heft was reassuring. And then, the sound came again. She would have thought something was blowing against the house, like a door that had been left unlatched. It seemed about that far away, but there was no wind. She waited.

She didn't register a sound behind her but sensed a presence. The hair on the back of her neck stood up. She spun around, her hand dropping instinctively to her revolver. There stood Clements on the other side of the barbed-wire fence.

"Did I take too long?" she whispered.

"No," he replied, also keeping his voice low. "I saw all I needed in about 30 seconds. People. They're getting washed up and going inside, maybe for lunch."

"Crusaders?"

"Seems likely," he replied. "I didn't hear any talking, but they were doing some heavy-duty, physical training. I called in backup, and the field office is scrambling some locals. They'll set up a line of containment outside the boundaries of the farm. Our guys should be here in a little over an hour. In the meantime, we're going in for a closer look at the house. Should be a good time, if everyone's eating. We go in here?"

"No," replied Rebecca, softly. "You'd end up in the pool area with no cover. Follow me." She started back to the spot she had entered previously.

When they reached it, she said, "If we go in here, we'll be in the middle of the side yard." She paused a beat. "So, what are we up against?"

Clements started climbing the barbed-wire fence. "I counted six—four males and two females—but there could be more. Their ages ran from about six or seven to maybe the mid-twenties."

"Six years old? You gotta be kidding."

"Wish I was," Clements said as they pushed through the outer row of trees. "Hopefully, they won't spot us. But if they do, we have to be ready for anything. Who knows what they've been trained to do to protect their home?" Reaching the chain-link fence, Clements pulled the wire cutters from a pocket and started to work.

Rebecca knew the truth of her partner's statement but didn't feel it. "It's just that a six-year-old boy would have no idea what he's doing, if Doc's right," she whispered to Clements's back.

Clements glanced up, giving her a strange look, but returned to his task without a word. Rebecca could see him doubting the specifics of Greenwood's methods; she had trouble believing all of it herself. But that the biologist had done something to these people seemed undeniable. And then, she understood Clements's look. "The six-year-old is a girl, isn't she?"

Clements looked up at his partner again and nodded. "Yeah, sorry. But no one needs to get hurt. We just need to get eyes on that house, figure out how to put a net around it before they get suspicious. If they do, the ring of local law enforcement around the outside of the farm should slow them down, but it won't stop them."

"OK, then, let's get it done."

Clements nodded and pulled back a section of the fence big enough for them to squeeze through. They crawled through the inner row of trees, pausing on the edge. Clements scanned the area. "Yeah, we should be able to position some men here. We'll need to ...."

He stopped mid-sentence, both agents freezing at the sound of a large vehicle in the distance. The engine roared, the noise coming from the direction of the gate. It was followed closely by a crash and the screeching of metal on metal.

"What the hell," growled Clements.

But his words were nearly lost in the wail of sirens, as police cars came barreling around the bend in the drive. Clements and Rebecca ran to the front of the yard and began waving their arms in the air. But rather than stopping, the drivers interpreted the gesture to mean spread out. The cars began peeling off to the right and left until six vehicles were fanned out across the front lawn. Doors flew open. Each vehicle held two or three officers, and they all took positions behind their cars, guns drawn.

"Hold your fire." Clements bellowed the command over and over. But everywhere Rebecca looked, officers were chambering rounds in their shotguns or training their revolvers on the house, fingers on the trigger.

She glanced back. Several individuals, all dressed identically in white T-shirts and gray shorts, walked around the corner of the building. The two in the lead were both male, tall and well-toned. One held a pole in his hand, a hook on one end. But the most relevant factor in Rebecca's mind was that it wasn't a weapon.

"FBI," she and Clements both yelled across the lawn. "Get down on the ground, hands behind your head."

The group exchanged puzzled looks, a few more coming forward from behind. Among them was a small girl, presumably, the six-year-old Clements had mentioned. Even from the distance, Rebecca thought she could read confusion in the child's large, blinking eyes. "Who are you?" Rebecca shouted as Clements again yelled, "FBI. Get down." Other than a few additional grunts and murmurs, their response was the same. As mind-boggling as Doc's guess had been, Rebecca now had no doubt it was true. These people were Crusaders, all grown in body and completely stunted in mind.

The group's unintelligible responses and its ever-growing size were apparently too much for someone behind her. Rebecca heard the sound of a round being chambered in a shotgun. She turned back to the line of police cars, holstered her firearm, and raised her empty hands to her sides. She started walking backward toward the house shouting, "Lower your weapons."

"Marte," Clements yelled, staring at her.

Rebecca glanced at him but never slowed her backward march or her commands to the officers. Clements squeezed his eyes closed, then turned and ran to the nearest man. "What the hell's wrong with you," he yelled just inches from the man's face. "That's my partner out there. Lower your weapon immediately." Slowly, the deputy complied.

When the last dark, open end of a barrel disappeared from her view, Rebecca turned to the Crusaders, not sure what to do now. The group was slowly drifting toward her, the murmurs growing. Rebecca couldn't pick out a single word, but she heard confusion and curiosity in the noise. She needed to get them out of the potential field of fire, but their forward progress as they milled about was measured in inches, not yards.

"Follow," she yelled, hoping it was a word they knew. Apparently, it was, as they all broke into a slow jog in near perfect unison, the group forming a single-file line. When they reached her, they jogged in place. She turned and started at a trot toward a large tree on the edge of the lawn. From the sound of their footfalls, she knew they were following without looking. She stopped on the far side of the tree. The massive trunk would provide some protection if the scene turned violent. "Sit," Rebecca shouted, guessing at a second command they would know. They did so, almost robotically.

Clements ran up beside her, followed by several of the local sheriffs and deputies. Four of them surrounded the Crusaders, their sidearms trained on the sitting group.

"They're unarmed," said Rebecca, concerned that this situation could still get out of hand. "They're probably well trained in hand-to-hand, so keep them on the ground."

Clements leaned close to Rebecca, whispering to keep his words private. "Damn it, Marte, what the hell were you thinking?"

"I was thinking that I don't want these innocent children, regardless of how mature they may seem, slaughtered in front of me," she said, returning the hard stare she found on Clements's face.

Clements stared a moment more, then released a long breath. "Me either, but this conversation is not over. Not by a long shot. We'll talk later."

Rebecca didn't answer, but knew if she did, she would have said, "I'm not sure there'll be a next time." She thought she'd prepared herself for the possible violence of the job—the serial killers, the pedophiles, the serial rapists. But this? She didn't even know what to call it. Serial mental murder? A fanatic had stolen these people's lives, disposing of them when they were no longer useful. Maybe she would get over it, but right now, she was reeling from Greenwood's cold-heartedness.

Clements stood back from Rebecca and waved the local officers closer. "OK, we're going to set up a secure perimeter and wait them out."

"These people," said one of the deputies, nodding at the seated group. "They're Crusaders?" His tone was tinged with disbelief, his eyes narrowed.

"Almost undoubtedly," replied Clements. "And they're probably not what you expected."

"Yeah, they're a bunch of retards," said another of the locals.

Rebecca could feel her anger grow, her pulse climbing. But the man's words had the same effect on Clements, and he was quicker to words.

"They've been drugged their entire lives," he snapped, glaring at the man. "And because of that, they don't know how to talk, don't know what's right or wrong. They're basically innocents, deserving of our protection. You raise a hand to them other than in self-defense, and you'll answer to me. Do I make myself clear?"

The man looked down. "Yeah. I didn't mean I'd hurt them."

Clements glare hadn't left the face of the deputy before another spoke. "Aren't we going to rush the house, while we have the element of surprise?"

Clements took a breath, Rebecca guessing he was concerned about correcting two of his volunteers even before he knew their names. But if so, he was spared by another officer. "Jenkins, I think the agent feels like we lost the element of surprise a while ago. And barging into a building with who knows how many armed men inside could be suicide."

Clements nodded at the man. "That's right. No one's life is in danger, so time is on our side. In a few hours, we can get a SWAT team here, start negotiations, maybe get plans to the house. But we do need to get a perimeter set up five minutes ago."

This time, all he received in reply were nods and murmurs of affirmation. "Agent Marte, you've had more time to study the left side of the house."

Rebecca quickly ran down the situation—a yard with some cover, a pool area with virtually none, and a side of the house that was all windows, no doors. Clements added the information he had on the right side and back of the property, then allocated his assets—two officers to the left and right sides of the home, four to the rear. The back, he knew from his brief reconnoiter, was a large space with an elaborate obstacle course and an area for calisthenics. While it provided a lot of cover for his men, it also left dozens of blind spots and places a Crusader could hide. Three officers would stay with the group that was being detained, while the last three took up positions behind their cars on the front lawn.

The local officers had just left for their assigned positions when Rebecca's phone buzzed. She almost pressed Ignore when she saw the name on the display. "Doc, you've got to make this quick," she said when she accepted the call.

"Sister Prudence is at the Biomedical Engineering Associates building, gun in one hand, a button connected to a small roller bag in the other. A dozen or so of us are trapped inside."

"Aw, shit."

11:55 AM – The Crusaders' Compound

"Hold a second." She pulled the phone from her ear. "Gus, it's Doc. Prudence has shown up at Veles's place of work, apparently armed with a bomb. Several people are trapped inside."

Clements's head dropped then shook slowly. When he looked up, he said, "Find out as much as you can about his situation and what he's done so far. But make it fast."

Rebecca started to raise the phone to her ear but stopped. "We're going in?"

"With lives in danger, yeah, that's my call. Hopefully, no one's inside, and we can find something that tips the scales back in our favor. I'm going to see if anyone here has been trained on clearing a building. Otherwise, it's you and me, partner."

Rebecca nodded and raised the phone. "Doc?"

"Still here," he replied. "Are you at Greenwood's farm? I could hear some of the conversation. Have you found any Crusaders?"

"We are, and yes, we've run into some. This appears to be their home and training ground. And before you ask, I'd say you're right about Greenwood keeping their brains undeveloped. None of them seem to know more than a few words."

There was a pause before Doc spoke again, and when the response came, it was tinged with the sound of determination. "Understood. Anyway, I'm wondering if the police showing up is the signal Prudence is waiting for, the signal for the next action. Any chance you or Agent Clements could ask them to set up a perimeter out of sight? They aren't listening to me." A pause. "Wait. Hold on."

"What's going on?" Rebecca asked into the phone, but all she heard was background noise. The sound of car engines on the street. Someone was yelling, but the sound was too distant for her to understand. A door slammed. There was more talk, shouting, and then the crack of gunfire came through the earpiece impossibly loud. "Doc?" Rebecca yelled. A pause. "Doc?"

It felt like a lifetime until he came back on the phone. "Everyone's OK. That was a warning shot into the ceiling when someone got too close to the front door. We're all around the corner now."

"Good. Stay out of sight. You still want me to call the police?"

"Not necessary," replied Doc. "They already showed up in force. I guess I should be thankful that wasn't the cue to blow the building. Anyway, we checked the backdoor. It's locked with a chain and some sort of device with a blinking light. It might be a fake, but that's something for the bomb squad."

Before Rebecca could agree with him, Doc started shouting at someone else. "Get under something."

At first, she didn't understand. And then, she recognized the sound of a clock striking in the background. One, two, three. Was this Prudence's signal to set off the bomb? Four, five, six. Never had a clock chiming felt so slow. Seven, eight, nine. She pressed the phone to her ear harder, straining for the sound. Ten, eleven, twelve. And then, silence.

Doc sighed loudly enough that Rebecca had no trouble hearing over the phone. "I don't mind telling you, Agent Marte. This is no damn fun."

"I'll see if I can get that clock turned off, just in case she's waiting for one o'clock. How many people are trapped in the building?"

"I don't know exactly," Doc replied. "Maybe a dozen, fifteen? I'll get a better count."

Rebecca went through everything she had learned about hostage situations, hoping she had something to give Doc, but nothing fit. The hostages couldn't make themselves seem "more human" to Prudence. She had no concept of humanity. They couldn't sow seeds of discontent among the takers. Prudence wouldn't understand anything that complex. In the end, the only tactic that was relevant was to wait her out. And that was fine unless the signal for the finale came before she tired.

"OK, move as far from Prudence as you can," Rebecca said. "Maybe you can find something heavy, like a desk to get under. Otherwise, just try to keep everyone calm, and if you come in contact with her, cooperate. The negotiators will do the rest."

"Will do, although I'm not sure they'll find much in their playbook that will help with Prudence."

Rebecca nodded, even though Doc couldn't see. He'd obviously considered his situation already and knew that negotiation was a hollow hope. She looked across the lawn. Clements and two other men were jogging toward her. "I have to go. We're getting ready to break into Greenwood's farmhouse. Good luck, Doc."

"Same to you, Agent Marte."

"Hey, Doc?" she said quickly.

"Yes."

"Maybe it's time you call me Rebecca."

"Talk to you soon, Rebecca." He disconnected.

When Clements and his cohorts arrived, he did the introductions. Both men had been trained in clearing buildings, and Clements quickly established their tactics. They formed two teams with an FBI agent on each. Each team would take a side of the house, preventing someone from getting behind them. One team member would search the room while the other provided cover. It was about as simple as it got, but the approach was complex enough for a group with different backgrounds, little time to prepare, and no time for practice.

They approached the house in a crouched run, using cover whenever it was available. On the porch, the two teams took positions on either side of the door. Rebecca glanced over her shoulder. Her partner was standing back, dangerously close to a window. She grabbed his wrist and jerked him closer. When he realized what he had done, he grimaced, his face turning red. He rubbed the back of his neck, his eyes now tracking over the porch and lawn as if seeking other threats that he'd missed.

The crack in his confidence was not what Rebecca wanted to see. She raised a hand for a fist bump, hoping it was a motion he'd recognize. It was, and he returned the gesture with a nod and a smile of grim determination. She returned the look.

Clements scanned the faces of his breaching team, each member indicating his or her readiness. He stepped out from the wall, and in a smooth, fluid motion, he turned toward the house, planted his left foot, raised his right leg, and kicked the door near the knob. It exploded inward, followed closely by the hastily formed clearing team.

12:27 PM – The Biomedical Engineering Associates Building

"What the hell are the police doing out there?" the man asked.

I thought the question was rhetorical, but one of Nicole's coworkers believed otherwise. "I'm sure they're doing everything they can," she replied. "We just have to stay calm."

The thirteen of us—I now had an exact count—had congregated in a small break area about as far from Prudence as we could get. For the first few minutes of our captivity, everyone had their phone out, frantically calling law enforcement and loved ones. In fact, we had placed so many calls to the police that they had asked us to identify one "official phone" that we wouldn't use. That way, they could call us should the need arise. So far, it hadn't, leaving several of the group huddled around the device, staring like vultures waiting for a dying animal to collapse.

The only other thing that was getting any attention was a small television set someone had brought out from an office. On it, we could see the street in front of the Biomedical Engineering Associates building, eerie because not a car was moving. There were police cars parked in a line, and occasionally, we caught sight of an officer or FBI agent scurrying behind the barricade, but otherwise, there was nothing to see. That fact, of course, didn't keep the news reporter from talking nonstop.

Initially, he had used the term, hostage situation. That was good news for us, as nearly 90 percent of those types of incidents end nonviolently. Then, it became known that the Crusaders were involved and phrases such as domestic terrorism, hate-motivated killing, and ritualistic execution came to the fore. In a matter of two minutes of commentary, we went from a nine in ten chance of walking away to all but dead already. We turned the television's sound off, only to find it replaced by the drone from a hostage negotiator out on the street and the ringing of a phone in the building's lobby.

Nicole was sitting apart with a male coworker, and when he left, I went over to join her. "How you holding up?"

She shrugged, the gesture saying it all. Earlier, I had told her everything I'd learned from Marte. It was a revelation that was weighing heavily on her mind.

"I'm still having a hard time believing Laura would do this," she said. "I thought we got along well, professionally and personally. Of course, now that I know, the way she finagled a dinner invitation seems obvious. Bologna sandwiches in her hotel room no less."

"What?" I didn't follow the reference.

Nicole just waved a hand at the question then asked one of her own. "How could I have been so wrong?"

"It's not just you," I said. "This has been going on for at least three or four years for Constance to be as old as she was. Greenwood hid it from everyone."

"Everyone except Conroy," Nicole added.

"Maybe, although I wonder if he knew." I started to explain my thoughts, mostly to have something to talk about besides our current predicament, but I stopped. Something was different. It took me a moment to realize what. It was quiet. The negotiator had stopped talking. The phone had stopped ringing. Then, the television's picture disappeared.

"They've shut off the power," said Nicole. "I wonder if ...."

She got no further as the "official" phone rang. With a half-dozen people standing around it, I thought someone would grab it before the echo of the first sound disappeared from the halls. But instead, everyone just stared. Now that there was news, no one was sure they wanted to hear it. Eventually, a man picked up. "You've got the hostages in the Biomedical Engineering Associates building," he said. "You're on speaker." He pushed a button.

"This is FBI Special Agent Stan Alban. We're working with the local authorities to secure your release. Who am I talking to?"

"Willy Bush," said the man. "No relation to the famous St. Louis family by the same name. Not even spelled the same." I doubted the agent cared who his relations weren't, but I couldn't fault the man. It was probably a line he used all the time, brought to his lips by the logic-crushing stress of our situation.

"Good to meet you, Willy. How many of you are there?"

"Thirteen. All here in a break area near the back of the building."

"Thirteen? You're sure that's an accurate count?"

Bush looked around the group, everyone either shrugging or nodding. "Yeah. Pretty sure. We've checked."

"OK," said Alban. "A group of people believed to be Crusaders has been arrested at a rural location. These people apparently don't speak much at all. We think the same may be true of Prudence, but we're still going to try to get her talking. I don't have the building floor plan yet but should any moment. Can you tell me if you can see Prudence from where you are?"

"No," replied Bush. "Does that mean you don't know where she is?" While there had been an undercurrent of nervousness in his tone before, his voice cracked with the question.

"We'll try thermal imaging of the building as soon as we can, but so far, she's been very careful to stay out of sight," Alban replied, matter-of-fact. "But even when we have that, anything you see, hear, or smell might help us."

"Smell?" said a woman standing nearby.

"They could be important," he replied but didn't explain. "So, call at this number if you have anything. Otherwise, just stay calm, stay out of her way, and let us work the situation."

"Should we try to get a look at her?" asked Bush.

Alban paused. He wasn't going by the standard, hostage-negotiation playbook if he had to think about that question. I found the thought simultaneously comforting and chilling—comforting because the FBI knew that Prudence wasn't the usual threat and chilling for the same reason. Finally, he said, "If you find yourself in a position to see what she's doing, retreat to safety as soon as you can and then, give me a call. OK?"

"Got it," Bush replied.

"Any other questions?" asked the agent. When he received none, he ended the call.

"Well, that was a bunch of BS." The comment was from the man who had just questioned what the police were doing. "Promises, but they aren't doing crap." His face was starting to turn red, his volume increasing. "Why the hell aren't they better prepared?"

Nicole and I were still standing by ourselves, and I glanced at her. "Gene Russo," she whispered. The woman next to him reached a hand over and placed it on his shoulder. At first, I thought he might throw it off, but eventually, he dropped his glare and moved away from the group.

Nicole stepped forward. "The people the police arrested?" she said in a voice that seemed a mere whisper after the man's rant. "The Crusaders?

They're probably the product of research Dr. Laura Greenwood has been doing."

The tight circle around the phone opened, and Nicole, Russo, and I moved into the gap. Over the next couple of minutes, Nicole summarized Greenwood's research. Then, she discussed the idea that the attempt on Greenwood's life was a smokescreen, making her appear the victim rather than the perpetrator. Nicole finished with the possibility that Prudence was simply responding to signals in her surroundings.

Somewhat surprising to me, every eye followed Nicole, every head nodded as she talked—even Russo's. But then, if there was an assemblage who would understand the implications of Greenwood's research, this was it. When Nicole finished, they only questioned the psychology—and they apparently knew the source of that bit of speculation. "How sure are you about this reaction to a signal idea?" The woman who asked was looking directly at me.

"If Prudence, Justice, and the others are products of Greenwood's research, then it's extremely likely they've been trained with methods used with lower primates, like behavioral chaining. That's not an airtight conclusion, but there aren't many other options."

"OK," said the woman. "I can accept that. What about the signal that Prudence is waiting for?"

I glanced at Nicole, not really wanting to answer. "I don't know. I do know the FBI is trying to get the clock stopped so it won't chime again, just in case. But for all I know, she's wearing a beeper. Or waiting for sundown."

"And there's no way to stop the signal if we don't know what it is," said the woman.

"Thanks for stating the obvious, Joan," said Russo. He turned and walked away again. I was beginning to dislike the guy.

"If we knew how she had been trained, we could give her the reinforcer now," I said, thinking aloud. "She might believe the sequence is over. Or maybe we could get her to think she was no longer in a chain. We'd have to make her think she was in a different setting, someplace where her scripted actions didn't apply—like back at Greenwood's farm. The FBI is there now. Maybe we could get a call through to Agent Marte and she could describe it?"

"Like the beach that's there," Nicole said. She was staring at some bags of concrete stacked in a corner, staying dry until they were needed for the lunch area project.

Everyone turned to her. "Dr. Greenwood told us she'd recreated a Florida beach at her farm. Sand. Beach balls. Lounge chairs. The whole nine yards around a pool in her back yard. If we could build something like it, maybe we could confuse Prudence. You think, Sam?"

"Yeah, it might work," I replied. I raised a hand to the bags of concrete in case the rest hadn't noticed the source of Nicole's inspiration. "The concrete would look like sand—really white sand, but it should do. Let me try to get Marte." I dialed, the call going directly to voicemail. "Sorry, no luck. But if we're going to do this, we'll need as many props as we can find."

"Jessica has that big ball she sits on sometimes in her office," said the woman who had tried to comfort Russo earlier. "And I've got some potted plants that look tropical."

"Agent Alban said we shouldn't approach Prudence," said Russo.

"No, Gene, he didn't," said Nicole sharply. "He said ...."

Russo raised a hand to interrupt, wearing my already thin patience with the man even further. "You're right, Nicole. He said report if we happened to get close, which just makes my offer to help build this beach a bit less dramatic than going against his wishes."

I replayed Russo's words, wondering if I'd misunderstood. And when I was certain I hadn't, my impression of the man did an about-face.

"Look, I can't just sit here until the sun sets or a black cat walks in front of the door or whatever she's waiting for," Russo said, looking around the faces staring at him. "I'm with Nicole and ... what's your name again."

"Doc," said Nicole before I could react.

"Ah, I hate to break up the party," said a man who to this point had been silent. "I'm not comfortable with this whole idea. We don't know what this beach looks like ... or even if Dr. Greenwood actually built one. And even if we get close, is that really going to stop her?"

Again, all eyes turned to me. "It should," I said. "Not every sunset or black cat's going to get a reaction from Prudence. Otherwise, she'd be searching for that roller bag every time it happened. It's that signal in the context of this office building. If she thinks she's in a different setting, there's no connection between the stimulus and her response."

"But this is all just theory," argued the man.

Nicole was well regarded at work, but she was also a relatively new hire. She wouldn't have built up a lot of credibility in the eyes of her coworkers. And me? I'd have only what came from association with her. So, I was relieved when another man answered, letting me conserve whatever goodwill I had left.

"Not really, Ben. It's the same thing they use to train animals at the zoo or a circus."

"Now that woman out there's an animal?" said Ben.

"Greenwood's treatment would keep her brain at a stage much like a lower primate," replied Nicole. There was a bite in her tone, probably reflecting some frustration at retreading this topic.

"Still, I don't know."

"Let's vote," said Russo. "And if we go ahead with the plan, we can stop if Prudence reacts."

"Unless her reaction is to blow up the building," said Ben.

When the hands were counted, it was seven in favor, six against.

But Ben wasn't done and pointed at me. "He can't vote. He doesn't even work here."

"And he'll be just as dead as anyone else if Prudence sets off that bomb," replied the woman who had comforted Russo earlier. "We've voted. Let's get going."

That settled it and Bush called Agent Alban, telling him we would be doing some work in the lobby. No one savored the idea of being shot by a police sniper. When Alban asked what we were up to, Bush merely said, "Creating a visual distraction because we don't think the verbal ones will do any good." I admired both the way he phrased it and the manner; it was a statement, not a request.

Alban put us on hold, but a few moments later, he came back on. "The FBI can't endorse whatever it is you're about to do," he said slowly as if picking each word with care. "But we'll hold fire unless we see Prudence threatening one of you." He paused a moment. "Unofficially, we agree. We don't think telling her you have a spouse and kids at home will have any effect. But anything you can do to appear ... well, more like her, the better. Good luck." He disconnected.

"Well, ladies and gentlemen," said Russo, rubbing his hands together as if he was actually anxious to get started. "We have a beach to build."

12:58 PM – The Crusaders' Compound

Rebecca stepped out onto the front porch of the farmhouse and called out, "All clear." Three officers stepped from behind their cars and started toward her. Farther up the drive, she could see the six Crusaders they had apprehended earlier being loaded into cars with other officers. By now, the ranks of law enforcement had grown to two dozen or more.

"Apprehended?" she muttered to herself. Was that the right word for the follow-the-leader game she'd played with them? When the trio of officers got close enough, she said, "Any of you have computer skills? We need to break into a password-protected system."

The officers shared a look then one said, "No, guess not."

"OK, one of you spread the word about the all-clear and see if anyone else might be able to hack into a computer. And we could probably use four more people inside to search offices and files."

"Sure, I'll get the word out," said one of the officers, turning back toward the cars.

"Thanks. The two of you, come with me." Rebecca started back into the house, turning slightly to speak to the men as they walked. "We have a hostage situation in St. Louis, a place called Biomedical Engineering Associates. Sister Prudence is involved. Greenwood and Justice are probably there, too. We need to find anything we can that might help with that standoff."

"And you think it's on a computer?"

"Probably," replied Rebecca. "We're sure they train here. We've found pictures of the Biomedical Engineering Associates building and notes on the people working there. We also found a scanner. It's possible that all of this information has been scanned into the computer so they could set up something like a video game. Then, they could go over it again and again, until they have it down pat."

"Because they can't talk, it has to be pictures?" one of the men asked. "One of the Crusaders had pictures of exercises."

"Yeah, that's what we're thinking," Rebecca replied. "But there's a lot of paper to go through, too." They had reached a door, and Rebecca paused. "This appears to be Greenwood's office. What I've seen in here is medical research and may not be related to the hostage-taking. But one of you should stay and look through it."

"I'll do that," said one of the officers.

"Thanks. When more help comes, take who you need and send the rest back."

Rebecca and the last officer continued down the hall until it opened onto a large room, perhaps a dining room originally. Now, it was filled with equipment. Three computers with monitors were lined up along one wall. Much of another was covered by a large, flat-panel display. A workstation sat in a corner. Shelves were filled with CDs, DVDs, and external drives. Two sets of head-mounted displays rested on a small table.

"Damn, this is like a game arcade," said the officer. "Except not cheap plastic. This stuff looks expensive."

"Probably is," said Clements. He was rifling through one of six, four-drawer filing cabinets.

"Anything yet?" asked Rebecca.

"Pictures of places the Crusaders have hit and a ton of places they haven't. But I'm not finding anything like signals and what to do when one occurs."

"That's got to be on the computers," said Rebecca.

"And you're sure if you lock up one of those machines with failed login attempts, that won't lock them all up?" Clements asked.

"I don't see how. There's no hard-wired network, and I shut down the wireless router. They can't communicate anymore."

"OK," he said, although, to Rebecca, he sounded skeptical.

"Agent Marte?" Rebecca turned to see the officer she had left at Greenwood's office. "You said this hostage situation was at a place called Biomedical Engineering Associates?"

"That's right."

He stepped into the room, holding out some photographs. "That name is on the back of these. Thought you should see them."

She took the pictures from the officer and looked at the first. It was the front entrance to the building. The second was a man she didn't recognize. The third was Doc, but it had been altered. The fourth was a young woman, the picture edited the same way. She shuffled through the remaining photographs, finding no others that had been changed.

She walked over to Clements and handed him the picture of the woman. "Is this Veles?"

He studied it, frowning. "Yes, but what the heck does that mean?"

"I'm not sure, but this is Sam Price," she said, holding out another picture. "And this is everyone else in the Biomedical Engineering Associates folder." She fanned out the remaining shots like a deck of playing cards.

"Aw, shit," Clements said, the color draining from his face.

"Can you call one of our agents in St. Louis? I'm going outside to call Doc." Rebecca started toward the door, not waiting for an answer.

At the Same Time – The Biomedical Engineering Associates Building

After the narrowest of margins of victory for our fake-beach plan, everyone had pitched in to implement it, and in short order, it was done. And now that it was, I had to admit ... it wasn't very convincing. At least, not when you were close.

The dust from the concrete had gotten everywhere, leaving a white sheen that looked like morning frost on the tables and chairs. But the tradeoff between lost realism from hurrying and being dead because the signal had come was heavily weighted toward the former. The aggregate in the concrete was also too coarse, many of the stones being the size of the tip of my little finger. I suppose there are pebble beaches, but I doubted Greenwood would have used anything but fine sand in her mockup. Our stand-ins for the beach furniture looked like a table and chairs from an office lunchroom because they were. And we had nothing for a volleyball net. But the plants looked good. And in addition to the large ball to sit on, we'd found a smaller, weighted medicine ball. Both looked the part of beach toys, even if the smaller one weighed several pounds.

While approaching the front door had warranted a warning shot from Prudence earlier, apparently puttering around on the other side of the lobby was irrelevant; she hardly gave us a second glance. So, we had moved two partitions in front of our beach-in-the-making. Seeing the work in progress, we reasoned, might spoil the illusion.

With everything now done, it was time for the reveal. Russo and I were going to pull back the partitions, then "frolic" in a subdued sort of way. Why subdued? With the power to the building turned off, the 75-degree, outside temperature had become almost 80 inside. Prudence appeared unaffected, not even bothering to remove the light jacket she wore. Russo and I, on the other hand, were sweating profusely. Any dust we raised was now clinging to our skin, forming a white coating on our arms, hands, and faces. We wanted to look like Prudence's friends at play, not a dance of ghosts.

We were ready. The only problem that remained was Nicole. "Babe, you need to join the others in the break room." Everyone except my future wife had readily accepted the suggestion to wait farther away from Prudence and her bomb.

"And let you and Gene have all the fun?"

My suspicion that I wasn't very good at scowling at my fiancé was confirmed when I tried, and she smirked in reply. "Gene and I have this covered," I said. "And if it starts to fall apart, I don't want to have to worry about you."

"Sam Price," she said. Her scowl, unlike mine, was perfect. "We've had this discussion. You are not responsible for me." She was the stubbornest person I had ever known, an endearing trait most of the time. At the moment, however, my emotions were an ever-changing mix of frustration and worry.

My look of defeat apparently got to her because when she continued, her tone was much milder. "What you're trying to do is sweet. I appreciate it. But it's not smart and you know it. We have no idea how Laura handled gender differences. Prudence may feel threatened with only males in sight. If there's only going to be one gender here, it should be female."

"She's right, you know," added Russo.

I blew out a long breath. Out-argued and outvoted, I started to concede when my phone rang. "It's Agent Marte." I raised the phone to my ear. "Rebecca, can I put you on speaker?" There was a trace of hope in my voice that was apparent even to me.

"No, don't do that." Her words came out in a rush. "I need to speak to you or you and Ms. Veles, but not anyone else."

I wasn't prepared for that answer, and it took me a moment to recover. I turned from Nicole and Russo and slowly walked away. "OK," I said softly. "What's up?"

"First, sorry, but nothing about the signals Prudence is waiting for. But we have come across several pictures labeled Biomedical Engineering Associates. One is you and Gus confirmed one is Ms. Veles. We think the others are probably coworkers. But there's something ... different about your two pictures." She paused, taking a breath. "There's a big, red X across your faces."

Marked for death, but why? I couldn't see the reason. If Greenwood wanted a victim with a fresh, young face to send a wave of fear into the industries surrounding medicine, Nicole was the perfect candidate. But what was the message in killing me? Even future families of medical workers aren't safe from the Crusaders' wrath? That felt like a stretch.

"OK," I replied, just to let her know I'd heard.

"Clements is passing the same information on to an agent there," said Marte. "So, don't be surprised if they offer you some additional protection when they take you out. Not that we're going to leave anyone exposed."

"And hopefully, we've got something that'll get the agents in the door," I said. "We've created a distraction for Prudence. And now that it's done, I hate to ask, but did you find something like a beach there?"

"Yeah, we did," she said after a pause that seemed minutes rather than the split-second it probably was. "Why?"

"Tell you later," I said, not wanting to take the time now. "Anything else?"

"Nothing, except let's make that a story over drinks with you and Ms. Veles. My treat. I'd like to meet this woman of yours."

"I'm sure she'd love to." I disconnected and walked back to Russo and Nicole.

"The FBI have any news?" asked Russo.

"Apparently, the Crusaders prepared for this operation at Greenwood's farm. They found pictures of the building, stuff like that. Unfortunately, they haven't found the actual plan. So, the next step is up to us. Ready?" Both nodded.

I considered pulling Nicole aside to tell her about the altered pictures, but I wasn't sure how much time we had left. Seconds might count. And besides, knowing that Greenwood wanted us dead more than she wanted everyone else dead wasn't very helpful anyway.

Russo moved to the end of one of the partitions while I took the other. Nicole took a seat at the table, complete with a drink at her elbow composed of nine-parts water and one-part concrete dust that had collected there. I glanced at Russo. He nodded, and we pulled the partitions apart.

Prudence rose to her feet, her eyes narrowing as she took in the scene. She moved from behind a column where she had taken cover, leaving the roller bag behind but still carrying a revolver in her right hand. She was exposed to the building's front windows. Agent Alban had said they wouldn't shoot unless we were threatened, but was that just something they told hostages? I tensed, wondering if a rifle shot was about to shatter the glass.

Russo and I stepped onto the concrete-covered floor. As planned, he picked up the large ball. But before he could toss it to me, it slipped from his hands, hit the floor in a puff of dust, and bounced away. I could see the outline of a partial handprint on its surface, the product of sweat from Russo's fingers and the concrete mix.

"Damn," he whispered, as the ball stopped only after reaching the far wall.

I looked at Prudence. If we'd created confusion, it was gone. She glanced at the window, and as if realizing what she had done, she dived behind the column. There, she retrieved the pushbutton attached to the roller bag.

But before I could consider whether we had just sealed our fate, Nicole stood up and removed the thin pads covering the chairs' wire-mesh seats. She climbed onto one. "In her head, she's a kid, not a killer," Nicole said.

She jumped across to the second chair. She turned and jumped back, this time releasing a faked squeal like a child might make on a playground.

"The medicine ball," I said to Russo. It was sitting a few feet from him. He retrieved it, then tossed it in a high, arching lob. I extended my hands in front of me, hoping to use the extra distance to slowly drain the ball's momentum. Even so, it hit my hands hard, and I staggered back a step. I stepped forward and returned the lob, Russo catching it in much the same manner.

Nicole paused her play to laugh and point at us. If she'd been up for an academy award, the critics might say it was forced, but I marveled at how natural it sounded. I added a few snorts, and Russo soon joined in our feigned merrymaking. I wondered what law enforcement watching from outside was thinking. Perhaps that we had succumbed to the pressure and were now exhibiting mass hysteria? But a glance at Prudence said it was working.

She stood and walked more purposefully from behind the column. Again, she left the roller bag behind. Again, she brought the handgun. Halfway to us, she reached inside her jacket and pulled out a second revolver. The room went silent. Russo froze, halfway in his motion to lob the ball. Nicole stopped jumping between the chairs.

Please don't raise those guns.

I didn't want to see Prudence die. She might have looked like a twenty-something-year-old, but she was innocent. She'd never even had the chance to have an impure thought. "Games not over, Gene," I said and forced the most natural chuckle I could muster from a parched throat.

"You sure you can handle my fastball?" he said, resuming his windup and laughing as he lobbed the ball to me.

I could almost hear a collective sigh of relief from the three of us as Prudence laid her firearms on the floor and came over to our playground. And as if in complete affirmation of Nicole's argument for staying, Prudence walked directly to her, climbed up on the other chair, and took her hands.

Russo and I both ran to the revolvers on the floor then turned toward the roller bag. But before we reached it, law enforcement was inside, surrounding Prudence and Nicole with drawn guns. I looked on, feeling helpless should Prudence decide to make a last stand. But then, making a decision was beyond her, and apparently, no trained behaviors fit the situation. She simply looked confused as the officers took her into custody.

The room became a scene of organized confusion. Someone asked where everyone else was, and I pointed them toward the break room. A couple of officers led Prudence out. Nicole joined me, and I locked her in an embrace. "I think she'll be OK," Nicole said. I smiled but never had the chance to reply.

"We need to get everyone out," someone yelled.

I looked out through the front windows, finding a corridor of officers in riot gear that started at the entrance to the Biomedical Engineering Associates building and continued diagonally across the street into another structure. It would take a sniper in a helicopter to get a shot into the narrow gap between the rows of men, and since they had been keeping the airspace clear, even that wasn't a possibility. They started lining us up for the evacuation.

"Dr. Price? Ms. Veles?" asked a man I didn't recognize.

"Yes," I replied.

"I'm FBI Special Agent Blewitt. I have an extra precaution for the two of you. Something to make you look a bit different than when you came in." He held out a blue, FBI windbreaker and cap. "Sorry, but you're going to need to share. I could only find one set on such short notice. Ms. Veles, you first."

"I don't understand," Nicole said, looking at the garments in the man's hands.

"I'll explain, as soon as we're safe across the street," I said.

Nicole frowned but donned the gear, and they left. In less than a minute, Blewitt returned. "Your friend's safe and secure on the other side. Now, your turn."

After putting on the makeshift disguise, the dash across the street passed in a blur, making me wonder if I was coming down hard from the adrenaline-fueled stress of the last hour and a half. I was looking forward to some peace and quiet, a bit of normalcy, even if it was in the lobby of a strange building surrounded by people I didn't know.

Agent Blewitt and I had just passed through the doors when a woman approached. She was either a nurse or her fashion sense ran to white dresses accessorized by a clipboard. Beyond her, there were about 20 others, men and women, all moving between pieces of furniture that appeared a cross between a folding chair and a cot.

"Let me get you something to drink," said the woman. "You must be dehydrated."

"I'll take a sip, but what I really need now is a bathroom."

"Sure. The bathroom is just past the reception desk." She gestured with a hand and smiled at me. "And you may want to wash your face while you're in there." I reached up and rubbed my cheek, bringing back a layer of gray on a finger. "Were you all trying to tunnel out?"

"Something like that."

After using the bathroom and getting cleaned up, I felt better. But even so, the lobby didn't feel less chaotic. I walked slowly back to my chair/cot, looking for Nicole but not seeing her. The woman with the clipboard, however, was there, this time with a cup of orange juice in the other hand. I sat, accepted the drink with thanks, and took a sip.

"Let me take your blood pressure, and then, we have cookies or bananas if you're hungry."

But rather than sitting back and raising an arm, I slid forward on the chair. "Is that a list of the hostages?" I pointed at the clipboard.

"The workers, actually. Often these things are over before we get onsite and the victims are taken to emergency rooms for treatment. But given what they do on the other side of the street, I think someone knew exactly who to call. We're here in force."

She looked pleased, but the scene felt wrong to me. I gazed around the lobby, again failing to find Nicole. "My fiancé is here, somewhere. I'd like to talk to her."

"Of course, but let me take your blood pressure first. You seem fine, but it'll only take a moment and we wouldn't want you collapsing halfway across the floor." Her words were reasonable, but my mind wouldn't be quieted. I started to lean back, just to get it over with so I could look for Nicole.

"You're probably just not seeing her because we came with so many people. The first estimate of hostages was thirty, not thirteen."

"Thirty?" I stood up from the chair.

"Sir, please sit back down."

"Who reported thirty hostages?"

"I don't know. Whoever called it in, I guess."

I'd estimated twelve to fifteen when I'd spoken to Marte. Maybe someone else had taken a guess and passed it on to the police, but no one inside would have been that far off. Besides, the company only employed about twenty full-time people, and several of them had been working from home. I frantically scanned the lobby but still saw no trace of Nicole.

"Sir, you really need to sit down. You're going to make yourself ill."

I ignored her and instead, cupped my hands around my mouth. "Nicole," I yelled. Most of the heads in the lobby turned, but no one answered. "Nicole." By now, the lobby was nearly silent. I yelled once more. "Nicole!"

"Dr. Price, what's wrong?"

I spun around to find Agent Blewitt. "Nicole's disappeared. Where'd you leave her?"

He blinked a couple of times, then said, "At the door. With the first nurse we met."

"What did she look like?" I asked.

Blewitt paused. "Tall, dark hair, but I didn't really see her face. She was looking down ... at a clipboard. She said something about your friend looking dizzy. Sure enough, next moment she slumps against the nurse. I started to help, but they walked off. So, I went back for you."

"Which way did they go?"

"I didn't watch, but they started towards the back." I looked the way he was pointing, spotting an exit sign over the heads in the crowd.

"You have an alert out on Greenwood?"

"There's been a multi-agency alert out since they found those people at her farm." Blewitt stared at me a moment. "You don't think that was Dr. Greenwood, do you?"

I didn't answer, now sure what I thought. "Nicole Veles is missing and probably a hostage. You need to have that added to the alert. Talk to Agent Marte or Clements if there's any pushback." I sprinted for the exit.

FRIDAY, MAY 31

2:21 PM – My Apartment in the Central West End

It started as a murmur. The reign of terror under which every doctor, medical researcher, and patient had lived was over. True, the demented individual responsible had escaped, along with at least Brother Justice, but her ability to inflict pain and death was gone. It had vanished with her reputation because it was her name that had opened doors. It had given her access to rural hospitals, where she had returned their trust by stealing at least three female newborns. Those babies, in turn, became the foundation for her mindless army. Her stellar record of research got her into the halls of higher education where she discovered gaps in their security and planned her deadly attacks. Her credentials were her calling card at research facilities, doctors' offices, health clinics, and hospitals across St. Louis, even the nation. But with the loss of her professional aura, those doors were now closed, locked to her forever. Dr. Laura Greenwood had been defanged.

By the evening news on the day the Crusader compound was found and the hostages freed, the murmur had become a triumphant chorus of relief. And throughout the next day, the tumult grew. Dancing in the streets would be an exaggeration but perhaps not that much; there was a largely impromptu parade in downtown St. Louis in support of medical science and in condemnation of Greenwood.

My personal experience during those two days, however, couldn't have been more different.

After I confirmed that Nicole was missing and got her name included in the FBI's alert—with a lot of help from Marte—I walked the streets, searching. I walked all that afternoon, slowly expanding the radius around her work. Through the night and into the next day, I looked. My only companion was my phone. All I needed was a call, a text that Nicole had been found, but it stayed obstinately silent on that topic.

After 26 hours of wandering, I returned home. I had found nothing, but I had dulled my rage and my pain with exhaustion. At least, I had for a few, fitful hours of sleep. And when I woke sometime after dark, the waking nightmare came crashing down on me again. And the cycle repeated.

Other than the press who had my name from the list of hostages, the only calls I received in those first days were from the parents. Both sets wanted to come and support me. I told both, no. There was no point in my folks coming to St. Louis; the help they could provide for my pain had been delivered over the years of my upbringing. As for Nicole's parents—the Kansas City authorities had told them that their public announcements, messages they hoped would elicit compassion from the kidnapper, could be as effectively delivered from their home as in St. Louis. I used that as an excuse to decline their offer, too ashamed to face them after I'd failed to protect their daughter.

I lived like that for two more days, a shadow roaming the streets, my phone refusing to deliver me from my hell. I had no objective beyond finding Nicole. And all the while, my head was filled with images I couldn't shake. On the fifth day, Agent Marte called and those distressing visions took a turn for the worse.

"Doc, you should hear this from me, rather than the news."

I had answered on the first ring, still clinging to the desperate hope that Nicole had been dropped at some remote bus station or highway rest stop once Greenwood had safely escaped. Marte's greeting, however, hit me like a punch to the stomach. I squeezed my eyes closed and forced a single sentence through my lips. "What is it?"

"I hate to say this, but you and Nicole weren't the targets when Prudence took the Biomedical Engineering Associates building. It was just the opposite. The X's meant that the two of you were to be spared at all cost. And unfortunately, with all the law enforcement and medical experts we needed to make sense of Greenwood's papers and research ... well, much of what she had planned got leaked to the press."

Over the next several minutes, Marte recounted the full story. At first, there was little I didn't know or hadn't guessed, but among the revelations were several involving Conroy.

After Greenwood learned of his sister's death, she made it a point to "accidentally" bump into him at a medical conference. That night over dinner, she convinced him that telling the story would honor his sister's memory, putting her cruel plan in motion. Then, she took him as a lover. She hadn't known about Conroy's illness, but like any new lover would, he confided in her. She used the fact to keep him quiet. She'd told him she'd keep him alive as long as her medical expertise allowed, but that some of her treatments would be illegal in this country. Absolute secrecy was required, and he agreed. Their lovemaking was also a lie. She used it to collect his sperm so that she could impregnate the female Crusaders. She even noted in one of her notebooks that with a near-genius sperm donor, she didn't have to worry about her troop's innate intelligence. And when Greenwood released Prudence and Justice on an unsuspecting professor and his students, it was in a fit of rage over Conroy's death. But it wasn't because she loved him; it was because the city had forgotten him much too soon.

Greenwood was back in control of her demented mind, however, by the time Prudence took the hostages at the Biomedical Engineering Associates building two days later. At this point, she was starting phase two, and everything Marte said was news to me. And each revelation rained blows on my already battered psyche.

When Greenwood, Justice, and Prudence left the Crusader compound that Wednesday morning, the plan was to let Prudence fail. Our ruse with the beach had worked, but it was completely unnecessary. Prudence had been drilled on scenarios that would end in her death—with a sniper's shot through a window, in a hail of bullets as she ran from the building, at her own hand. The roller bag itself was a decoy, meant only to hold law enforcement at bay until the medical team was in place across the street—an unnecessarily large team that Greenwood had called in.

And why were Nicole and I to live? Because in the twisted logic that was Greenwood's reality, I was to become the first of several new spokespersons for medical freedom. I was to carry forward the message of James Conroy. And I'd do that tirelessly and passionately after I had to stand by and watch Nicole die a slow and painful death. Because in the chaos of treating the hostages, Greenwood was going to infect her with an incurable illness.

It was at this point in Marte's monologue that I made my only comment, a plea made in pain and disbelief. Infecting people this way had to be impossible. But Marte assured me that their panel of medical experts considered Greenwood's list of afflictions nothing short of evil genius. All the illnesses were terminal but only after prolonged periods of painful deterioration. And all were close to but just beyond the reach of current medical practice. Short periods of remission were possible, but they would only delay the inevitable and further intensify the suffering of those forced to endure it.

Marte asked for a moment, saying she needed a drink of water, but I never heard her set the phone down. I had the feeling she was steeling herself. And as she detailed how Greenwood had selected Nicole and me as her future pawns, I felt sure I was right.

The day Greenwood and Nicole first met, my fiancé's rather effusive description of my ability to explain complex concepts had piqued Greenwood's interest. Then, Nicole had apparently mentioned her love. That surprised me as Nicole shied away from public displays of emotion. But then, generating trust seemed as easy to Greenwood as breathing. She had certainly fooled me. The FBI even played their part in our selection. By suggesting I might be associated with the Crusaders, Greenwood manipulated Marte into checking into my background, where she found nothing anti-medicine.

The act that had sealed our fate, however, was mine. It was that innocent kiss I had placed on Nicole's cheek, not knowing that Greenwood was standing behind me in the kitchen. With that gesture, she wrote in one of her notebooks, she had all the proof she needed. Hearing the cold, calculated way the woman had verified our vulnerability to her evil design was almost more than I could bear. Fortunately, the tale was almost at its end.

When Marte and Clements were staking out the farmhouse, Greenwood was already in St. Louis, setting her scheme in motion. But when the locals broke down her gate due to a miscommunication of Clements's strategy, she knew her plan had been foiled. At that point, Greenwood and Justice would have ad-libbed their escape, and somehow, taking Nicole figured into that plan.

When Marte finished, I hung up without a good-bye. Her tale had forced a whole new set of grim possibilities into my mind, all ending with Nicole's death, and I was powerless against their sadistic pull. Once discovered, did Greenwood infect Nicole anyway? If the illness was slow acting, Nicole could still be the insurance she sought. Or was Greenwood prepared with something else that had only sedated her? And if Nicole was only insurance, why hadn't she been released? In five days, Greenwood could have driven to either coast and be halfway back to St. Louis by now.

As my brain churned away at the unthinkable, I was finding it increasingly difficult to form an image of my fiancé walking into a bus station disoriented but unhurt. Now, the only vision that came when I closed my eyes was Nicole dead in a ditch, animals picking at her lifeless corpse.

As Marte had warned, Greenwood's story of horror and our place of honor in it made the news. I became a virtual prisoner in my own apartment. What do you say to a reporter who asks, "How do you feel about your girlfriend being kidnapped by a madwoman?" The only response I had wasn't fit for a 10-second sound bite on the evening news. But while Greenwood's intentions were known, the kidnapping was a matter of speculation. She had never been positively identified at the scene. Lacking proof, the reporters eventually gave up and disappeared from my sidewalk and alley.

With the media gone, I went out and bought a handgun. It just felt like I should have one—or at least, that was the justification that came from behind the curtain of my unconscious. As I understood the law in Missouri, the background of the buyer was checked in the FBI's NICS (National Instant

Criminal Background Check System). Having the unblemished record that my security clearance at work required, I had no concerns about the outcome. If Agents Marte or Clements had known of the malevolence growing in my heart, they probably would have amended the FBI records. But they didn't know.

I studied Greenwood's life online—anywhere she had lived, taught, studied, completed a residency, done research. She had lived a lot of places, and I recorded each on a map, figuring if she had a past connection, she wouldn't return now. Then, I removed any of the big cities that were left. She was too well known to wander around a Chicago or a Denver. And I crossed off the extremely remote locations—the middle of nowhere Montana. She wasn't the pioneer who could repair a broken generator in the middle of a blinding snowstorm. Maybe I was being naïve taking this approach. Maybe an experienced investigator would laugh at me, but I had to start somewhere. And I was reasonably smart and driven by demons that showed me no quarter. I'd learn. I'd find Greenwood.

After a week and a half of missing work, I called and resigned over the phone. I said my remaining vacation time would cover the two-week notice. That was a lie, but I figured I needed the practice; I could see a future filled with them. "Hi, I'm looking for Andrea. She's my second cousin on my mother's side and I wanted to say hello." And besides, I didn't care what Ruger-Phillips thought anymore. That was another life, now dead and gone.

After quitting, I sold a few of my possessions and tossed the rest in the trash dumpster behind my building. That had made the task of packing a half-hour job—one that I had just completed. I was about to close and lock the door for the last time when my phone rang. It was Marte and probably her third or fourth call this week. I hadn't answered any of the others. I had heard too many times from too many people that I should leave the matter to the police. Or that time heals all wounds. Or that I was going down a slippery slope. Or some other crap. To hell with all of that.

But even so, Marte had listened when she didn't have to. She had shared all she could, and she acted on my concerns. I admired and respected her. I should say good-bye.

"Agent Marte."

"And I was about to suggest you use my nickname, Becca. But it sounds like you've reverted to old habits."

"Sorry. Never updated my phone display," I replied as if that explained everything.

"Given where I work, I guess you're not surprised I know you're leaving." I wasn't, but it felt pointless to say so.

"Anyway, I'm not going to repeat anything I said in all those long messages I left. And I'm not going to pretend I know what you are going through. I don't. But I did want to say, be careful. And if you ever need someone to talk to, call me. I understand I'm a good listener."

"You are."

"Hey, I don't think I mentioned this, but we had this massive raid planned for some church in south-central Missouri till we found the Crusaders using your tip." She said the final words in her most official-sounding voice. I knew, however, that they'd already decided to investigate Greenwood, and I'd merely been the emergency they used to justify breaking into her home.

"Anyway," she said, "after we got the Crusaders at Greenwood's, we scaled back to six agents. Probably only needed two, since the Reverend and his wife were still in bed when the agents got there. Turns out, they weren't Crusader supporters. The minister just used the medical controversy to stir up his congregation, so when he dipped his hand into the collection plate, no one would notice the missing cash. The team got some idea what they were getting into with all the elaborate gardens outside—lots of exotic plants, meticulously maintained. The missus apparently had groups of church women competing for that honor. But what they found inside the private quarters was nothing short of a palace—expensive furniture, antiques, valuable paintings. He wasn't involved in the crime we thought, but it still felt good to stop him from ripping off all those hardworking people."

Perhaps it was a sign of how far I had dropped from humanity because my first thought was, why the hell are you telling me this? But after a moment I said, "Another small victory for justice."

"And we were looking into a realtor too—a dirt pimp as a friend called him—as a possible handler for the Crusaders. But he was just collecting money for another group down south, so they could build their own meeting hall. Not even a crime there."

"Can't win 'em all," I said.

With two terse and somewhat trite responses, I think Marte read my mood, as both her tone and topic changed. "You know, it's already afternoon," she said, sadness tingeing the words. "Why don't you stick around and leave first thing tomorrow?"

"Can't. The new renters start moving in today."

"You can stay at my place, crash on my couch. It's not bad."

She didn't understand. When I gave up each day, it made no difference if I was floating on a cloud or lying in the mud. I'd be up in three hours, the guilt, rage, and pain returning to eat at my soul. "Sorry, but I need a change of scenery."

"I thought you might say that. Guess Gus and I will have to solve the next one ourselves. Take care, Doc."

"You too, Becca." I disconnected.

I started to take a final look around the apartment but couldn't. Even empty, Nicole was everywhere. I turned off the light, then closed and locked the door on my first life, never expecting to return.

ACKNOWLEDGMENTS

This book would not have been possible without the help of a number of talented individuals. I'd like to thank Ms. Janet Harrison, Ms. Elaine Neale, and Ms. Olga Iordache for reading and providing numerous helpful comments on earlier drafts of the manuscript.

Special thanks go to Dr. Liz Gehr for helping me watch my technical Ps and Qs. Any inaccuracies are mine; hopefully, they're all intentional to build the fiction.

The diligence of my editor, Ms. Laurel Heidtman, is greatly appreciated. I'd never find all those pesky, extra commas without her help ... not to mention all the other slipups that are so easy to overlook when you know a story by heart.

Finally, thanks go to my talented daughter, Ms. Courtney Perrin, for the design and creation of the cover art. Maybe I can build a picture with words, but I could never do what she does with graphics software and a computer.

ABOUT THE AUTHOR

Bruce Perrin has been writing for more than twenty-five years, although you will find most of that work only in professional technical journals or conference proceedings. After receiving a PhD in Industrial/Organizational Psychology and completing a career in psychological research and development at a major aerospace company, he's now applying his background to writing novels. Not surprisingly, most of his work falls in the techno-thriller, mystery, and hard science fiction genres, examining the intersection of technology and the human mind now and in the future. Besides writing, Bruce likes to tinker with home automation and is an avid hiker, logging nearly 2,500 miles a year in the first six years of Fitbit ownership. When he is not on the trails, he lives with his wife in St. Louis, MO.

Thank you for reading *Mind in Chains*. If you'd like to help others find this story, please consider leaving a review on Amazon, Goodreads, or the website of your favorite bookseller.

For all the latest on my new releases, promotions, and book reviews, subscribe to my blog: BruceMPerrin.blogspot.com